THE GIRL IN THE CASTLE

JAMES PATTERSON

& EMILY RAYMOND

GRAND
CENTRAL

New York   Boston

Grand Central Publishing
Hachette Book Group
1290 Avenue of the Americas, New York, NY 10104
grandcentralpublishing.com
twitter.com/grandcentralpub

Originally published in hardcover and ebook by Little, Brown Books for Young Readers in September 2022
First trade paperback edition: January 2024

Grand Central Publishing is a division of Hachette Book Group, Inc. The Grand Central Publishing name and logo is a trademark of Hachette Book Group, Inc.

The publisher is not responsible for websites (or their content) that are not owned by the publisher.

The Hachette Speakers Bureau provides a wide range of authors for speaking events. To find out more, go to hachettespeakersbureau.com or email HachetteSpeakers@hbgusa.com.

Grand Central Publishing books may be purchased in bulk for business, educational, or promotional use. For information, please contact your local bookseller or the Hachette Book Group Special Markets Department at special.markets@hbgusa.com.

Library of Congress Cataloging-in-Publication Data

Names: Patterson, James, 1947– author. | Raymond, Emily, 1972– author.
Title: The girl in the castle / James Patterson & Emily Raymond.
Description: First edition. | New York ; Boston : Jimmy Patterson Books/ Little, Brown and Company, 2022. | Includes author's note. | Audience: Ages 14 and up. | Summary: "Eighteen-year-old Hannah experiences danger in the past and present, as college intern Jordan tries to uncover the truth about Hannah and her memories." —Provided by publisher.
Identifiers: LCCN 2022016602 | ISBN 9780316411721 (hardcover) | ISBN 9780316411929 (ebook)
Subjects: CYAC: Mental illness—Fiction. | Psychiatric hospitals—Fiction. | Psychic trauma—Fiction. | Time travel—Fiction. | LCGFT: Novels.
Classification: LCC PZ7.P27653 Gk 2022 | DDC [Fic]—dc23
LC record available at https://lccn.loc.gov/2022016602

ISBNs: 9780316411820 (trade paperback), 9780316411929 (ebook)

Printed in the United States of America

LSC-H

Printing 1, 2023

I measure every Grief I meet

With narrow, probing, eyes—

I wonder if It weighs like Mine—

Or has an Easier size.

—EMILY DICKINSON

THE GIRL IN THE CASTLE

CHAPTER 1

It starts with a girl, half naked and screaming.

Even though it's midtown Manhattan, in January, the girl is wearing only a thin white T-shirt over a black lace bra. She slaps at the air like she's fighting an enemy only she can see.

A gangly teen, halfway through his first-ever shift at the Gap, watches her nervously through the window. Every other New Yorker just clutches their phone or their Starbucks cup and pretends not to see her.

Maybe they really don't.

She lets out a tortured cry that strangles in her throat, and then she crumples to her knees. "How do we get out of the castle?" she wails. "They're going to kill us all!"

A police car speeds up to the curb and two officers step out. "Are you hurt?" the first asks. DUNTHORPE, his name tag reads.

The girl's answer is more wordless screaming.

"We need you to calm down, miss," his partner, Haines, says.

"Are you hurt?" Dunthorpe asks again. He thinks he's seen this girl around the neighborhood. Maybe she's one of the shoplifters or the dopeheads—or maybe she's just some scared, crazy kid. Either way, he can't just let her stand here and scream bloody murder.

When Dunthorpe moves toward her, she drops to her hands

and knees and starts crawling away. Haines tries to grab her, but the minute he touches her back, she spins around at the same time her right foot flies out, smashing into his chest. Haines loses his balance and falls backward, cursing. The girl stands up and tries to run, but she stumbles over her backpack and goes down on all fours again.

"Help me!" she screams. "Don't let them take me! Call off the guards! They'll kill me!"

As Dunthorpe moves toward her with one hand on his Taser, she launches herself forward and hits him in the face with a closed fist. He reels backward, roaring in surprise, as Haines springs into action and gets her into a headlock.

Dunthorpe rubs his cheekbone and says, "Call the ambulance."

"But the little bitch hit you."

Dunthorpe's cheek smarts. "That'll be our secret."

"You sure you don't want to book her?" Haines's arm tightens around the girl's neck and her knees buckle. Quick as a snake, Haines gets behind her, grabs her hands, and cuffs them behind her back.

"I'm sure," Dunthorpe says.

The girl keeps quiet until the ambulance comes, and then she starts screaming again. "Don't let them take me!" she yells to the passersby as the two cops and an EMT wrestle her onto the gurney. "I have to save Mary. Oh, my sweet Mary!"

Strapped down, the girl wails over the sound of the ambulance siren.

"You can't take me! I need to save Mary! No, no, you can't take me!"

But of course, they can take her wherever they want to.

Half an hour later, the ambulance pulls up to the hospital, where a small but powerfully built nurse stands with her hands on her hips, waiting.

Arriving at the exact same time—but on foot, and voluntarily—is a handsome young man of nineteen or so. "Excuse me," he says, peering at the nurse's badge, "are you Amy Navarre? My name's Jordan Hassan, and I think I'm supposed to shadow you—"

"You'll have to wait," Nurse Amy says curtly as the ambulance doors open.

Jordan Hassan shuts his mouth quick. He takes a step to the side as the EMTs slide a metal gurney out of the back. Strapped onto it is a girl, probably right about his age, with a dirty, tear-streaked face. She's wearing a T-shirt and pair of boots but little else.

The nurse, who he's pretty sure is supposed to be his supervisor for his class-credit internship this semester, walks toward the girl. "You can take the straps away," she says to the EMT.

"I wouldn't—" he begins.

The nurse looks at the girl. "It's okay," she says.

Jordan's not sure if she's reassuring the EMT or the girl. In any case, the EMT removes the restraints, and the nurse gently helps the girl off the stretcher. Jordan watches as the girl shuffles toward the entrance.

As the doors slide open automatically, she feints left and bolts right.

She's coming straight for him.

Acting on reflex, Jordan catches her around the waist. She strains against his arms, surprisingly strong. Then she twists her head around and pleads, "Please—please—let me go! My sister needs me!"

"Keep hold of her!" Nurse Amy shouts.

Jordan has no idea what to do or who to listen to.

"I'm *begging* you," the girl says, even as Amy advances, radioing security. Even as one of the girl's sharp elbows jams into his solar plexus. Jordan gasps as air shoots out of his lungs.

"Just let me go," the girl says, quieter now. "*Please.* I need your help."

Jordan's grip loosens—he can't hold her much longer, and he doesn't want to, either. But then two uniformed men come running outside, and they grab the girl's arms and drag her into the hospital, and all the while she's fighting.

Nurse Amy and Jordan follow them into a small room off the lobby. The guards get the girl into a geri chair and strap her down, and Jordan watches as Nurse Amy prepares a syringe.

"Your first day, huh?" she says to Jordan, her face looking suddenly worn. "Well, welcome to Belman Psych. We call this a B-52. It's five milligrams of Haldol and two milligrams of Ativan, and we don't use it unless it's necessary for the safety of patient and staff." She injects it intramuscularly, then follows it up with an injection of diphenhydramine. "Don't worry. It'll quiet her down."

But it's not like in the movies, when the patient just slumps forward, drooling and unconscious. The girl's still yelling and pulling against her restraints. It looks like she's being tortured.

"Give it a few minutes," Amy says to Jordan.

Then she touches the patient's hair, carefully brushing it away from her gnashing teeth. "You're home, sweet Hannah. You're home."

DELIA F. BELMAN MEMORIAL
PSYCHIATRIC HOSPITAL
INTAKE & EVALUATION

PATIENT INFORMATION

Name: Hannah Doe
Date of Birth: 1/14/2005
Date Service Provided: 1/17/23

FUNCTIONING ON ADMISSION

ORIENTATION: Confusion w/r/t to time,
place, identity; pt believes herself to
be in a castle, possibly as a captive

APPEARANCE/PERSONAL HYGIENE: Pt presents
disheveled, dirty, with clothing missing.
Underweight. Superficial contusions and
excoriations on legs and arms

PSYCHOSIS: Pt experiencing auditory and
visual hallucinations

MOOD: Angry, upset, incoherent, uncooperative

LABORATORY RESULTS: Lab evaluation within normal limits. Toxicology report negative, and pt does not have history of substance abuse.

NOTES: After a breakdown on 44th St., pt was brought by ambulance at 9:34 a.m., mildly hypothermic from cold exposure. She attempted escape before being admitted. She was unable to answer orienting questions and insisted security staff wanted to kill her and her sister. Tried to attack security guard. We were unable to complete intake interview due to her delusional state; we will conduct further evaluation tomorrow if she is coherent.

Chapter 2

My name is Hannah Dory. I am eighteen in the year of our Lord 1347, and God forgive me, I am about to do something extraordinarily stupid.

I crossed myself, stood up, and threw a heavy cape over my shoulders.

"Hannah!" cried my sister, Mary. "Where are you going? Mother won't like—"

I didn't wait to hear the rest of the sentence. I marched down the narrow, frozen lane toward the village square, my jaw clenched and my hands balled into fists.

It was deepest winter, and there was misery everywhere I looked. A boy with hollow cheeks sat crying in a doorway of a thatch-roofed hovel, while a thin, mangy dog nosed in a nearby refuse heap for scraps. Another child—a filthy little girl—watched the dog with desperate eyes, waiting to steal whatever it scavenged.

I had nothing to give them. Our own food was all but gone. We'd killed and cooked our last hen weeks ago, eating every bit of her but the feathers.

My hands clutched over my stomach. There was nothing in it now—nothing, that is, but grief and rage. Just last night, I'd watched my little brother Belin die.

Mother hadn't known I was awake, but I was. I saw him take his last awful, gasping breath in her arms. He'd been only seven, and now his tiny, emaciated body lay under a moth-eaten blanket in the back of a gravedigger's cart. Soon he'd be put in the ground next to his twin, Borin, the first of them to come into the world and the first one to leave it.

My name is Hannah Dory. I have lost two brothers to hunger, and I will not lose anyone else. I am going to fight.

Have you ever felt a beloved hand grow cold in yours? If not, then I don't expect you to understand.

"Blackbird, Blackbird," crazy old Zenna said as she saw me hurrying by. She winked her one remaining eye at me. "Stop and give us a song."

She called me Blackbird for my midnight hair and my habit of singing through a day's work. She didn't know that my brothers had died—that I'd rather scream than sing. I bowed to her quickly, then hastened on.

"Another day, then," she called after me.

If we live another one, I thought bitterly.

Mary caught up with me a moment later, breathless and flushed. "Mother wants you at the spindle—I keep over-twisting the yarn."

"What use is spinning when we're starving?" I practically hissed. "We'd do better to *eat* the bloody wool."

Mary's face crumpled, and I instantly regretted my harsh tone. "I'm sorry, my sweet," I said, pulling her against my chest in a quick embrace. "I know Mother wants us to keep our hands busy. But I have…an errand."

"Can I come?" Her bright blue eyes were suddenly hopeful.

My Mary, my shadow: she was four years younger than me and four times as sweet, and I loved her more than anyone else in the world.

"Not today. Go back home," I said gently. "And take care of Mother and little Conn." *The last brother we have.*

I could tell she didn't want to. But unlike me, Mary was a good girl, and she did what she was told.

Down the hill, past the cobbler's and the bakehouse and the weaver's hut I went. I didn't stop until I came to the heavy wooden doors of the village church. They were shut tight, but I yanked them open and stumbled inside. It was no warmer in the nave, but at least there was no wind to run its cold fingers down my neck. A rat skittered into the corner of the bell tower as I grabbed the frayed rope and pulled.

The church bell rang out across our village, once, twice—ten times. I pulled until my arms screamed with effort, and then I turned and went back outside.

Summoned by the sound of the bell, the people of my village stood shivering in the churchyard.

"Only the priest rings the bell, Hannah," scolded Maraulf, the weaver.

"Father Alderton's been dead a week now," I said. "So I don't think he'll be complaining."

"God rest his soul," said pretty Ryia, bowing her head and folding her hands over her large belly. She'd have a baby in her arms soon, God willing.

Father Alderton had been a good man, and at my father's

request, he'd even given me a bit of schooling and taught me to read. He'd never beaten me or told me I was going to hell for my stubbornness, the way the priest before him had.

Now I just hoped God was taking better care of Father Alderton's soul than He had the priest's earthly remains. Wolves had dug up the old man's body from the graveyard and dragged it into the woods. Thomas the swineherd, searching the forest floor for kindling, had found the old man's bloody, severed foot.

Do you see what I mean? This winter, even the predators are starving.

"What's the ringing for?" said Merrick, Maraulf's red-cheeked, oafish grown son. "Why did you call us here?"

I brushed my tangled hair from my forehead and stood up as tall as I could.

My name is Hannah Dory, and I am about to save us—or get us all killed.

Chapter 3

I jabbed my hand in the direction of the graveyard. "Tomorrow, my little brother, Belin, will be taken there to join his twin," I yelled. "He was weak from months of cold and hunger, and he couldn't fight the fever when it came for him. Our mother knew this, and so she lied to him: she told him that he should sleep, and that he would be better in the morning. But in the morning, he was *dead*." Tears had begun to stream down my cheeks, and I angrily wiped them away. "But maybe my mother was right. Maybe Belin *is* better, because he's not suffering anymore. And maybe death is the only way to escape our torment. Who among us has not buried someone this winter?" I heard low murmurs: they all had lost fathers, children, sisters. Fever, hunger, the bloody flux—they were killing us, one by miserable one. "How much longer until there are more of us *under* the ground than above it?"

"Winter is always a hard season," said Morris, the wheelwright, stupidly.

"This one's the worst I've ever known," said ancient Zenna, who'd managed to stagger her way toward us. "Death himself has settled in our village, hasn't he?" She let out a strangled-sounding cackle. "He tells me he finds it very much to his liking."

"Hush, you old witch," said Maraulf roughly, and she jabbed him in the foot with her walking stick.

"Drunken softsword," she replied with a sly smile.

"Be quiet and listen to me!" I said. "I know what we need to do."

"We must pray harder," said the wheelwright.

"Yes, we could ask God for help," I said viciously. "But my mother and I tried that for the twins, and all it got us was sore throats and dead boys." I lifted my skirt and climbed to the top of the churchyard's stone fence. "I propose that we take matters into our own hands."

From that height, when I shielded my eyes and squinted, I could see the thing that had haunted my dreams ever since Borin first took sick.

The baron's castle. It loomed on the horizon like a squat, black mountain, and it was full of everything we lacked.

"I know how to get food. Maybe medicine, too," I said.

"Oh, get down from there before you fall," Serell, the cooper, said. "You're mad."

Of course they doubted me: I was the girl who always had a fanciful story to tell or a rosy song to sing, my voice as sweet as a lark's.

But that was the old Hannah. The new one was as sharp and cold as a knife.

"Baron Jorian died in battle last summer," I said. "And his son, Joachim, is young and untested. Now is our time to act."

"And what would you have us do?" scoffed Maraulf. "Knock on the castle doors, ask for scraps, and hope he's kind enough to give us some?"

"We shouldn't ask for anything," I said. "We should *take* it!"

Zenna began her crazed cackle again. Her eye, cloudy with mucus, rolled around in delight. "Death finds this notion very interesting indeed."

Suddenly I felt like telling her to shut up. "Maybe I'm asking you to risk your lives," I said, gazing down at the hungry, desperate villagers. "But what are lives like ours worth, anyway?"

No one spoke. No one wanted to be the first one to say *Nothing. Our lives are worth nothing at all.*

Chapter 4

*I*n the end, four men agreed to my outrageous plan. "We'll either be fed, Blackbird," Maraulf had said, clapping me on the shoulder like a brother, "or else we'll be dead."

I'd smiled grimly at him, knowing that he was right. "And in one way or another, our troubles will be over," I'd agreed.

It was late afternoon by the time I started back home. My steps were lighter than they'd been in months. I actually felt hopeful. Or was I—as Serell said—simply *mad*?

I'd just passed the bakehouse when arms grabbed me from behind, grasping tight around my waist. I reacted, letting out a cry as I crashed my elbow into a rib and stepped down hard on a leather boot.

"Ooff," said a laughing voice. "That hurt!"

My heart leapt with relief—I knew that voice. Big hands spun me around, and I found myself looking up into the leaf-green eyes of Otto Rast, eldest son of the town doctor.

"You—you *beast*," I said in mock anger, striking him on the chest. "You scared me."

"I did, did I?" Otto smiled and backed me up against the wall of what had once been the carter's cottage. He kept his hands on my hips as he pressed himself against me and one of his thighs pushed itself right between mine. "But I thought you were so fearless," he said, his voice a low growl.

His touch sent a shiver through my whole body, and my breath quickened. "Where did you get that idea?" I looked away from him—his face was almost too handsome for me to bear.

"I heard your speech," he said. "I know what you're going to do."

"I looked for you in the crowd, but you weren't there!"

"I arrived just in time to hear you promising that you could get food and medicine. Before that, I was at Ferrick's near the churchyard, putting leeches to his son's neck."

"Please, say no more—"

"We gave him gall of boar and bled him for hours, but he's raving and purple with fever. I don't think he'll last until cockcrow." Otto said this as calmly as if he were predicting that it would snow. He was more used to death than I ever wanted to be.

I reached my arms around his neck and pushed my face into his chest. I felt sadness crushing me all over again. "Belin died," I whispered. It was hard to even breathe.

"No! Not Belin, too," he said. He pulled me closer and held me as I wept. "You should've called for me."

Why? I knew there was nothing you could do.

He pressed his mouth to the top of my head. "My love, my love, I'm so sorry," he whispered into my hair.

I shivered and leaned into him, wanting to forget everything. *Aching* to. I felt blood suddenly rush to my cheeks—and to every secret part of me. How could I desire him like this when I was so full of sorrow? And would he desire me enough to help take me away from here, even for a few stolen moments?

"Come inside with me," I urged.

Otto hesitated. "Hannah," he began.

"Shhhh," I said.

I reached behind me and felt for the door of the cottage, and blindly I unhooked the latch. Pulling Otto along with me, I moved into the dark chill of the abandoned room.

Otto put his fingers to my lips, and I kissed them. He bent toward me, tipping my chin up and pressing his mouth to mine. Heat flooded my body as one of his hands cupped my breast and the other reached up to the nape of my neck. I shook with desire as our soft, open-mouthed kiss grew harder, more insistent. I could feel him stiffening against me, and I grabbed his hips and pulled them tight against mine. There was a pile of clean straw in the corner, and we stumbled together toward it.

Then Otto pulled back, gazing at me urgently with eyes as green as summer. "Are you sure?" he whispered.

"We are as good as wed," I reminded him, "having promised ourselves to one another."

"We'll be married right after the Maying, Father says." Otto's voice grew hoarse with lust as his hand slid between my legs. "And we shouldn't forget," he added, "that we have already *given* ourselves to each other on many delightful occasions."

I kissed him. "Stop talking," I said.

I knew I should go home to my family, but the truth was that I needed this. I lay back in the straw, sighing as he lowered himself down beside me.

Here, at last, was a hunger that could be satisfied.

Chapter 5

I returned home flushed and breathless. My lips felt bruised, and I could still feel the warmth of Otto's skin on mine. As I took off my linen headwrap, bits of straw shook loose and fell to the floor. Thankfully, no one noticed.

But whatever happiness I'd stolen in Otto's arms quickly vanished. Mary sat huddled in a corner, miserably twisting yarn on a wooden spindle, and the air was heavy with Belin's absence.

"Where did you go?" my mother asked, stirring a pot of gruel over the hearth's feeble fire. "There's the darning to do, and the thatch in the south corner is rotten...." Her weak voice trailed off.

I made a show of hanging up my cape and brushing dust from my skirt. I kept my eyes away from the corner where Belin had breathed his last. Where did I go? I couldn't tell her.

My name is Hannah Dory, and I am a traitor and a tramp.

"She just went for a walk, didn't you, Hannah?" Mary said quickly. "I told her to, Mother. I thought it would make her feel better."

I gave her a grateful look. Though I always thought of myself as Mary's protector, she looked after me, too.

My mother sighed wearily. "I hope it did, since supper will be small comfort." She reached out and took my hand in her rough fingers, to show that she forgave me for running off. "Call Conn in to eat, please."

I walked out to our frozen garden, where I expected to find my brother playing with his friend Vincy, who lived with his widowed father a little ways up the lane.

Vincy was there all right, dancing around in the dirt and stabbing invisible monsters with a pointed stick. But Conn was nowhere in sight.

"Where's my brother?" I asked.

"He went down to the river," Vincy said, viciously striking the air. "Take *that*! And that, you slavering beast!"

The river? Alone? Panic rose in my throat. "When?" I demanded. The river took a life every season—in spring floods, a summer drowning, or a winter plunge through the ice.

Vincy shrugged and dropped the stick to his side. "Don't know," he said. "Haven't seen him in forever. Is it suppertime? Do you have food?"

Ignoring him, I rushed back inside to get my cape, trying not to let my terror show. *Dear God we can't lose another boy.* "He's gone to the river," I said. "I'll fetch him."

My mother gasped and her face went white. "*Run*," she said.

But even as I was moving toward the door, it burst wide open, and in came Conn, soaked to the skin and blue with cold. My mother shrieked and ran to him, clutching at his sopping clothes and trying to pull them off before he froze.

But Conn wasn't half drowned. He was grinning ear to ear. In his small hands he gripped a black, snakelike fish—a winter eel.

"I broke a hole in the ice," he said. "I sat there for hours and hours, Mama. And then I caught him!"

My mother clasped him to her chest, her thin face radiant with relief. "Hannah, gut the eel."

The moment I touched its cold, slimy flesh, I could tell that it had been dead for days. Poor little Conn, thinking himself a great fisherman, had plucked a decaying thing from the frigid river and brought it home for us to eat.

And I was nearly desperate enough to cook it.

But with Conn by the fire now, getting rubbed pink and dry by my mother, I went to the door and threw the eel into the street. The dogs would find it quickly enough, and they had stronger stomachs than we did.

Then I dished out our meager slurry of cabbage and a few grains of barley. It was pale and watery, seasoned with the last of our salt. I knew that we'd slurp up every drop, and that when we went to our beds, we'd still be hungry. We'd wake in the middle of the night with empty guts twisting.

As if she could hear my thoughts, my mother looked up at me. "The harvest will be better this year," she said. Her lovely face was lined and her brow etched deep with worry. She was trying so hard to keep us alive, and it just wasn't working.

"We can't wait that long," I said. I put down my spoon. "But I'm going to make sure we don't have to."

My mother frowned. "I don't understand."

I pushed my soup bowl over toward Conn; I was past feeling hunger. "I'm going to do something, Mother," I said. "It's dangerous, but it has to be done."

STOP

Anyone entering this area must check in at the nurse's station before entering a patient room

- This door is locked 24/7
- Access via key swipe only
- High elopement risk

Make sure door is shut and locked behind you

Thank you

Belman Staff

CHAPTER 6

I woke, fell asleep, and then woke again. In the dim artificial light, a shadow tiptoed toward me. I tried to get away from it, but I couldn't. The shadow stuck something small and sharp into the crook of my elbow. I screamed.

"Hush, Hannah, dear," the shadow said. "It's okay."

I didn't believe the shadow at all. How did it know my name? I tried to speak, but my tongue was too big for my mouth. In my head there was confusion and darkness and a roaring that sounded like a terrible wind.

The shadow touched my cheek. "You just need to get some rest. You'll feel better in the morning."

Lies! I wanted to say. *Lies!*

I was afraid to fall asleep again because I didn't know what the shadow would do to me while I was unconscious. But sleep was coming. I could feel it rising like a huge black wave, getting closer and closer, no matter how I tried to run from it. When it crashed over me, it obliterated me. The shadow vanished. *I* vanished.

I dreamed of sharp things. Needles. Knives.

Blood.

CHAPTER 7

When I woke again I couldn't move.

I opened my mouth to yell, but the scream died in my throat. Crying out wouldn't help. To be released, I had to be quiet.

Good.

Sane.

I heard footsteps in the hall, then the sound of low, concerned voices. *Let me out, let me out!* It took all my self-control not to beg, but I kept my eyes and mouth shut tight. Kept my body utterly still, except for the peaceful rise and fall of my stomach, even as my mind crackled with frenzied thoughts. I'd had a breakdown. I was at Belman Psychiatric Hospital. I was strapped to the bed.

Again.

The voices moved on down the hall, and then I opened my eyes.

I was slowly trying to work one of my wrists out of its restraint when I heard a bright, familiar voice call out. "Oh, Hannah, you're awake!"

Nurse Amy came bustling into the room. "You're good now, aren't you, hon?" she asked. She patted my immobile arm. "You know we hate doing this to you, but you weren't being cooperative, not in the least." She clucked her tongue at me and smiled. Nurse

Amy wore too much eyeliner and too much perfume, but she was young and pretty, with broad, soft shoulders and tiny perfect teeth.

"I'm good," I lied.

How could I be good? I was in a freaking mental hospital!

But Amy's definition of good was different than mine. She didn't mean was I happy, healthy, and 100 percent right in the head. She meant was I going to try to punch someone anytime soon. She meant was I going to try to run.

I wasn't.

"You can let me out," I said. "I'll behave this time, I swear."

After Amy undid my restraints, I sat up and rubbed my wrists, which were an ugly red. My head felt fuzzy, and my tongue was heavy and thick, like it had grown bigger overnight somehow.

"Better now?" she asked, smiling kindly at me.

"Yes," I said around my fat tongue. "But honestly, that isn't saying much."

CHAPTER **8**

N urse Amy patted my shoulder. "It's okay, sweetheart. Let's get going—it's time for group."

That meant I'd slept through breakfast. My stomach was growling loud enough for Amy to hear it as I got up and followed her down the hall to the therapy room, where a dozen or so people had pulled their chairs into a sloppy circle. I flopped down into an empty one as Lulu, the therapist, looked up at me and blinked. Her face fell.

Gee, Lulu, you aren't happy to see me? No? That's okay, I'm not super happy to see you, either.

Don't get me wrong—Lulu was nice. And I think she actually liked me. But every time I showed up on the ward, she had to wonder a little bit more about the effectiveness of Belman's treatment protocols.

"Well, everyone, it seems we have another person attending group this morning," she chirped.

You'd think this would be too obvious to mention, but in my experience, psychiatric patients sometimes need someone to point out the obvious. Otherwise, everything that's going on inside their minds can drown the rest of the world out.

Most Belman patients fell into four main categories. Either they: (1) moved through the ward in a medicated haze, (2) practically vibrated with manic, psychotic, or otherwise chaotic energy, (3) withdrew into themselves, or (4) seemed totally with it and totally cool, and were only in the hospital for hardcore therapy because their family could throw money at a "problem" kid.

And then there was me.

I didn't fit into any of those categories, and I didn't belong here. But when my mind went to the past and my body stayed in the present, in what I'm *told* looks a lot like a psychotic episode, I got sent to Belman.

I learned a long time ago not to fight it. At least the beds were warm and the food was mostly edible.

When Lulu turned back to me, her expression had returned to its usual brightness. "Why don't you introduce yourself?"

"Hi. My name is Hannah Do—"

"Hold it, hold it! Only first names, Hannah. You know the rules." She wagged a finger at me.

"Sorry," I mumbled. "I forgot."

"Blame the B-52 ass-jab," the bone-thin girl next to me whispered. Her name was Michaela, and I hadn't forgotten *her*. We'd been roommates the last time I was here, and we'd become friends. Had she been readmitted? Or had she never left? I knew I wouldn't—shouldn't—ask.

"Hi, Michaela," I said. "Again."

"Welcome back, babe," she said smoothly. I couldn't entirely tell if she was being serious or sarcastic. It was probably in bad taste to welcome someone back to a locked psychiatric ward anyway.

I looked around the room at the heavy, pleather chairs, the faded Impressionist posters behind unbreakable glass, and the tall windows that were too narrow to jump out of. I hadn't forgotten about any of those. I hadn't forgotten how cold it was on the unit, either, or how it smelled like air freshener and latex gloves and disinfectant and maybe something like despair.

I really, truly, deeply can't believe it. I'm back on Ward 6, and I don't have any idea how I got here.

"Did you say something, Hannah?" Lulu asked.

I shook my head. Did I? I hadn't meant to.

Maybe she can hear your thoughts.

No she can't, that's ridiculous.

"Well, would you like to take your turn?" Lulu said.

I looked down at my lap. I was wearing a faded hoodie and ugly sweatpants, neither of which were mine. I still had my boots, but someone had removed the laces. There was a long cut on the back of my hand, and the dirt underneath my fingernails had the brown-red tint of dried blood.

Did I hurt someone? Did I hurt myself?

Everything that had happened in the present time, before I woke up strapped to a hospital bed, was a blank.

"Can I pass?" I said. "I feel... sort of woozy."

Lulu didn't like it when people skipped their turns, but she decided not to force anything. "All right. Sean? How about you?"

Sean was a skinny guy with long, greasy hair. "I don't belong here," he said. "This place is fucked. I want to go home."

Beside me, Michaela made a little groaning sound, because *everyone* said that when they were new. (I seemed to be the only one who *kept* saying it.)

"Let's talk about why you think you shouldn't be here," Lulu said gently.

Across the circle, a pimply kid dug his finger deep into his nose. The intercom made a staticky burp. "Paging Dr. Klein," it said. "Paging Dr. Klein."

I leaned back in my ugly chair. Most likely Sean *did* belong here, because it wasn't like you could just waltz into Belman and ask for a room. I didn't know what his problems were, but I knew what he had to look forward to during his stay on Ward 6. In addition to group therapy, he'd have meetings with a social worker, check-ins with therapists and doctors, art therapy, cognitive behavioral therapy, and optional classes for breathing, yoga, and stress management. There would be mushy cafeteria food and supervised walks outside, an ever-changing cocktail of prescription medications with unfortunate side effects, and endless bad television shows blaring from the lounge.

The thing about Belman was, it was about as nice as a psychiatric hospital could get. Ward 6 was a special adolescent/young adult ward, staffed mostly by people only a few years older than us. There were no sadistic nurses, no senile old men drooling in wheelchairs in the hallway, no fully grown addicts withdrawing from what Nurse Amy liked to call "street drugs." Belman wasn't a scary place at all. It was just sort of depressing.

"Like I said, this is bullshit. But if I gotta stay, I just hope I can get into someone's pants," Sean said. "I hear crazy girls do it like—"

"I'm going to stop you right there," Lulu said quickly. She was a pro. "For starters, we don't use the word *crazy*."

I closed my eyes. I really was woozy. My head felt…well, *soggy* was the best way to describe it. If someone could show me a picture of my brain, I was sure it would look as wet, sloppy, and useless as an old kitchen sponge.

Blame the B-52 ass-jabs, okay.

Just breathe. In and out, in and out.

I must've drifted off, because the next thing I knew Michaela was poking me in the ribs. "What?" I grumbled.

"Not what, *who*," she said, cocking her head toward the door.

I swiveled around in my chair and I saw him. He was very tall, wearing jeans, a wrinkled button-down, and a slightly nervous expression. He had dark hair and olive skin, and his nose was on the large side, and maybe just a tiny bit crooked, but even in my tranqed-out state, I could see that he was unquestionably and uncommonly hot.

"His name," Michaela said, "is Jordan." She fluttered long eyelashes in his direction as she put her arm loosely around my shoulders to whisper in my ear. "He's, like, an intern or something, he goes to Columbia, and everyone's already in love with him."

Lulu called, "No physical contact, Michaela!"

Michaela shot Lulu an evil look as she let her arm fall back to her side. Then Jordan nodded at me, almost like he knew me, and his eyes were the startling green-gold of agates. I quickly turned away.

"He was working when you got here," Michaela whispered. "You came in strapped down. But then I heard you tried to make a break for it."

Blink. Breathe. Try to remain calm.

"You were screaming about a castle when they brought you up here. You thought people were dying."

I don't feel good. I wish she would stop talking. Everyone's staring at me.

"You seem okay now, though," Michaela went on. "You probably got more meds this morning."

My hands twisted in my lap as Lulu moved on to the next patient.

I seem lucid, right? Do I belong in the psych ward? You can be the judge of that. Just as long as you know that your opinion doesn't matter.

But don't feel bad, because neither does mine.

CHAPTER **9**

O h, my god, you're back." A grinning, skinny, black-haired guy came running up to me, waving his arms around his head like he was trying to hail a taxi in a downpour. "Don't ask me to pretend I'm not glad. It's awful here without you. It's awful here with you, too, but it's just a little bit better. Who brought you in? Was this your idea or someone else's? How long are you staying? Do you have a roommate?"

"Indy," I said, overwhelmed. "Give me a minute."

"Sure, of course," he said. He shoved his hands into the pockets of his sweatpants. "Commencing backing off." He took a couple tiny steps away from me. "Is this better?"

Indy—called that because he wore an Indianapolis 500 T-shirt most days of the week ("ironically," he insisted)—was loud and funny and irreverent. When I hung out with him and Michaela, I could sometimes forget we were on a psych ward.

"What happened to your eyebrows?" I asked.

He put his hand up to where little patches of hair were starting to grow back. "I thought they were snakes and so I shaved them off." He shrugged. "That was right before my parents brought me back. You know, paranoid delusions, suicidal ideation, NBD."

"I'm sorry," I said.

"Thanks," he said.

I noticed his fingers were ink-stained. Last time we were here together, Indy spent most of his time drawing labyrinthine M. C. Escher–like rooms on paper scraps, then filling in the margins with microscopic writing that Michaela swore contained the secrets of the universe. Once, when one of the aides made like he was trying to decipher it, Indy punched him.

"Walk with me?" Indy said. "Tell me everything about the other side." He leaned in and sniffed my hair. "You smell like freedom."

"I smell bad is more like it. I need a shower."

"Well, you'll have to wait," he said, tapping an invisible watch on his wrist. "Because right now it's slop time."

Of course. That was another thing I hadn't forgotten. If there was a higher power in a mental health unit, it wasn't God: it was the Almighty Schedule.

At Belman Psych, you ate your meals when it told you to. You went to group therapy when it told you to, and to individual therapy when it told you to. You took your medicine when it told you to, got your vitals checked when it told you to, and turned your lights out when it told you to.

And you did all those things again and again, day after day, until some doctor decided that you were better.

Or that you couldn't be helped.

Together Indy and I walked down the long, white hallway. There were a bunch of double rooms for patients on the right-hand side. On the other side was the nursing station, a few therapists' offices, and a small lounge with a kitchenette. We used to be able to use it to make popcorn, but then two patients got into a fistfight over the microwave and the nurses declared it off-limits.

At the end of the hall was the big room that served as the ward cafeteria on one side and the lounge on the other. The walls were painted a color that one of the nurses told us was called Serenity Peach.

An obvious example of wishful thinking, Indy had said.

Michaela called to us from a table in the corner, and we walked over and sat down with her. "It's lasagna day," she said.

Indy rubbed his hands together. "My favorite."

I couldn't tell if he was being serious, but my stomach was growling, and I was ready for whatever rolled up to us on the food cart. I watched its slow progress around the room, as a girl not much older than any of us passed out the plastic trays to all the ward residents. When she finally made her way over to us, I took my tray gratefully. There was the promised lasagna, plus yogurt in a plastic cup, a few pieces of broccoli, a packet of Oreos, and a carton of milk.

"Are we sure this is lasagna? Because it looks like a square of vomit," Michaela said mildly.

"Oh, shut up," said Indy. "You aren't going to eat it anyway."

"Not if I can help it," Michaela said.

Once Michaela had told me that she wanted to live on water and sunlight. It sounded so poetic and pretty, but the reality of starving herself was anything but: her skin yellowed, her fingernails turned brittle, and when she showered, clumps of her hair fell out.

She was doing better now, though. She didn't look as frail as she used to, and she was willingly depositing spoonfuls of yogurt into her mouth.

Me, I shoveled the food in like I hadn't eaten in days. And for all I knew, I hadn't. The lasagna was salty, tomatoey, cheesy—honestly, it was delicious.

Indy stabbed his spork ineffectually at a tough broccoli stem. "I hate plastic utensils. It makes every day the *worst* kind of picnic." He abandoned the spork and picked up the vegetable with his fingers. "We really did miss you, Han," he said.

"Indy left, too, you know," Michaela told me. "Then I was all alone."

"First of all, I was only gone for a month, which is pathetic. And secondly, you weren't alone," said Indy. "There's Beatrix and Kevin and Jade, plus Andy and Skye and Cayden...."

I knew a couple of the patients he pointed to; others I'd never seen before.

"You know I don't talk to them," Michaela said.

"What's stopping you?" Indy asked innocently.

"Gee, I don't know," Michaela said. "Beatrix creeps me out, Kevin can only talk about *World of Warcraft*, and Jade doesn't talk at all. Ugh, do I have to go through the whole list?"

"No." I opened my milk and drank half the carton in one gulp.

"What Michaela is trying to say is that she missed you, too," Indy said.

I swallowed, nodded. It was definitely weird to be welcomed back to a psychiatric ward. The way I saw it, being readmitted meant that normal life was a test you'd failed again.

Not that my life was what you'd call normal. But I knew that Indy and Michaela were trying to be nice.

"I missed you guys, too," I said.

"Julia died," Michaela blurted.

There was a sudden roaring in my ears. I closed my eyes and

clenched my fists as a wave of nausea flooded through me. These were words you never wanted to hear.

Julia had roomed with Michaela, too, once upon a time. Julia was from a little town in Connecticut, but she'd always talked in a British accent. She used to call me *Dahling* and *Duck*. She had the most beautiful copper hair I'd ever seen.

I remembered the last conversation we had. It was spring, and we were sitting in the hospital garden.

"I don't want this anymore," she'd said.

"You don't want what?" I'd innocently asked. Like she was talking about the granola bar Amy had given her.

She gestured to the trees, the flowers, the sky. To herself. "Life," she'd said. "I mean, I'm done. I don't know why no one can understand that."

I crumpled the juice cup in my hands.

"She killed herself on Christmas Eve," Michaela said.

I put my forehead down on the cool table and let all the feelings—sadness, resignation, and an awful, unexplainable relief—come over me in a rush.

Julia was dead and I was alive. This place was terrible. This place was home.

DELIA F. BELMAN MEMORIAL PSYCHIATRIC HOSPITAL PATIENT LOG

Date: 1/18/23, 8:35 p.m.
Name: Hannah Doe

PROGRESS REPORT: Pt fully lucid and
    cooperative but convinced she does
    not need to be hospitalized. Informal
    exchange in lounge prior to bedtime went
    approximately as follows:

    HD: I don't belong here, you know.
        I'm fine. Perfectly fine.

    RN: They found you screaming on a
        street corner. You didn't know
        where you were. You couldn't tell
        us your name.

    HD: Maybe that's true, but I'm great
        now. Today is January 18th, we're
        in New York City, and you can get
        70% off sale items at the Gap.

RN: You were barely dressed.

HD: It was a nice day.

RN: It was 29 degrees. Where did the scratches come from?

HD: Who cares? Put a Band-Aid on them and discharge me.

RN: If you're released and you have another episode, there might not be anyone around to help you.

HD: I'm willing to try my luck.

RN: You were screaming about the castle. People were dying.

HD: Sounds to me like a good reason to be screaming.

Pt angry at not being "let go." Stormed off with other pt, Adam "Indy" Rivera.

CHAPTER 10

J ordan Hassan is being followed.

Not by one of Belman's actual patients—that was Day 1—but by the unit's supervising psychiatrist, Dr. Francine Klein.

It doesn't take him long to decide that he'd rather be trailed by someone who thinks demons have put microchips under his skin than by someone with multiple advanced degrees and the ability to dismiss him from his brand-new duties with a single word.

Does it matter that these brand-new duties are, in effect, being a glorified volunteer? That's what his professor had called him. *You're there to learn whatever you can, but mostly to help the patients feel like they can interact with the outside world*, she'd said.

She'd also said that Jordan could learn a lot from Dr. Klein, who's one of New York's top psychiatrists. But right now Dr. Klein isn't saying anything to him. She's just … *walking right behind* him, silently, which is utterly nerve-racking.

But Jordan knows he'll never pass his Abnormal Psych class, let alone get into med school, if he can't last a week in his hospital internship, so he straightens his shoulders and walks into the patient lounge with his bag of tricks, a.k.a. the puzzles, card decks, and simple board games he's brought to make free time with the patients pass a little faster.

A young man comes lurching toward him, dragging one of his feet behind him.

"Good morning, Andy," Dr. Klein says amiably. "How are you feeling today?"

Andy is maybe nineteen years old, with greasy blond hair and watery blue eyes. "I'm dead," he says. "I can feel the damn bugs inside my skin. They're eating my liver."

When he careens away, Dr. Klein turns to Jordan. "Cotard's syndrome," she says. "He believes he died last week."

Jordan nods, like, *Yes, I am completely familiar with that diagnosis.* He makes a mental note to look it up later.

Then, to his utmost relief, Dr. Klein gives him one last look—her eyes so piercing he swears she can see right into his subconscious—and moves on, going to consult with one of the psychiatric nurses.

Jordan's about to see if a kid with acne-scarred cheeks wants to play Connect Four when Brittany, a mental health tech just a few years older than he is, comes over and pulls him aside.

"Come on," she says, "you can watch me do safety checks. They're a big part of our days around here."

Patients at the Delia F. Belman Memorial Psychiatric Hospital have to be checked on every thirty minutes, day and night. It's obvious why this level of monitoring is important—the whole point of a locked psych ward is to keep struggling, unhappy people *safe*—but Jordan still feels weird just walking down the hall and opening people's doors.

Brittany chatters about the current residents as they go, and he tries to keep their names and diagnoses straight. Andy: schizoaffective disorder. Beatrix: dissociative identity disorder. Sean: bipolar disorder, rapid cycling.

Brittany reaches for a door handle, which is specially designed so that no one can tie something around it and use it to strangle themselves. Soap dispensers, showerheads, grab bars, towel hooks: everything at Belman is what they call "ligature resistant."

"Safety check," Brittany calls as the door swings open to reveal a small, dim room. It's empty except for a wooden dresser and a low, narrow bed. Lying curled in a ball on the bed is the girl from yesterday morning.

The one who tried to run. Hannah.

Her cheeks are flushed pink, and her dark hair spills across the pillow.

He can't help remembering the way he grabbed her around her thin waist. How she'd struggled in his arms like she was fighting for her life. And how he had wondered, for a moment, if he should just let her go.

Her breathing comes slow and even now. Sleeping, she has no idea that he's staring at her, and for some reason knowing that feels even more invasive than walking in on the naked burpees in Room 3. She seems so small and so vulnerable. Jordan looks away, embarrassed.

"She's probably still tired from her...episode," Brittany says. "Plus the cafeteria lasagna is a lot of work to digest." She laughs.

"Do you know her?" Jordan asks.

"Yeah, she's what we call a frequent flyer. So are Michaela and Indy. The three of them are thick as thieves."

"Can I ask—" he begins, then stops. Does he want to know what disorders they've been diagnosed with, too?

But Brittany's already filling him in. "Michaela's been diagnosed with depression, body dysmorphic disorder, and anorexia.

Indy's got obsessive-compulsive disorder, experiences suicidal ideation, and is probably Bipolar two." Brittany gently shuts the door. "And Hannah—well, she's an odd one. But she's got schizophrenia in her chart."

"What do you mean she's an odd one?" Jordan asks.

Brittany sighs and suddenly looks older than twenty-two. "Let's just say that diagnoses are not necessarily a perfect science. Anyway, she's been on the ward dozens of times over the years." Her brow furrows. "But somehow, we know almost nothing about her. And we can't figure out how to help her."

They finish the rest of the safety checks in silence, and Jordan's on his way back to the lounge when he hears a piercing shriek— one that he immediately recognizes.

CHAPTER 11

He turns around and races back into the hall. He sees Hannah outside her room, kicking at the walls and pulling at fistfuls of her hair. She's crying and yelling something about a castle, and his heart starts pounding.

"Hey, you in the button-down! Give me a hand, man," says a nurse called Ron, who's trying to hold on to Hannah's arm.

Jordan hurries over, instinctively following directions. It hits him that for the second time in two days, this underfed, dark-haired girl is about to fight against his grip. It makes him feel awful, even as Ron looks at him expectantly and Jordan tells himself that this is to help a patient. He steels himself, then reaches out and catches her elbow. He puts his other hand reassuringly on her shoulder. She tries to shake him off.

"I'm sorry," he says, not that she hears. He's close enough that he can see her pulse beating in her neck. She's freaking out, and he's terrified.

"No!" she screams. "You can't keep us down here!"

"Come on, kiddo," Ron says. "Let's go to the quiet room." He looks to Jordan. "We're just gonna pick her up, okay?"

Jordan balks. You don't touch a girl *anywhere* without her consent: he's known this forever. The rules of the hospital world are different by necessity, everyone tells him that—but it doesn't matter. He doesn't want to do this. It doesn't feel right.

"Come on, man!" Ron says. "Help me out!"

Jordan grits his teeth. He's got to try. He watches the way Ron loops Hannah's arm around his neck, and he's willing himself to try it, too, when Amy comes barreling down the hall and nearly shoves him out of the way. He watches as Amy grabs Hannah's hand, ducks down and wraps Hannah's arm around her shoulders.

Hannah's feet are kicking wildly as they pull her down the hall. Her screams pierce his eardrums.

With a nurse on either side of her, Hannah is carried down the hall to the seclusion room. It's a tiny space, with nothing in it but a vinyl mattress pushed into the corner. It looks like a jail cell.

"Let's go, Hannah," Ron says through gritted teeth. "You can do it."

Hannah fights blindly. Chaotically. Jordan can barely stand to watch. It's just too awful. He came to Belman to help people—not to stand by while they're dragged screaming into a place they don't want to be. Amy lets go as Ron slides around behind Hannah and picks her up around the waist. It's an ugly struggle, but he gets her all the way in. Once she's in the middle of the room, he releases her.

The next thing Jordan knows he's hearing the click of the lock as Ron comes back out, wiping sweat from his forehead.

"So…she just *stays* there now?" Jordan asks. He's shaking. They're going to leave her in that *cage*?

"Some patients like it," Ron says. "They can't scream in the TV room, but in there they can yell as much as they want to." He shrugs. "And they eventually calm down. I mean, what else is there to do in there?"

Through the tiny window, which is reinforced with chicken wire, Jordan watches Hannah fall to her knees on the mattress. Is she...*praying*?

Mitch, another RN, comes up beside them. "A bit of Haldol would make it all better."

"Dr. Klein doesn't want us to administer another chemical restraint unless absolutely necessary," Ron says.

Mitch turns to Jordan. "Welcome to the loony bin," he says. "Having fun yet?"

Jordan feels his shoulders slump. Even with the heavy door shut tight, he can hear when Hannah starts screaming again.

Chapter 12

*M**y name is Hannah Dory, and I am a traitor and a thief.*

It was just past dawn when the castle guards lowered the drawbridge and the gatehouse's iron portcullis rose with a metallic shriek. The crowd of merchants and laborers waiting to enter surged forward. I slipped in at the back, behind a rickety hay cart and a pair of skinny, devil-eyed goats led by a boy no older than Conn.

Just keep your head down, I told myself, *and the guards won't even notice you.*

This morning there were two of them, clad in mail and armed with daggers and pikes. Their cold eyes swept the crowd for beggars, pickpockets, and anyone who didn't have proper business in the baron's domain. Every few moments they called out, halting the line's progress.

"State your business," said the bearded guard to a man hunched under a basket of fabric.

The man tried to bow, even though he was halfway to the ground already. "Silks for the table, sir."

The guard yanked out bolts of shimmering red and purple cloth like they were rags. Peering into the basket and seeing nothing out of order, he grunted and shoved the sullied cloth back into the man's arms. "Go!"

The line moved forward again, and I shuffled along at its rear, keeping my eyes lowered. I heard the guards greet a merchant by name, then turn away an old beggar by threatening to throw him into the dry moat.

I was getting closer.

"Halt," the nearest guard called to the driver of the rattling hay cart.

The whole line stopped as the baron's men came forward. The bearded one grabbed the horse's harness while the other stabbed into the hay with his weapon.

"Do they always do this?" I whispered to the woman nearest me.

She spat onto the ground. "Always got to search for sommat what shouldn't be in there," she said. "The baron don't trust no one."

I thought of the rope I'd coiled tightly around my waist, hidden beneath my kirtle. If the guards stopped *me*—

I didn't finish the thought, because someone shoved me from behind. The guards had found nothing; it was time to move again.

Keep your head down. You're nothing and no one. You're invisible.

I watched the twitching tails of the goats, but as I neared the castle entrance, I allowed myself a quick glance up. Through the gatehouse passage, I could see the courtyard beyond.

I was almost inside.

Suddenly the bearded guard was in front of me, blocking my way. "And who might you be?" he asked in a rough, ugly voice.

Fear nearly closed my throat. "I'm a—I'm a washerwoman," I said. "Sir."

He put his hand on the knife at his hip. "No, you're not. I know 'em, and they're all ugly cows."

"Not that it stops you from ruttin' on 'em day and night," yelled the other guard over the heads of the crowd. "Ya hairy old bull!"

A soft ripple of laughter made the bearded guard flush with anger. "Piss off, Finnet," he growled. He turned back to me. "Who are you, and what do you want?"

My name is Hannah Dory, and I am a thief and a liar.

"I'm old Berna's niece," I said. "You must know her. She's been washing for the baron since before I was born."

The guard narrowed his eyes. "And where's good old Berna today?"

"She's taken ill, so she sent me in her place."

"Is that so? A pretty thing like you to wash the baron's underthings?"

I nodded as meekly as I could bear to. "Yes, sir."

He took up a fistful of my skirt and gave it a tug. "Maybe I'll find you later, Berna's niece," he said leeringly. "You can show me what's under these rags."

Gritting my teeth, I nodded as though I thought this was a fine idea. *I just need to get through the gate.*

"You and your prick are holding up the line, Gorn!" said the second guard. "There's ale in that cart back there, damn it, and it'd better be inside for breakfast."

The guard called Gorn was so close to me now that I could feel his hot, foul breath on my cheeks. "You can pass by for a kiss, little niece."

My stomach twisted in disgust. *It's just a kiss,* I told myself. *And a small price to pay to save your family.*

I pursed my lips. Gorn leaned in, grinning. His teeth were black and half rotted. "That's a good girl," he said. His hand reached up and grabbed my breast.

And then—*dear God please help me, though I know you won't*—I spat in his face.

Chapter 13

S houts rang out behind me as I flung myself past the guard and ran forward into the passageway. Pushing my way through the crowd, I knocked the silk seller sideways. Hands reached out to stop me but I dodged them all, bursting out of the gatehouse and into the courtyard of the outer bailey.

I stopped and looked around wildly. Where to now? There were people and livestock everywhere, and the air was so full of noise that I couldn't even hear the shouting guards. But I knew they were close behind me, and that I couldn't run more without being spotted.

In the shadow of a towering battlement, I scanned right and left for a hiding spot. Then, just a little ways up ahead, I saw the battered hay cart slowly rolling away. Bending down low, I hurried toward it as quickly as I dared. When I reached it, I clambered into the back and covered myself with the itchy golden stalks. The driver continued on as if nothing had happened.

Perhaps, as far as he was concerned, nothing had.

My heart was beating so hard it seemed like it could leap right out of my chest, and I willed it to slow as the cart clattered its way toward the stables.

When a groom called out, the cart jolted to a stop. I slithered to the back of the cart as the men began to haggle over the price of the fodder. Lifting myself over the rails, I dropped to the ground and scurried into the stable. I ducked into the corner of the nearest empty stall, shaking with fear and praying no one had seen me.

I stayed in the stall until the weak sun had climbed well into the sky. Then I got up, brushed the hay from my clothes, and walked into the courtyard as if I belonged there. I saw no guards—only blacksmiths, farriers, and groomsmen. High on the wall, stone-masons were repairing a damaged drum tower.

"Where are the kitchens?" I called to a serving boy hurrying past.

He slowed down, just barely. "In the inner bailey, where else?"

When he saw my blank look, he flung his arm out to the left. "By the gardens. In the *keep*." Then he raced on, muttering about stupid girls who couldn't understand directions.

Rude little git.

Continuing deeper into the castle grounds, I passed a handful of men loading logs into a kiln, and others building what looked to be a huge wooden cage. Servants brushed by me on either side, carrying fresh rushes and armfuls of linen.

All this, to serve one man, while we'd brawl in the street for a single loaf of bread!

At the far end of the outer bailey was another stone wall and another gate. This one was narrower, with two guards at either end, but I passed through without incident. Once inside, I was in the castle's innermost grounds. To my left was the baron's chapel, which was ten times the size of our village church, with windows of colored glass. Beyond that, casting its long shadow on the ground, was the keep itself: a narrow tower of black stone, its dark face brightened by blood-red flags emblazoned with a golden stag.

To its right lay the vast garden, its leafless fruit trees and grapevines waiting for spring. Chickens pecked here and there in the dirt. A handful of sheep, clustered in a narrow pen near the butcher's wooden lean-to, shifted nervously as I neared.

They seemed to know they were doomed, but I wasn't the one with the knife.

To my left, on the keep's ground floor, I saw the castle's kitchens. I crept closer and peered into the larger one. Spitboys turned freshly butchered animals over crackling fires, while cooks chopped winter vegetables for stew. The smells—of spices, roasting onions, and charring meat—were overpowering. I was a stray dog, drooling at food that was never meant for me.

"More turnips," shouted the red-faced cook nearest me.

A small boy who'd been lurking in the corner leapt up as if struck. A moment later, he scuttled down a set of stairs just to my left.

Silently I followed him.

After a few paces down a dark, narrow hall, we entered a cellar storeroom. Humming tunelessly, the boy moved among sacks and barrels, hunting for the turnips by the light of a small candle.

I, meanwhile, began to look for something else.

Somewhere below the kitchens lay another passageway, one that ran beneath the castle walls and ended in a small opening above the moat. Before years of drought narrowed the Vernet River and dried up the moat, boats had brought meat and grains from the fertile south, which was lifted from their hulls and pulled through the tunnel straight into the cellar storerooms.

That, anyway, was what crazy old Zenna had promised. And I prayed that she was right.

Chapter 14

*I*f sneaking into the castle had been terrifying, waiting in the frigid underground was a thousand times worse. I'd found the mouth of the tunnel—Zenna hadn't been crazy about that—but I was certain that the men from my village would change their minds. They'd never approved of me or my wild ideas. What if they simply went to bed hungry again, convinced this was another one of my fancies?

Otto will come, at least, I thought. *Won't he?*

From the tunnel I watched as darkness spilled down the hill and into the valley. The cold seemed to seep into my bones, and my hopes sank as the hours passed. Pressed against black stone, I listened to rats scuttling in the cellars and the sound of my heart beating in quiet terror.

My name is Hannah Dory, and I have made a terrible mistake.

At some point, I must have fallen asleep, because I woke to the churring call of the nightjar. I got up with a start, banging my head against the low ceiling. It was Otto's signal! He'd come!

I scrambled over to the opening. I could see nothing below, but I let down the rope that I'd smuggled in around my waist, the other end of which I'd tied to the grate at the tunnel's entrance. I held my breath as the rope tightened, bearing the weight of a climbing man.

I could hear his torturously slow progress. Every scrape of shoe against rock sent a shiver of dread through me. Could the guards, high on the castle walls, hear it, too? Any moment might come the hiss of arrows.

Fed or dead, fed or dead, I whispered. *Either way, our troubles will be over.*

Moments later, hands appeared at the mouth of the tunnel, and Otto's straining face appeared in the opening as he pulled himself the rest of the way up. For a moment he lay sprawled on the stone, breathing hard.

"That's more difficult than it looks," he said, righting himself.

"You made it!" I whispered, relief flooding my body. I wanted to fling myself into his arms.

He leaned forward and took my face between his hands. "You are a mad genius, Hannah Dory," he said. And then he kissed me with warm, soft lips until I pushed him away, breathless. "We have work to do," I reminded him.

We moved deeper into the tunnel as Maraulf and Merrick clambered up to join us.

"Just Vazi now, right?" I asked.

Otto looked away.

"Is he not coming?" I asked, panicked. "He's the strongest of all of us!"

Otto still would not look at me. "Oh, he's coming," he said.

Sure enough, the rope was pulled tight, and soon I could hear the grunting final effort of his ascent.

"Almost here," Otto said softly.

But when I saw Vazi, I gasped in horror. Because on his back he carried my sister, Mary.

Chapter 15

*W*hat on earth possessed you?" I hissed as we crept through the tunnel leading to the storeroom. "I *know* you always want to be included, but this is dangerous!"

"I want to help," Mary said firmly. She sounded so much older all of a sudden. Was this what losing two brothers had done to her?

Though I couldn't see her face, I could easily guess her expression: her jaw set firm, her pretty brows in a stubborn frown. *I'm here*, it said, *and there's nothing you can do about it now.*

She was right, of course, and all I could do was pray our mother wouldn't wake from one of her nightmares to find all but one of her children gone. "You have to keep close to me the whole time," I said. When she didn't answer, I said urgently, "Mary—promise me! I can't let anything happen to you."

"Yes, Hannah, I promise," she said. "I'll stay close."

I gave her hand a quick squeeze, and she squeezed back, hard. My heart swelled in my chest. I loved her more than anyone. I would keep her safe, no matter what.

Only the rats were awake as we crept out of the storeroom and climbed the stairs. Even giant Vazi was as quiet as a shadow.

I barely allowed myself to breathe as we entered the kitchen.

Coals in the hearth lit the walls with a dim red light. I scanned the room, peering into the corners for sleeping cooks or spitboys.

The way was clear, and my breath came out in a rush. Maraulf, whose sack was already bulging with apples, root vegetables, and nuts from the cellar, shouldered his way in and gave a low whistle. "There's enough to feed the village till June."

His son hurried over to a low table along the wall, on which lay the remains of the night's dinner: meat suspended inside a jelly made of calves' hooves, smoked fish, dove pie, pears boiled in wine, spices, and honey.

"Someone didn't do the cleaning up," Merrick said reproachfully.

"Well, then, it's a good thing we're here to help out, isn't it?" said Otto. "The baron should thank us."

Maraulf tore a hunk of bread from a loaf as he looked over the offerings. "Take all the food you can fit in your sacks," he said, "but be sure you can still carry them. We're a long way from home."

"Baron Joachim eats all this?" Mary whispered to me in wonder. "Is he even bigger than Vazi?"

I swept a wedge of cheese into my sack. "When I saw him, he was a boy hardly bigger than Conn."

That was ten years ago now at least, when he rode through our village beneath his father's banners, wearing a child-sized suit of gleaming armor. Baron Jorian was giving Joachim a tour of everything he'd one day inherit: forests, villages, meadows, lands that stretched even farther than the eye could see.

We villagers went out, dressed in our finest, to greet him. And I'd never forget the way he'd looked down at us from the back of his shining black horse—like we were lower than livestock. Like we might as well have been mud.

As Joachim's procession passed, Otto had reached down, picked up a handful of horse manure, and flung it after them. It missed the mark, or else Otto would've been flogged in the square. It wouldn't have mattered that he was only eight; they would have stripped the skin from his spine. As it was, his own father beat him cruelly, because a boy—even a doctor's son—must know his place in the world.

The incident had terrified me, but I didn't know if Otto even remembered it.

"The baron has many, many men to feed," I said to Mary. "Knights, guards, men-at-arms, craftsmen, gardeners—"

"And gong farmers," Otto whispered, appearing at my side and grinning.

"What's that?" Mary asked him.

Otto slung his arm around her thin shoulders. "A job you wouldn't want if it fed you like a queen," he said. He bent close to her ear and said, "A gong farmer goes down into the privies and cleans 'em out with his shovel."

Mary shuddered; she hated filth of any kind. But then she said, "I'd do it if it would help my family."

Otto laughed. "Ah, you're right to say so, Mary. Any of us would serve the baron, however he wanted us to, if it meant our survival."

"But as it is, we must steal to live," I said. "So let's hurry up and finish what we came for, shall we?"

Chapter 16

I was shoving salted bacon into my sack when I noticed Merrick huddled in a corner, ripping enormous bites out of a leg of roasted peacock. I could even hear his teeth cracking the bones.

"Merrick," I said. "We eat *later*!"

He shook his head. "Too hungry," he said, his mouth so full he could barely speak.

Otto, laughing, held a piece of pale white bread close to my lips. "We need strength for the stealing, love! Open up."

My mouth watered. I couldn't resist. Against my better judgment, I let him feed it to me. I closed my eyes at the soft, sweet wonder of it. I'd never had anything so fine. It tasted like hope. Like life itself.

"The baron would surely be pleased to see you enjoying his bread so much," Otto said. "Too bad he's asleep in his fine bed, ignorant of the peasants helping themselves to his leftovers!"

"I'll wager he's a drunk, like his father," said Maraulf.

"I'll wager he's a spindly weakling, with a prick no bigger than this," said Merrick, holding a limp, cooked parsnip between his legs.

Vazi's shoulders shook with laughter, and Otto covered his mouth to stifle a guffaw.

"Enough talking! More stealing!" I said, now grabbing at

whatever I could reach. Bread, cheese, sausages all got swept into my sack, and the heavier the sack got, the better I felt. My plan was *working*. We wouldn't have to starve.

The others were quiet now, swiftly taking all that they could. I tucked eggs into the bodice of my dress and lowered a block of salt into my bag.

My name is Hannah Dory, and I have saved us.

When my bag was full to bursting and I had to bend under its weight, I called to the rest of them softly. "All right, we've been here long enough."

Maraulf nodded, slinging his sack over his shoulder with a grunt. I looked around for Mary—she was in the corner, pulling little wheels of cheese from a basket. "Mary," I said. "We need to go!"

She turned around, her face alight with relief. "Yes, Hannah, *let's*," she whispered. "I'm scared."

"We'll be safe outside in a matter of minutes," I assured her.

Then Vazi, reaching for a flagon of wine, knocked a poker into a kettle.

It rang like a bell.

For a moment, we froze where we stood. From across the room, Mary's frightened eyes met mine. Her sack dropped from her trembling hands with a thud. I started inching toward the stairs, motioning for her to follow. *Leave it*, I silently begged. *Come with me. Now!*

The castle was quiet, and for a moment I allowed myself to hope that no guards had heard.

Into the tunnel, and then we'll be safe!

I was at the top of the stairs when the night exploded around us—shouts, footsteps, and the hiss of knives drawn from their sheaths.

"Run!" I shouted.

It will naturally be asked by what sign is a man or woman to know when they are threatened with a breakdown.

By no one sign in particular. One cloud does not make a wet day. It is only when other clouds begin to gather and we feel a certain change in the atmosphere that we surmise that rain is coming. The signs which warn us of the approach of a storm are almost too indefinite for words.

from *Nervous Breakdowns and How to Avoid Them*
by CHARLES D. MUSGROVE, MD
NEW YORK, FUNK & WAGNALLS COMPANY, 1913

CHAPTER 17

The soft, breathy voice blows right into the ear of Belman Hospital's newest intern. "She's not *going* anywhere, you know."

Jordan Hassan spins around to see Michaela from Room 12 standing barely an inch away from him. Her skin is yellowish—is it malnutrition?—and her eyes are such a pale blue that they seem almost drained of color. She gives him a sideways smirk because she's snuck up on him. Because she's caught him peering into the quiet room again.

"I'm just checking on her," he says quickly. "It's part of my assignment."

Michaela nods slyly, like, *How come I haven't seen you checking on* me *every two-point-five minutes?* Then her expression softens. "It sucks in there," she says quietly. "It's so lonely. And it's always freezing cold."

Jordan hazards another glance through the window. Someone took Hannah's shoes and socks away, and this morning, when Jordan asked if she could have a blanket, the nurse had told him no.

"We can't have her trying to strangle herself with it," she'd said matter-of-factly. "Or stuffing it into her mouth to try to choke herself." Seeing the alarmed look on his face, she'd added, "People can hurt themselves with just about anything. Blankets, a staple, paper towels, a plastic spoon, you name it."

Jordan can see Hannah darting around inside the room now. Her bare feet make little slapping sounds on the tile floor.

"I take it you've been in?" he says to Michaela.

She nods. "I hate it. It's also haunted."

Now she must be messing with me, he thinks. "What do you mean?"

Michaela exhales in a long, slow sigh and says, "Not to be, like, super dramatic or anything, but that room is basically filled with the echoes of mad girls' screams." She steps up to the glass and looks in on her friend. "When you're alone in there, you can hear them."

"That sounds . . . spooky," Jordan allows.

"Those walls know our secrets," Michaela says. Then she spins around and flings her arms up in the air. "So whatever! Who cares! Let's go get some Paxil!"

"Didn't you get some at med pass this morning?" he asks.

"Sure, but it's *always* time for medication," Michaela says. "Drugs! Can't live with 'em, can't live without 'em! Wouldn't you enjoy a pop of Ativan right now?"

Jordan's wondering whether to feel amused or worried when Hannah's voice comes ringing through the door.

"Run!" she screams. "Run!"

Jordan pushes Michaela out of the way so he can see in again. Hannah is crouched down in the corner, pleading with someone only she can see.

"Mary!" she cries, and there's terror in her voice. "Oh, god, oh, god—don't hurt my sister!" She collapses. Then she's still. Silent.

Jordan gives an involuntary shiver, and Michaela puts her hand on his arm. He lets it stay there for a moment before he steps away. *No physical contact.*

"I'm going to get Dr. Klein," he says.

"She won't like to be bothered," Michaela warns.

Too bad, Jordan thinks. He's not going to pretend like something terrible's not happening in that room.

Dr. Klein looks up from her desk when Jordan walks in, and Michaela was right: she's not at all pleased by the intrusion.

"I'm sorry to interrupt you," he says, "but Hannah's really upset. She's saying—"

"I'm not Hannah's therapist," Dr. Klein says smoothly. "That's Dr. Nicholas, and she'll see him tomorrow." She taps something into her computer, and Jordan stands there, waiting, feeling like an idiot. "And I'm not her RN, either," she adds. "If Hannah needs PRN medication, per her chart, a nurse can take care of it."

"But she's saying her sister's been stabbed."

Dr. Klein says, "Who, Mary?"

Jordan nods. How'd she know?

The doctor picks up a pencil and points it right at him. "To be successful here, Jordan, you'll need to be able to tell when a patient is delusional."

"I'm not saying her sister has actually been *stabbed*," he protests. "I just meant—Hannah's really upset."

"That's what the quiet room is for," Dr. Klein says.

But it's a prison, he thinks.

Dr. Klein tucks the pencil behind her ear. "We've found that Hannah actually does better if we let her work through these… episodes, I'd call them, in a safe space," she says. "One minute she's here with us, aware of everything around her, and the next moment it's like she's gone, her body left behind. There's no getting through to her, no awareness. You can even see the moment it happens. When Hannah goes deep down into her mind, she goes into a place we can't understand. A place we can't reach her, no matter how hard we try."

"And is that...typical of a schizophrenia diagnosis?" Jordan asks hesitantly.

"We've come to understand that schizophrenia is not a single disease or a unifying diagnosis," Dr. Klein says. "It's better understood as a group of mental health disorders with a set of co-occurring psychotic symptoms." She takes a sip of coffee from a chipped old Zoloft coffee mug. "And believe me, it's a good thing that our understanding of schizophrenia is evolving. Up until the fifties, *lobotomies* were considered an answer to the diagnosis. A miracle cure, in fact."

Jordan shudders. Just last week he'd read about the transorbital lobotomy, which was when a doctor took an ice pick, hammered it into a patient's eye socket above their eyeball, and then stirred the pick around in the brain's frontal lobes.

"Hannah has extended periods of lucidity," Dr. Klein goes on. "But then some stimulus—external or internal, we can't really predict—can send her into her fantasy world."

"Where is that fantasy world?" he asks.

"The more interesting question is actually *when*," Dr. Klein says. "If memory serves, the year is 1347. England, perhaps, or maybe some other part of what's now the UK. Now if you'll excuse me, I need to get back to work."

Chapter 18

A scream tore itself from my throat as guards burst into the cavernous castle kitchen.

"Run, Mary!" I cried. *"Run!"*

It was too late. I pressed myself against the wall as two men charged past me in pursuit of Maraulf, who was trying to slip out the back passageway. His son, Merrick, grabbed a poker from the hearth and swung it like a sword. Another guard lunged at Otto, who flung his heavy sack into the side of the man's head, knocking him to his knees.

"Go, Hannah—leave us!" Otto yelled.

The cellar staircase was only inches away, but I couldn't go without my sister. Mary was somewhere in the dark, invisible behind the attacking enemy. I tried to weave my way toward where I'd last seen her.

"Mary!" I shouted. *"Mary!"*

Plates and kettles crashed to the ground as Maraulf struggled against two burly men who had him by his arms. Merrick had bloodied his assailant with the poker, but then another guard slammed him up against a wall and pressed the tip of a dagger into the skin of his throat. Before I could reach him, a guard grabbed me, spinning me around at the same time his other fist smashed into my temple.

Stars exploded before my eyes. Blindly I reached out for a weapon, my hands scrabbling across the table until my fingers closed around the neck of a wine decanter. I struck the guard across the nose with the leaden jug. Blood mixed with wine dripped down his face, but he laughed as if I'd tickled him. He grabbed for me again, and his grimy fingers caught the bodice of my dress, ripping it almost to my waist.

I kicked his knees and clawed at his eyes. I felt his skin shredding beneath my nails, but he was so much bigger and stronger. He struck me again, and I felt the skin on my cheek open up. When I staggered forward, he caught me, pulled me up, and punched me again.

Out of the blurry corner of my eye I saw Otto and a guard circling around each other, each holding a knife and dancing away from each other's swings.

"Mary, where are you?" I yelled.

The guard kept hitting me on the arms, the chest. He could have killed me right then and there, but he seemed to enjoy raining his fists down onto my body. I could hardly see from the blood in my eyes. Every blow pushed air out of my lungs. I fell to the ground, bracing myself for another attack.

Then I saw the cook's knife, gleaming dully on the floor. I flung myself toward it. When the guard tried to catch me, I leapt out from under the table and sliced the blade across the front of his shins. As he backed away in surprise and pain, I rose up and cut him straight across his midsection. He fell screaming, fingers clutching madly at the wound as his entrails spilled themselves onto the floor.

"Mary!" I sobbed, the dripping red knife still clutched in my hand. "I'm coming!"

I thought I saw her—her pale dress, her golden hair—dodging the blows of another guard. "Go! Run to the tunnel!"

If we could just shut the grate behind us, it would buy us enough time to get out. The forest was a stone's throw away on the other side of the moat, and once we made it into the trees, they'd never find us.

I saw a guard's blade fall in a savage arc and cut Merrick's hand off at the wrist. I ran forward, jumping over Maraulf, who was writhing on the floor in agony. Where was Otto? Where had Mary gone?

We are all going to die.

Finally I found my sister. Her dress was torn, and she was shivering and pleading in a corner. Her little hands were raised in a gesture of surrender to the guard who loomed menacingly over her. "Please," she gasped. "Please no."

I rushed forward, aiming for right between his shoulder blades. But even as I lifted my knife, he plunged his dagger down.

"Mary!" I screamed.

When she fell, her mouth open in horror, I fell, too. I clawed my way across the blood-slick floor toward her.

I was nearly to her—she was almost in my arms—when something struck me from behind, and all the world went black.

CHAPTER 19

I awoke, rigid with terror. There was cold bright light everywhere, and I was alone.

Am I hurt?

Am I dead?

"Mary!" I cried out. "Mary!"

There was no answer. As my eyes adjusted to the light, I understood that my sister was gone.

Or maybe I should say that *I* was gone.

I wasn't in the baron's castle anymore. I was in the quiet room on Ward 6.

I didn't know what time it was, or even what day it was. I only knew that I was lying half on the bare floor and half on a thin, hard mattress.

I sat up and put my hand to my cheek, feeling the unbroken smoothness of my skin. There was no gash, no blood.

It's because the other world isn't real, Hannah: that's what everyone told me.

They were wrong. It *was* real. It was real and true and I needed to go back. I needed to make sure Mary was okay.

But I couldn't get there by wishing, no matter how hard I tried. I'd have to wait until the way into that world opened up again.

I just never knew when that would be.

I plugged my ears so I could yell as loud as I could. "Get me out of here!"

Pretty soon I heard footsteps coming down the hall. A few seconds later, the concerned face of the new hospital intern appeared in the window. What was his name again? His black hair tumbled over his forehead, and he pushed it back with the easy grace of habit.

"Are you okay?" His voice was muffled through the door.

Do I look *okay?* I thought. "I need help," I said. "I need to get out of here."

"I talked to Dr. Klein," the intern said. "She says you'll see your therapist this afternoon. Do you need PRN meds? I can ask Nurse Amy…"

PRN stood for pro re nata, or "as needed." In other words, did I want a blast of tranqs or something? The answer was no.

"I don't want pills and I don't want to see Dr. N!" I said. "I want to…" I paused. How could I possibly explain it to him?

I closed my eyes. I just wanted to go back to Mary. But I couldn't make it happen, and I hated feeling so helpless. Tears pricked hot behind my eyelids. When they spilled over, I opened my eyes and wiped them away.

"What's the matter, Hannah?" the intern asked. He actually sounded concerned. Not like Mitch, who'd just wave to me through the window as he walked by on his rounds, like, *Have a nice day, nutjob!*

I couldn't stand being alone in here. So I said, "Come inside and I'll tell you."

"I don't know if that's a good idea," he said.

"Why not?"

"Well, the last time I saw you, you were fighting the staff."

I crossed my arms in front of my chest. "I'm not going to attack you," I said, "if that's what you're worried about." I held up the first three fingers of my right hand. "Scout's honor. Anyway, you could totally take me in a fight. You're a foot and a half taller than I am."

He gave a nervous smile. "I just...I think you're supposed to be taking it easy."

That made me laugh. Take it *easy*? In the quiet room? A person could go seriously insane in here.

But I could tell my weird sense of humor wasn't helping my case, so I sat down on the mattress and smiled as reassuringly as I could at him. Was that sympathy I saw in those agate eyes? I hoped so.

"Please come in," I said. "I need you to understand. I think you might be the only one who can."

CHAPTER **20**

What do I do now? Jordan thinks. This is way above his pay grade. He looks up and down the hallway, but no one else is coming to help.

Meanwhile Hannah's in there, pleading with him to listen to her, and he can't just walk away. She looks so distraught. So alone.

The door is locked. But he has a keycard, so nothing's stopping him from going in. And so, a moment later, he does. He realizes instantly that Michaela was right: it's freezing in there. And yeah, it's spooky, too.

Hannah pats the vinyl mattress, and Jordan hesitates only for a second before sitting down next to her.

"Hi," he says, and then he doesn't have any idea what to say next.

"What's your name again?" she asks.

"Jordan," he says. "Jordan Hassan."

"Well, Jordan Hassan, I'm Hannah. It's nice to meet you," she says. "I wish it could be under different circumstances, of course." She flashes a sudden and surprising smile. "Like, it'd be better if we started talking because we were next to each other on the F train. Or what if we'd met because we wanted the same apple from the fruit cart on 45th? That'd be nicer, right, than you letting yourself into my jail cell?" Her voice is low and lilting—musical, even.

"Maybe," Jordan says, smiling back at her, oddly charmed. "But I don't think the F's so great, do you? Maybe we should have met in a coffee shop. Or in line for a movie."

"That sounds great," she agrees. "As long as it's not a horror movie."

He shakes his head. "No way. I saw *Sinister* when I was a kid, and then I was scared for two whole weeks."

"That's cute," Hannah says. "Did you learn your lesson?"

"Yeah, I stuck with Disney movies for about a decade after that." It's an exaggeration, but barely.

Her laugh's even more musical than her voice. "*Jungle Cruise* is your jam, huh?"

"I'll see anything with The Rock in it," he says, and this is definitely *not* an exaggeration.

He's surprised at how easy it is to sit in the quiet room with Hannah, and how perfectly *regular* she seems right now. She could be a girl in one of his classes, or down the hall in his dorm. How is it that only yesterday she was carried into the room kicking and screaming?

She fiddles with her tangled hair. "So you're new here," she says.

He nods. "Very." *And don't tell anyone, but it's kind of overwhelming.*

"I'm going to let you in on a little secret," she says.

"What?"

"I don't belong here," she whispers.

Jordan's not surprised to hear this. He's been interning for less than a week, and this is the twentieth time someone has spoken that sentence. He asks, "At Belman? Or in the quiet room?"

"I mean in this *century*," Hannah says.

To be successful here, Jordan, you'll need to be able to tell when a patient is delusional...

Maybe Hannah sees a flicker of doubt cross his face, or maybe she just changes her mind. She says, "Actually—forget that. Never mind."

"No, please," he says, not wanting to shut her down. *Engage with the patients*, Amy had said to him. *Be open and friendly.* "I wish you'd keep going."

She sighs. Her shoulders slump. "Do you know what it feels like to not be believed?"

Jordan gives a half shrug. "The summer before college, my brother hid a handle of whiskey in my closet, and my parents couldn't be convinced it wasn't mine. Does that count?" he asks.

Hannah rolls her eyes. "Barely," she says. "But if that's what we have to work with…" Then she gets up and goes to look out the tiny window into the hall. Jordan sees her wave to someone. "That's Mitch on safety check," she says to him. "I'm just letting him know that I'm fine."

"Nice of you," he says.

"Not really, I just don't want him bothering me," she says. She smiles again. "Bothering *us*." She sits back down next to him. "I might like talking to you, Jordan Hassan. Is that weird?"

He feels a nervous jolt of pleasure. Already he can tell that he likes talking to her, too. For one thing, it makes him feel like he might be able to do a good job here. For another, she's surprising and curious and crackling with energy. Despite the fact that she's locked in a room, wearing shapeless, invalid clothes, with hair that hasn't seen a brush in weeks, there's an aura of assurance about her right now. Of charisma—power, even.

"So do you want to hear what I have to say?" she asks.

"Yes, I want to hear what you have to say," he says. "And I want to believe it, too."

CHAPTER **21**

O kay," she says. "Basically what you need to understand is that I live *here*, in the twenty-first century, but I also have a life in the fourteenth century. And it's as real as this one."

Even though Dr. Klein had warned him, he's surprised to hear her say it.

"I know how that sounds," she goes on, "but I promise I'm not insane, and I'm not lying. It's been happening for years. I've lived two lives, in two different centuries, for almost as long as I can remember."

Hannah's voice is so calm and matter-of-fact; it's like she's telling him that her favorite color is blue. Jordan stares at the blank wall of the quiet room while he tries to take this in, but he can tell Hannah is looking at him. Trying to gauge his reaction.

I want to hear what you have to say, he'd just told her. *And I want to believe it.*

He keeps his face open. Neutral. Whatever happens, he wants her to trust him. He's on her side.

Hallucinations are perception-like experiences that occur without an external stimulus, says the *DSM-5*, the bible of mental disorders. *They are vivid and clear, with the full force and impact of normal perceptions, and not under voluntary control.*

"Basically," Hannah says, "I'm able to go back and forth in time."

Without meaning to, Jordan blurts, "But that's impossible."

"A lot of things seem impossible," Hannah says, unperturbed. "But it's really just because they can't be explained. No one knows why a muon does what it does, for example."

"A what?" he says. He suddenly feels like his head's spinning.

"It's a subatomic particle that basically disobeys the laws of physics. Scientists can't figure out what's going on with it. Just like doctors and therapists can't figure out how I go back and forth in time."

"Okay," Jordan says cautiously. Maybe he should ask the dark-haired girl in his dorm, the one who's always reading a physics textbook, if she knows anything about muons. Or maybe he should ask Hannah if the Middle Ages are as awful as his high school history class made them sound—like they were nothing but privation, bloodletting, and lice.

"Life's definitely a lot easier here," Hannah goes on, almost like she's just read his mind. "I'm not hungry all the time, for one thing. There's running water and electricity, which are basically miracles, and I don't always have to wear the same filthy dress." She gets up and begins pacing around the room. "But in my other life, we have a strip of land we plant in spring, and this year we were going to get a goat—Mary wanted to name her Sally—and Mother said we might be able to get a pig we can fatten up on acorns..."

Her eyes have a distant look in them now, and her hands flutter in the air as she speaks. "I don't have anyone here," she says. "There, I've got a family. We have a little cottage. My father's gone, but there's my mother and my brother and my sister..."

Suddenly Hannah's crying, and Jordan doesn't know what

to do. He wanted to help her by listening, but it seems to have backfired.

"It's winter now, and everyone's dying. There's sickness in the village. I've lost two brothers already—"

"But you're here now, aren't you?" Jordan interrupts, his voice gentle. "And I'm here with you. You're not alone. You're safe."

She clenches her fists. "But *they* aren't safe! My family's starving, I don't know what happened to Otto, and a guard stabbed Mary! She's going to die if I don't get back to help her!"

Hannah's volume rises by the second; she looks like she's about to get hysterical. Jordan fingers the Call button on his lanyard—should he press it?

He doesn't have to. A passing nurse hears Hannah's screaming and comes into the room. When the nurse tries to lay a calming hand on Hannah's arm, Hannah spins away and takes a swing at her.

"I have to get to Mary!"

Jordan backs away. Hannah's gone again, caught up in whatever hallucination she keeps having.

The nurse tries to talk her down, but that doesn't work. Another nurse appears with a needle. Hannah cries and slaps at them. She fights them, but she can't win.

"I'm sorry," the second nurse says as she plunges the needle into Hannah's glute. "You poor, poor thing. I don't know how else to help you."

DELIA F. BELMAN MEMORIAL PSYCHIATRIC HOSPITAL PATIENT LOG

Date: 1/20/23, 10:25 a.m.
Name: Hannah Doe

BACKGROUND: Pt placed in QR 1/19 and remained there overnight. Pt delusional in the early morning but later was reported to be alert, lucid, and cooperative. Pt briefly conversational with volunteer before beginning to hallucinate suddenly. Speech became loud, rapid, nonsensical. High degree of agitation.

RESPONSE: Attempt to calm pt with verbal de-escalation strategies ineffective. Pt deemed immediate physical threat. Administered Haloperidol 10 mg IM. Pt now sleeping in QR.

Chapter 22

*H*annah, please wake up!" Mary's whisper was urgent.

Groggily I opened my eyes. There was blackness all around, and a cold stone floor against my cheek. When I tried to sit up, my head spun.

What happened? Where am I?

I breathed in the metallic scent of blood and the dark, foul odor of shit. And then I knew—instantly, horribly. We were in a dungeon beneath the baron's castle. And *I* was the reason we were here.

Nausea overwhelmed me, and I retched. But there was nothing in my stomach except for the tiny bit of bread Otto had fed me. I coughed up bile until my throat burned. When the spasm passed, I wiped my swollen, bloodied lips and put my hand out in the dark.

"Mary, I can't see you."

"I'm over here."

Painfully I dragged myself toward the sound of her voice. "I'm coming, love," I said. I'd been hit so many times that it was agony to talk. But my eyes began to adjust to the darkness, and I thought I could see a small, forlorn lump in the corner of the cell. *Mary.*

Just a few more feet.

Every bone and muscle in my body ached as I crawled. Then I was beside her, touching the hard, warm knob of her shoulder. "Are you hurt?" I whispered.

There was a pause. "Just a little," she said.

But her voice cracked as she spoke. She was lying.

As if of their own accord, my fingers flew over her body, searching for the wound. "Where? Where?" I demanded.

"Oh," she gasped, "be careful—"

I froze. I'd touched her side where her kirtle was ripped and wet, and her skin was feverishly hot. When I pulled my hand away, it was sticky with gore.

I felt like I was falling from darkness into a deeper darkness, and there would never be any way out. *Dear God, no.*

"Hannah, it doesn't pain me too much," Mary whispered.

But I knew it was another lie.

"This is all my fault," I said fiercely.

"No, it isn't," she said. "I wasn't…supposed to come. I know that."

"But you did, because you believed in me. And Otto did, and—" I couldn't bear to say their names. My grief was suffocating me. "Where is everyone else? Are they here?"

"I don't know," Mary said. "I think they might be in another cell." She reached for my hand and squeezed it weakly. "Hannah, will you…sing for me?"

"Sing?" I cried. "Mary, what reason do we have to sing? I've brought suffering to all of us!"

"It will comfort me," she said. "Please."

I didn't think I could do it. Icy fingers of panic squeezed too tight around my heart. *I cannot bear to lose her. If she dies, I will die, too.*

"I want to hear the song you used to sing to me when I was little," she said. "The one with the dancing stars."

I took a deep, shuddering breath, trying to fill my lungs. *All right, Mary. I'll sing.* But when I opened my mouth, out came a wordless, animal shriek.

Chapter 23

H annah!" Mary gasped. "Don't—"

"Guards, help us!" I screamed. "We need a doctor! My sister's hurt!"

Laughter came back to me, as hard and brutal as a blow. "Good for her, then! If I was you two, I'd get my dying done now, too," growled someone on the other side of the wall. "For if you don't, you'll soon hang before a crowd."

I was about to scream again—to plead for our lives, to promise anything in order to save us—but Mary put her small hand on my arm.

"Hannah," she said softly. "Please, just sing."

I didn't want to sing. I wanted to save her. To save *us*. "Mary, let me bind the wound first," I urged. "It'll only hurt worse for a moment. We have to stop the blood."

She shook her head. "Please," she said. "The lullaby."

I licked my swollen lips. My mouth was dry, and my throat throbbed in pain. But Mary was telling me, without saying so outright, that singing was all there was to do. That it was the only help I could give.

I gently pulled her close, smoothing the tangled hair from her forehead as tears slipped down my cheeks and fell onto hers.

I'd sung the song to her for years, and together we'd sung it to

Belin and Borin when they were little, cradling their soft heads in our laps the way I now held Mary's.

> *Close your eyes, for night is nigh*
> *A thousand stars dance in the sky*
> *The redwing sings a song so sweet*
> *There is no sorrow when you sleep*
> *Hush my sweetling, and do not cry*
> *God keeps you safe, and so do I.*

I sang that single verse over and over again as my body began to shake with sobs. *God keeps you safe, and so do I.* I wanted more than anything to believe it. But it was just another awful lie.

Mary's breathing grew quicker and more shallow. She shivered in my arms as her life's blood flowed from her side, running slick along the dungeon's stones.

"Sing it with me," I begged.

> *The redwing sings a song so sweet*
> *There is no sorrow when you sleep*

"I can't," she gasped.

I bent down and rested my head on her chest. Her heart was beating as fast as a bird's. I kept singing as her breathing slowed, and as it began to come in ragged, irregular gasps.

"Mary, Mary, stay with me," I begged.

She didn't answer. Her little body strained against itself, and her spine arched. She was fighting with all her strength, but she couldn't win. She let out a tiny, halting cry. And then she died in my arms.

Chapter 24

The sound of my grief ricocheted against the cold stone walls. I screamed until my throat felt raw, and then I slumped down over my sister's body. "You can't leave me," I whispered. "I won't let you. I'm older, and you must do as I say!"

Something thudded against the door. "Shut your damn mouth, or my fist'll shut it for you!"

His threats meant nothing to me. The worst had already happened.

"Mary," I cried, "come back to me, come back—"

She didn't obey. Her skin was already growing cold. I felt my heart shattering into thousands of pieces. I clutched her limp body and screamed again.

More banging came from outside my cell. One of the guards growled to the other, "I say we just take her to the gallows now."

"And have him hang us, too? You bloody fool, we'll stay here with her until we're summoned."

"If she don't shut up, I *will* kill her before the hangman does."

"I beg you, do it!" I said.

The second guard gave a mirthless chuckle. Heavy footsteps struck the stones as he walked to the door and pressed his mouth close to the bars. "Scream as much as you like," he said. "Personally, I like the music."

I was still crying, cradling my sister's body, when they came for me. One brute grabbed me by the armpits and lifted me, pulling me from Mary's side. Her stiff little hand was in mine, but when he dragged me away, her arm fell to the ground with a soft, sickening sound.

"Come like a good girl, and I won't hurt you. I'll leave that to the hangman."

I kicked and struggled against him. "Leave me here with her!"

He cuffed me hard on the side of the head, and the pain made me go limp. He snarled, "Now you've gone and made me hit you already, stupid girl. Quit your whining. You'll be seeing your sister soon enough. You can hold hands again in hell."

"In the meantime," the other said, "you'll go where the baron tells you to and you'll die when the baron wants you to."

And they pulled me out of the cell and into the underground hall. The flickering light of pitch torches turned their faces into demons' masks.

I yelled in protest, but it didn't matter. They hauled me away like I was already a corpse. My last view of Mary was of her bare feet, glowing pale and small in the terrible dark.

CHAPTER 25

How long will she sleep now?" Jordan asks. He isn't outside Hannah's door anymore, but he can't stop thinking about her. Worrying about her.

Nurse Amy is busy logging everyone's vitals from the morning. She shrugs. "No telling. She was agitated again last night."

"Will she be better when she wakes up?"

Amy glances up from her work. "What if I give you the exact same answer again? You know, 'no telling'?"

"I was kind of hoping you'd have a different one," he admits.

Amy smiles benevolently at him. "You're new," she says. "You're eager and optimistic and all of that stuff. It's cute."

Jordan rolls his eyes. He resents being called cute.

"Hey now, don't make that face. We need people like you," Amy says earnestly. "I mean, deep in our hearts, we know there's hope for these patients. But it's so hard here. Last month there was a sixteen-year-old so charming and amazing that I couldn't understand what she was doing here. Then one night she took out a smuggled razor blade and made so many slashes on her thighs it looked like she was wearing goddamn red plaid pants." Amy's brow wrinkles. "Things like that can break you if you let them."

Jordan lets this awful story sink in for a minute. Then he asks, "Do a lot of patients here try to self-harm?" *Does Hannah?*

"Some definitely struggle with urges," Amy says. "That's why we don't give patients pens with sharp tips or actual silverware. But for some of these kids, it's not about them hurting themselves. It's more about who hurt them." She sighs. "Like Hannah, for example."

A chill runs up Jordan's spine. "What do you mean?"

"Hannah hasn't ever tried to hurt herself," Amy says. "I think she was the one who was hurt." She shakes her head. "Something really bad happened to Hannah before she came to us, that's what I think. But we can't get her to talk about it. Sometimes I'm not even sure that she could, even if she wanted to."

Chapter 26

The guards dragged me into the courtyard and dropped me onto the dirt. For a moment I lay there, shivering uncontrollably. My breath came in painful gasps.

Hundreds of people had gathered in the courtyard, and they were whispering and gabbling in anticipation. It was just as Father Alderton used to say: *Not even God can draw a crowd the way a hanging can.*

When I'd pushed myself to standing again, one of the guards grabbed my hands and roughly tied them behind my back. Then he shoved me between the shoulder blades, sending me stumbling forward. The crowd parted so quickly, you'd have thought I was a knife slicing through it.

As I walked, the women cursed me and the men spat at me. I felt more than one slimy glob hit my cheek and slide down my face.

"Traitor," yelled a toothless, ancient man. "Thief!"

I held my tongue. He was right.

As I got closer to the center of the courtyard, I saw a wooden cage guarded by men in chain mail and boiled leather. Inside it was Vazi. He was bloody and bruised, his eyes rolling in confusion and terror. Through the bars, children jabbed at him with sticks, taunting him like they would a wild animal.

"Oh, Vazi," I cried. "Don't let them—"

"Shut your mouth, girl." The guard struck me across the shoulders with the shaft of his halberd.

Vazi threw himself against the bars of his cage, wanting to protect me, but two soldiers shoved him back. He let out a high, strangled squawk, the only sound I'd ever heard him make. Then he pointed at something behind me. I turned around, and my heart stopped.

Otto was twenty yards away from me, and he was already standing on the gallows platform. His wrists were bound in front of him, and a rope was looped around his neck. His feet were bare and streaked with filth. There was blood caked all along the side of his head, and a horrible dark and empty circle where his left ear had been.

"Oh, my love," I gasped.

I had kissed that ear, whispered promises into it. Otto's beautiful mouth was battered and purple. His eyes were so swollen he could barely open them.

Otto, what have they done to you?

"He's been there all night with th' rope round his neck," my guard said. "Deserved worse, if you ask me."

"I didn't ask," I said through clenched teeth.

I didn't want to look, and yet I couldn't tear my eyes away. Looming over Otto's shoulder was the executioner, a massive man with a face that could've been carved from wood. Only his small black eyes raked hungrily over the crowd, as if he hoped to find more men to hang.

Then, with a curse, he turned back and tightened the rope around my beloved's neck.

"Otto," I cried, struggling to get closer to him. "I'm here!"

At the cracked, raw sound of my voice, Otto turned. His summer-green eyes seemed already lifeless. But then his mangled mouth opened. "Fed or dead," he called to me. He spread his fingers in a helpless kind of way, and he smiled sadly. "I love you, Hannah."

And then, before I could answer, the executioner sprang the trapdoor.

Otto dropped through it, straight as an arrow.

I shrieked in horror as Otto began to shake and convulse on the end of the rope. I lunged toward him, but the guard swept my legs out from under me with an easy kick. With bound hands, I couldn't break my fall. I fell sideways, striking my cheek on the ground and sending an explosion of pain through my head. All around me the crowd cheered.

"Look at 'im dance," someone yelled.

Even from the ground I could see Otto's legs shaking and his feet spasming. It was the most awful thing I had ever seen. But then they went still—and that was even worse.

My guard kicked me in the side. "You're next," he said.

Chapter 27

The guards wrenched me to my feet and dragged me up the steps to the gallows. The noise of the crowd grew even louder as I was led toward my beloved's swinging body, and to the empty noose waiting beside him.

"You'll look pretty with a rope necklace," my guard whispered mockingly into my ear. "Of course, that'll change after you're dropped. You'll look like *that*."

He turned me, forcing me to look directly at the man I thought I'd marry. Otto's face had turned a livid purple, and the sweet hands that had caressed me were limp and lifeless.

It felt like a sword had been driven into my heart. Tears swam in my eyes, and the crowd blurred into a dark, shouting mass. *First my sister, and then my love.*

Trumpets blared suddenly, and I looked up. The baron had appeared on a wall above the courtyard. He was dark-haired, beardless, and dressed in blood-red silk with a heavy cape of black wool fastened with a silver clasp. He looked nothing like the child I'd once seen riding through my village.

The crowd hushed, waiting for him to speak, while children clambered onto barrels and carts, the better to see what would happen next. But the baron only gazed down at us silently, his expression stony and indifferent.

I felt like screaming at him. Damning him. But I knew that my words—my fate—could not matter to him less.

Then something hit me hard in the arm and fell with a thud at my feet. I looked down to see half a rotting cabbage. Soon great handfuls of food were being thrown at me: leeks, carrots, turnips. A mutton bone with ragged strips of meat and tendon still attached.

If I weren't about to die, I would've laughed at the irony—I was being pelted with *soup ingredients*.

I kicked the cabbage back into the crowd. "If you would have brought this to my village," I shouted, "I wouldn't be standing here with an executioner slobbering at my back!" I ducked as a hunk of moldy bread came flying at my head. "You strike me with more food than I eat in a week!"

"Shut up, girl," my guard growled, pushing me toward the noose.

"I came here to steal, I do not deny it! But I didn't do it because I'm wicked, I did it because I am *starving*. My brothers are dead, and my mother drowns in her tears." I glanced up toward the wall where the baron stood, his face utterly impassive. "Tell me," I yelled, "how do we survive when we must give the lord of this castle half our crops and livestock as tribute? How do we feed ourselves on the scraps we have left?"

The executioner's knuckles struck my cheek with a sharp crack. My head snapped around and I started to fall, but he grabbed my arm and righted me, throwing the rope around my neck. I felt his thick, hot fingers digging into my flesh as he adjusted it.

I'm coming, Mary, Belin, Borin! Father—I will see you soon.

"Say your prayers, thief. *Silently.*"

For once in my life, I was obedient. *Dear God in Heaven, my name is Hannah Dory, and I pray you will have mercy on my—*

But I couldn't finish. A sudden, surging life force rose up inside me, and I threw myself at the executioner with all my strength. My forehead connected with his chin, and he stumbled back, arms flailing as he careened into Otto's body and nearly fell through the trapdoor himself. When he regained his balance, he came at me, his lips curled in a snarl and his face black with rage. The crowd cheered wildly. This was so much better than a hanging! They were going to watch him kill me with his filthy bare hands—

"Stop!" cried a smooth, rich voice. "Stand down."

The executioner turned away from me with a furious curse.

"Silence!"

Suddenly it seemed as if the whole courtyard was holding its breath. Stunned, I gazed up at the man who had just saved my life. The baron stared back at me.

"We only wanted to be like you," I cried. "To wake each morning to bread and ale, knowing that we would live through the day. As you would fight for your king, so I would fight for my family. I stole, and I am not sorry." My throat ached with tears I couldn't shed. "Death will be easier than what I've lived through. I welcome it."

The baron's arms were folded across his splendid red doublet. His expression was still cold. But something else glimmered in his eyes. "You will not meet it quite yet," he said. "Take the rope from the girl's neck."

The crowd let out a collective gasp. And with barely repressed fury, the giant man moved to do as he was bid.

"No," I said.

"No?" repeated the baron in surprise.

"If you spare me, you must spare my friends. And if you won't, then let your man have what he wants. Let him see me twirl on the end of his rope."

Though I'd just dared the baron to have me killed, my heart was strangely calm. I didn't care whether I lived or died. But if there was a chance to save Maraulf, Merrick, and Vazi, then I had to take it.

The baron turned and began to walk away, back toward the tower. Right before he vanished from view, he looked back and his eyes met mine.

"Done," he said.

CHAPTER 28

The Columbia dorm lounge is quiet as Jordan passes through on his way to his shift at Belman. The girl who always studies physics at the table by the window is—surprise—studying physics at the table by the window, a giant cup of Starbucks steaming by her arm.

She looks up as Jordan walks by, and his breath catches. For a split second, she looks just like Hannah.

Of course, her hair isn't messy and her clothes aren't ill-fitting hand-me-downs, but there is something in her eyes that seems familiar. A mix of wariness and piercing intelligence.

"Morning," he mutters, but she's already looking down at her book again.

On the bus to Queens, he stares out the rain-streaked window, wondering if Hannah will be awake and lucid today. If she is, will she try to convince him again that she's perfectly sane? That she's a time traveler rather than a schizophrenic?

You're not supposed to call someone that. You say "someone living with schizophrenia." Because language and labels matter.

But what if he thinks of Hannah as having altered perception disorder, or disconnectivity syndrome, or any of the other new names for schizophrenia that he's heard proposed—does it make a difference? Does it put her any closer to being better?

"No, no, no!" a voice calls out.

Jordan looks up. A few rows in front of him on the bus, an old woman in a violet wig is waving her arms and carrying on a heated conversation with someone who isn't there. "No," she's saying, "I don't want to do that."

Jordan wonders if working at a psychiatric hospital has made him start seeing mental illness everywhere, or if the city is just full of garden-variety misfits. But the woman is getting more and more agitated, so when the bus comes to the next stop, he goes up and sits down across the aisle from her. He's ready to help.

"Ma'am?" he says quietly. "Are you okay?"

"I've told you," she says. "I'm not interested in the parrot!"

"Ma'am?"

Finally she turns to him. Her wig's on sideways and she doesn't have any teeth. She looks ancient and terrifying. "Can't you see I'm in the middle of a conversation?" she demands.

And suddenly, he can. Because there are Bluetooth earbuds in her ears and a phone in her hand.

Jordan goes red from neck to crown. "So sorry," he says. "Have a nice day."

And then he gets off the bus three stops early.

CHAPTER 29

D ude, your favorite psycho's finally awake," Mitch says, elbowing Jordan in the ribs as he heads out on the floor to do 10 a.m. safety checks. "You can take her to her new room if she's ready. Number 5A."

"Don't call her—" Jordan begins. But Mitch is halfway down the hall already, laughing.

"I'm just kidding," he calls over his shoulder. "Don't be such a snowflake."

"I'm being *human*," Jordan mumbles.

Of course, Mitch is right about one thing: Hannah *is* Jordan's favorite Belman patient. He's played a lot of cards with Indy, and Michaela destroyed him in Connect Four, but so far only Hannah has seemed to truly want to talk to him.

Over and over again, he remembers the first time he saw her, and how he caught her like she was a wild animal. If he hadn't been there, would she have made it back to wherever she lived? Would she have been better off?

Maybe that's why he feels such a bewildering kind of responsibility for her. He's the reason she's here in this cage.

That it's probably the best place for her strangely doesn't make him feel better.

Now, when he knocks on the door of the quiet room, Hannah looks up and shrugs one thin shoulder at him. If it's an invitation to enter, it's an extremely half-assed one. He lets himself in, offering her a clementine he swiped from the break room. "How're you feeling?" he asks.

She holds the fruit in her palm for a minute, thinking. "I feel like…" Hannah's voice trails off. She rolls the clementine away into the corner, like it's a ball she doesn't want to play with.

Jordan retrieves it and shoves it back into his pocket. *Don't fill the silence*, he reminds himself. *Let her do the talking.*

"Shit!" she exclaims.

"What?" he asks, suddenly alarmed.

She laughs. "I was answering your question," she says. "I feel like shit." She speaks slowly, as though she has to search for the right words. "Like a zombie: unalive, and also…paradoxically undead."

Jordan squats down by the mattress so he's not looming creepily above her anymore. And he sees, for the first time, two large scars beneath Hannah's collarbone, one on each side of her chest. The ghosts of old stitches surround the scars like tiny white seeds.

God, he wants to say, *what happened to you? Is this what Amy was talking about when she said she thought you'd been hurt?*

But he doesn't ask those questions. He says, "Can you tell me more about what that's like?"

"You sound like my therapist," Hannah says dryly. "I don't need another therapist, believe me. I've had a million of them, and none of them have helped."

"I just thought you might like to talk," Jordan says.

Hannah sighs. "Sorry, I know. You're not being nosy, you're being helpful."

"Well I'm *trying* to be," Jordan says. "I don't know how well it's working, though."

"Are you fishing for compliments, Jordan Hassan?" Hannah asks. Her voice is suddenly lighter—almost playful.

"No," he says earnestly. "I'm just—"

"Trying to be helpful, I know," Hannah interrupts. "I appreciate it, I do. I'm glad you're here. And I'm especially glad you're not trying to shove pills down my throat or make me paint a self-affirmation mandala."

Jordan laughs. "I'm not qualified to dispense meds, and I don't even know what a mandala is."

Hannah rolls her eyes. "Stick around here long enough and you will."

"But do you want to talk about it?" Jordan asks. "About how you're feeling? Or about...the other world?"

Instantly her demeanor shifts. She drags her fingers through her tangled hair in agitation. "It isn't good."

"Now you seem upset," he says.

"Duh," she snaps. "Could it be because my sister is dead? And Otto, too?"

Jordan's taken aback. Mary was alive when he last talked to Hannah, and he still has no idea who Otto is. Too late, he realizes that his confusion is all too visible on his face.

"I thought you might be the one person who'd believe me, but I guess I was wrong," Hannah says. She gazes up at the tiny window that's covered in heavy wire mesh. "Maybe you think I should talk about how I feel after getting another ass-jab and spending the night in psych ward jail. Well, I want to talk about the fact that my sister is dead, the man I loved is dead, and both of these things are my fault."

She seems so certain—of Otto and Mary, and also that Jordan won't believe her. That he's like everyone else. But Jordan's not going to doubt her right now. If she believes in this so strongly, there's got to be some kind of truth to it. Maybe not *literal* truth, but emotional truth. She's got a family she cares about. Thinks about. Longs for.

And what are the possibilities? Either she's the reincarnation of a medieval peasant, or she's a time traveler, or she's a person caught up in a persistent, vivid, and overwhelming hallucination who nevertheless has periods so lucid that Jordan can talk to her like he would anyone in his dorm.

She's like a case study in a psych book, where the symptoms are wildly complex and the diagnosis can't be determined. Hannah has secrets—he knows that. Everyone does. But hers are deeper and darker than most. She's starting to trust him, though, and maybe this means he'll be able to help her bring them to light.

"It's not that I don't believe you," he says firmly. "That's not it at all. I just didn't know...I didn't know about Mary. I'm so sorry."

Hannah looks up at him, startled. "Thank you," she says. "That actually means something to me."

CHAPTER 30

S uddenly I didn't want to talk only about terrible things—I wanted to remember the good years I'd had. So I told Jordan about the communal fields we planted twice a year, and the forest where we played and hunted for mushrooms and berries, and the songs we used to sing while we worked. I told him the names of all the villagers, and the way the river looked in the spring rush, and how we'd once found a litter of snow-white kittens mewling in the straw of our chicken coop.

I must've rambled on for half an hour before I had to lean over and snap my fingers in front of Jordan's face. "Hello?" I said. "Earth to intern, hello?"

His cheeks turned a bright, embarrassed pink. "I'm so sorry," he said. "I—I was trying to picture it and spaced out for a minute."

"You had the thousand-yard stare I usually associate with a high dose of tranquilizers," I said. "Anyway, it's okay. Listening to me talk about my other life is probably as boring as listening to people talk about their dreams."

Jordan flashed a quick grin. "'I dreamed I was in my house, but it didn't *look* like my house....'"

"Exactly. 'When I got to school, I realized I wasn't wearing any pants!'"

"Classic dreams, but they don't sound like they're 'simply and undisguisedly realizations of wishes,' do they?" Jordan asked.

"Nope. Nor the 'royal road to the unconscious.'"

Jordan looked surprised. "You've read *The Interpretation of Dreams*? By Sigmund Freud?"

"No," I said. "Just the one by Dr. Seuss." When his expression changed from surprise to confusion, I couldn't help grinning. "I'm kidding," I said. "I've read Freud. I've read a shitload of books."

"That's pretty impressive."

Was it, though? Since no one else seemed to care about educating me, I'd basically had to do it myself. It helped pass the time. "Sure," I said. "I guess."

"I know Freud was doing groundbreaking work and stuff, but I feel like he got a few things wrong," Jordan mused.

"He got a *lot* wrong," I said heatedly. "Dreams don't have anything to do with wish fulfillment. They're more like—well, like your mind takes a giant dump every night, and the result is a bunch of weird, nonsensical stories that happen to you while you're sleeping."

Jordan laughed, and then I suddenly started laughing, too. How wild was this? I was having a normal conversation with a cute, normal guy, and I'd managed to say something funny. I couldn't remember the last time something like that happened. Maybe... never? Yeah, never sounded about right.

"Freud probably shouldn't have done so much cocaine," Jordan said, tossing the clementine back and forth between his palms.

"It was over-the-counter medicine back then," I reminded him. "And if you want to talk about drugs, I've done gobs of them." Without thinking, I began to tick off names on my fingers. "Let's see, Thorazine, Stelazine, Moban, Haldol, Seroquel, Zyprexa—"

"Amy says you sometimes won't take them, though."

And just like that, the conversation wasn't normal anymore. We were back in the present reality that I was so sick of—the one where 99 percent of the world's population was sane, and I was in the 1 percent that was truly nuts, which was why I had to be in a locked ward of a famous, highly regarded psychiatric hospital that kept taking me in like some kind of charity case.

Some kids get scholarships to college; others get scholarships to mental wards. Who said life was fair?

"Yeah, well," I said, "a lot of the drugs make me feel flat and dull and exhausted. I gain weight, I've gotten facial tics, and sometimes my brain feels like it's turning into some giant wet dishrag. I'm not *me* anymore. I'm a different person."

That this other Hannah was the one that everyone wanted me to be—quiet, obedient, leaving my loves in the past and living only one, dull life—didn't make her more appealing to me.

Jordan looked like he was going to say something, but then he stopped and held out that stupid clementine again. "Are you sure you don't want this?"

"I'm only starving in the Middle Ages," I said dryly. "Here, I can wait until lunch."

"Okay," he said. He stood up and walked over to the door. "Well, do you want to go to your new room?"

"New room?" I repeated. I looked at him doubtfully. "I've been here twenty times. I promise, there's absolutely no such thing."

CHAPTER **31**

I followed Jordan down the hall and around the corner to Room 5A.

"Here we are," he said as brightly as if he were some kind of tour guide. He knocked, then pushed open the door. "Good morning," he said to whoever was inside. "Come on in, Hannah."

I sighed, straightened my shoulders, and walked into a room I was sure I'd stayed in before. Then again, they *did* all look exactly the same, so who could really tell?

"OMG, look at you! You could be Lily Collins's twin sister, and I can already tell that we're going to be great friends."

This baffling sentence was spoken by the curvy redhead sitting cross-legged on one of the room's twin beds. She had a heart-shaped face, bright blue eyes, and—I could already tell—way too much energy for this place. For *me*.

"Hannah, this is Sophie," Jordan said. "Sophie, meet Hannah. You guys are going to be roommates for the, uh, foreseeable future."

"Hi," I said, barely even politely. Just because I hated being locked in the quiet room didn't mean I was interested in a psychiatric institution slumber party. And if I had to have a roommate, why couldn't it be Michaela? We understood each other's issues, and we gave each other space. Plus sometimes her grandma sent her care packages of brownies and Doritos. Since she never wanted to eat them, she'd give them all to me.

I fell facedown onto my new-old bed. "I don't know who Lily Collins is," I said into the pillow.

The other bed creaked as Sophie bounced up and down. "Really? *Emily in Paris? Les Misérables?*"

I rolled over onto my back and stared up at the ceiling. The only thing uglier than a bare hospital wall was the fluorescent light and acoustic tile of a hospital ceiling. I remembered the second or third time I'd come to Belman, when one of the patients ripped out a bunch of those tiles because he thought they contained hidden microphones. *They're listening!* he'd screamed. *They're always listening!*

When a nurse asked him *who* was listening, he'd shaken his head. He was too scared to say. He thought they'd come and kill him.

"Hello? Yoohoo!" Sophie said. "Have you ever had Yoo-hoo, by the way? It is so, so gross, but our doorman drinks it by the case. Pretty soon all his teeth are going to fall out."

Aaaaand...the only thing worse than being stuffed into the quiet room was being forced to share your sleeping quarters with someone who can't shut her mouth.

"Lily Collins is also Phil Collins's daughter, but I'd excuse you for not knowing who that is," Sophie went on. "Maybe your parents know his music."

"I saw *Les Mis* the musical," Jordan offered, either trying to help break the ice or else get Sophie to be quiet for one second. "Have you, Hannah?"

"I've read the *book*," I said. "It's by Victor Hugo. Incidentally, Hugo's daughter was committed to an insane asylum. Supposedly she was driven mad by unrequited love."

The way I might be driven mad by my new roommate!

Sophie flicked her hair over her shoulder. "That's fascinating, but it doesn't tell you who Lily Collins is," she said. "I'd show you her IMDb page, but they took my phone away, so I guess your ignorance will persist. Very few people know as many things as I do, anyway. I don't know why I forget this sometimes. Your minds aren't as powerful as mine is, and I feel sorry for you. But I also feel a lot of love for you—I have love for everybody, even the people I hate."

I stifled a sudden laugh. Sophie's rapid-fire monologue was giving me a headache, but she was funny. Was she as messed up as everyone thought I was? Only time would tell. I wouldn't ask her what she was here for, of course. That was rude. But Indy—who, like me, was a frequent flyer at Belman Psych—would.

What are you, he'd go, *a suicide risk or something?* And, as if asking wasn't enough already, he'd do it at the top of his lungs. He got in trouble for stuff like that, but he didn't care. Indy liked pissing people off. "It's one of the symptoms of my mental illness," he'd say. I wasn't really sure that was true, though. It might've just been an excuse to be a dick.

"I haven't slept in three days," Sophie went on. "Maybe four or six. Sleep is for plebeians." She got up and began pacing from the window to the door and back again. "I bought ten thousand dollars' worth of handbags on The RealReal because I'm going to start my own high-end retail shop in Bushwick. Then my mom said I had to finish high school, which is ridiculous because my school's just a holding pen for rich assholes before they go off to a college where they can become frat brothers with even more rich assholes. I'm rich, too—well, my parents are, I only have like two million to my name—but I promise I'm not an asshole. I can tell I'm talking a lot, I'm aware of that. But I have so much to say and all of it is interesting! Because of my prodigious memory I know a lot of good jokes, and everyone says I'm the most charming person they've ever met—"

"You two have group therapy in half an hour," Jordan interrupted her. "Hannah, do you want to show Sophie around before that?"

"Do I look like a tour guide?" I asked him.

"You look like Lily Collins, we've already established that," Sophie said. "I mean, if Lily Collins stopped showering and got her clothes out of a Kohl's dumpster. But I know we're going to be friends! I don't know about the other people in this place, though. I think I will only like you. You have beautiful cheekbones. Have you ever used filler? My mom says I'm too young but everyone at school does it. I want a Botox lip flip like Marilynn O'Connor. She's a senior, and everyone says she had sex with Harry Styles—"

"Anyway," Jordan said, "see you guys later." He gave us a wave and raced down the hall.

I couldn't exactly blame him.

"Are you voluntary?" I asked. The question was bordering on rude, but I was curious.

Sophie shook her head. "My mom made me come here. I mean, I did threaten to kill her, but I didn't mean it." She was still walking back and forth; I could hear her hurried footsteps. "I know I could ride this out—I'm very powerful. But she's driving me crazy.

If it weren't for her everything would be really wonderful, I think. Being here is, like, R&R or whatever—some time apart. I'll be out in a day, after everyone here sees that my mind is incredible and I have perfect clarity and self-awareness."

By this point I definitely didn't need Indy to yell *What's wrong with you, new girl?* Because I'd seen manic episodes like this before. I'd bet money that somewhere in Sophie's chart was a diagnosis of Bipolar 1 or 2.

If I had any money, that is.

"My mom hates my boyfriend because he's twenty-eight," Sophie went on. "Like he can help what year he was born? He has a Tesla Roadster. God, I wish I had my phone."

Sophie didn't seem to notice that I wasn't really listening. I could feel myself sinking down deeper into the mattress. A fog began swirling around in my mind, and her voice got quieter, like it was coming from farther and farther away.

Then the temperature in the room started dropping, and I shivered in the sudden dampness.

It's happening.

The white hospital walls were receding, and other walls were taking their place. I could hear my heartbeat as loud as a drum.

"Hannah?" Sophie said. But she was calling me from the other side of the world, and from the other side of centuries.

The shadows are advancing.

They're turning into men with dark, cruel mouths.

"Hannah has a visitor in the castle," I heard myself say. "You'll never guess who it is."

Chapter 32

I was dreaming of Otto. His hands—always warm, even in winter—slowly eased my dress from my shoulders, pulling it down the length of my body. His fingers, touching me everywhere, were roughly callused but infinitely tender. Desire burned beneath my skin, hot as flames. He was whispering, but I couldn't make out the words—

"Rise and thank the baron for his mercy!"

The beautiful dream vanished. I lurched to my feet. "Is mercy what you call it—to bring me back to the dungeon and leave me here to die? The baron should have had me hung," I said.

"Well, that remains a possibility," came the smooth voice.

I felt a jolt of sickening surprise. On the other side of the cell door, the baron stepped into view, the torch he held illuminating his haughty face.

I would've torn out his eyes if I could have. Instead I spit out my words like poison. "How dare you come here and think I will thank you! *Mercy?* You have no mercy. You killed my sister, and you killed Otto!"

"I did not kill them. Others did."

"Under *your* orders."

"I was only protecting my castle," he said, "and the resources within it. Surely even your limited mind can understand that."

"Being born poor doesn't make me stupid," I hissed.

"It does seem to make you defiant, however. I had hoped for a touch of gratitude for sparing your life and those of your friends, not to mention an apology for the inconvenience you and your unwashed companions caused my men by ransacking my kitchens in the middle of the night. But since I'm obviously not going to get what I want, perhaps I should take you back to the courtyard gallows."

"Do it, if it pleases you."

He sighed as his fingers ran up and down one of the window's iron bars. "There is often little pleasure in duty."

"So you would look at it as a duty to kill me? Tell me, why was it not your duty to help the people in my village? Why have you let us starve and die?"

"Surely thievery was not your only option."

"Imagine being so hungry that you'd want to eat meat you knew was rotten, just to fill your belly for an hour before you retched it up again!" I said. "But you can't, can you? You are castle born and castle bred. You wouldn't last a day living the way I have. You can't even fathom it."

The baron lifted an eyebrow. "If village life is so difficult, my dungeon should be a pleasant change."

"I'd rather starve in freedom than dine like a king in your dungeon. But it isn't up to me, is it?"

He gave a low, silky chuckle. "No, it is not. But I don't make a habit of keeping people in underground cells, no matter how mutinous they are. As a punishment for wrongdoing, hanging is much more efficient. Even if you add in a little torture beforehand, it's all over very quickly."

I had the distinct feeling that the baron was mocking me. Once again, I wanted to do him grievous bodily harm. "Is that what you've done to my friends?"

"No," he said. "I have freed them, as I said I would."

Please God, let him be telling the truth.

"What about me, then? Will you free me, too?"

"No, I have something else in mind." He turned and began to walk away, but he hadn't taken ten steps before he was suddenly back. "Oh, look," he said, the barest hint of a smile on his lips, "I found this in my pocket." He dangled a narrow strip of dried meat through the bars. "Fallow deer, if I'm not mistaken."

I didn't want to take it from him—I was too proud. But my hand shot out and snatched it from his grip, and I'd shoved it into my mouth before I even knew what I was doing. The meat was tough and salty, and nearly impossible to chew. It didn't matter. It was food.

"That was meant for my hound," the baron said. He sounded amused. "Who, I might add, has better manners than you."

My mouth was full, but I managed to speak around the gristly strands. "I'll gladly show you my manners," I said furiously. "All you have to do is let me out."

The baron merely bowed, and then he walked away without turning back.

Chapter 33

*W*hen the baron left, he took his guards with him, and I was alone in the frigid, stinking darkness for hours. Days, maybe. Armies of rats skittered ceaselessly along the stones, and sometimes I could hear what sounded like low, inconsolable moaning. Was I imagining it, or was someone dying in a cell not far from mine?

I didn't know, and I realized with a dull sense of shock that I didn't even care. I was freezing, starving, and so thirsty that I'd licked the damp, slimy walls just to get a few drops of moisture on my tongue. If the baron's plan was to break my spirit, it was working. Every time I closed my eyes, I saw Mary's pale, bloody face and Otto's livid, lifeless hands. I heard Otto's last words to me and Mary's final, agonized gasps.

All of this was my fault.

Dear God in Heaven, my name is Hannah Dory, and I am ready to die. I beg you to bring me home.

But either He didn't hear me or He didn't want me in his kingdom. My stubborn heart kept beating, and my chest still rose and fell. There were no words I could say to make it otherwise.

When the men finally came back and stopped outside my cell, I didn't move. I had gone past hunger, past terror. I was a shell of the girl I'd been.

"Is she dead?" one of them whispered.

"Kick her and find out."

The door swung open and a guard strode in. When his boot connected with my hip, I let out an involuntary cry of pain.

"She's alive all right," he said. He reached down and caught me by the ankle, then started to drag me across the floor. When he'd got me through the doorway, he gave me another kick. "On your feet."

"Where are you taking me?" I rasped as I tried to stand. The light of their torches blurred and swam in front of my eyes.

"Back to the gallows." He grinned at me with black teeth. "You'll hang for a week or so, just to get good and ripe, and then we'll cut you down and put your head on a pike."

"Crows'll eat your eyeballs," said the other, a bald man with a long horse's face.

So, I was to be hanged after all.

Even if you add in a little torture beforehand, the baron had said, *it's all over very quickly*.

I was so weak that I could barely walk, so the guards dragged me through the subterranean hall and up a set of narrow, curving stairs. At the top, they opened another heavy carved door, and sunlight exploded all around me. Through my streaming eyes, I saw not the gallows, but long, empty garden rows and leafless fruit trees. We were in the inner bailey, near the castle's tall keep.

"I think you're lost," I muttered. "The gallows are the other direction."

My answer was a hard slap to the face, and my mouth filled with blood. When I stumbled, the black-toothed guard picked me up and threw me over his shoulder like a sack of grain. My head bobbed dizzily upside down as he ducked in through a door, trudged up more stairs, and then headed down another hallway.

Maybe they're going to hang me inside, I thought dully. *Or maybe it's where the torture happens.*

He turned and entered a room off of an upper passage. Still upside down, I saw a barrel-vaulted ceiling, a blur of tapestries on the walls, a fire blazing in the hearth. The heat on my face was sudden and wonderful. The guard pushed me off his shoulder, sending me crashing onto the floor and knocking the breath from my lungs.

I lay still, waiting, as pain flooded every inch of my body. When I could speak again, I asked where I was.

"Don't you know what a bedroom is, *milady*?" said the bald one mockingly.

The guard who'd carried me took an exaggerated sniff and said, "No, and I don't think she knows what a bath is, either."

"You're both very funny," I whispered. "But I was kept in a dungeon for days. What's your excuse for smelling like pig shit?"

The bald one raised his hand to strike me, but the black-toothed guard caught his wrist. "She's not to be touched anymore," he said. "Baron's orders."

The bald one spat angrily at me. "You'd best hold your tongue, or I'll yank it out with my bare hands, orders or no."

I just closed my eyes, listening to the fire as it popped and crackled. I could feel its heat beginning to seep into my bones. I was overcome by a fatigue so deep that I could not even move a finger.

If I lie very still like this, I thought, *maybe they will leave me.*

And soon enough, they did.

Chapter 34

I must have slept. When I opened my eyes, the fire was lower and a blanket had been draped over my shoulders. I sat up and pulled the warm wool tighter around me to cover my ripped, bloodstained dress.

I was still alone, and the castle was quiet. I looked numbly around the richly decorated chamber. To my left was a huge four-poster bed, its wine-colored velvet curtains pulled back to reveal a mattress covered in more velvet and bearskin. The dark stone walls were softened with tapestries showing forests of flowering trees, multicolored birds, and horses with horns protruding out of their heads. Thin white candles flickered in iron sconces.

The room was beautiful, but there was a staleness to the air, as if no one had slept in here for years. I saw delicate cobwebs in the corners, a thin fur of dust across the windowsill.

Am I still dreaming?

I went to the door and pulled. It was locked from the outside.

I knew then that it wasn't a dream. I'd simply been brought to a new kind of prison.

I pressed my forehead against the door as a wave of grief overwhelmed me. I had made mistake after mistake, and people I loved had paid for them with their lives. The guilt made my stomach feel like it was filled with stones.

Then I turned away and walked to the window on the other side of the room. Opening its shutters, I gazed into the winter night. The sky was a huge, cold darkness. Though I could see fires flickering in the courtyard, there was no other sign of life.

I thought of Otto out there in the cold, and I shivered, clutching my arms, fingers digging into my skin. Father Alderton, our village priest, always claimed that dying was a blessing. "We go home to heaven," he would say, "where there is no such thing as sin or pain." But how could I believe him when he'd fought death the way he had? The whole village had heard him calling out to God from his sickbed, begging Him to spare his life.

Did God deny him—or simply not hear the old man's pleas? It was blasphemous to even wonder such a thing. All I knew was that we'd buried Father Alderton in the churchyard, and two days later, the wolves had dragged his corpse from its grave.

Horror shuddered through me. Where was Mary now? Had they buried her, or left her deep in the dungeons to be eaten by rats?

I couldn't bear to think of it. Instead I cast back to when we were younger, before our father went to war and when the summers were sweet and endless. How we'd lie on our backs on the edge of the meadow, watching twilight bats swoop and dive, and together, Mary and I would sing.

We rest upon the great green earth as night comes
dropping down
And above the forest the moon shall rise, wearing a
silver crown

It was a song I'd written for her on her sixth birthday.

Now's the time to be at peace, our day's long work is done
And mothers are calling their children in, one by one by one.
Come home, my son, come in, my love
The night grows dark and wild
Lay your cheek upon your bed
And by sweet dreams be beguiled—

"That's a fine tune for such a stinking bag of bones," said a voice.

Chapter 35

I whirled around to see two women standing at the threshold of the room. Their hair was the color of straw, and their eyes were so pale blue they were almost colorless. They would have been indistinguishable from each other if it weren't for their expressions. One of them looked at me with curiosity, and the other with contempt.

"Please excuse Agnes," said the curious one. "Mutton doesn't agree with her."

"My stomach has nothing to do with it," Agnes said, looking darkly at me. As she closed the door behind her, I heard a bolt slide into place from the outside.

I pressed myself against the wall as they came into the room. "What do you want?"

The friendlier servant gave a quick curtsy. "I'm Margery," she said. Her glance flicked up and down my wrecked and filthy dress. "Did they drag you behind a horse?"

"She's the one that was supposed to hang," muttered Agnes. "And should've, if you ask me."

Margery shrugged. "Far be it for us to judge, sister," she said. "Our job is to serve."

Sister. The word pierced my heart like a knife, and a vision of

Mary flared in my mind. I saw her sweet lovely face, contorted in pain. I saw her hands clutching mine in a dark cell. I saw her life-blood pooling on the stones.

"Are you all right?" Margery's voice pulled me back.

No, I am not all right. I am not all right at all.

"She's alive, isn't she?" Agnes said. "If she's not on the end of a rope, she's got no reason to be complaining."

Margery shot her sister a look but said nothing as she pushed aside a midnight-blue curtain and disappeared through a doorway I hadn't noticed before. Agnes remained in the room with me, glaring. I stared back at her. If she thought her scorn could wound me, she was wrong.

"Ready," Margery called from the other room.

"Go on, then," said Agnes.

When I didn't move from my place, she strode over and grabbed me roughly by the arm, yanking me through the curtain into a small room warmly lit by dozens of candles. In the center of the room stood a round, wooden tub of water.

I looked up at Margery in alarm. "No," I said. "Please!"

But Margery only laughed. "I know you've never had a proper bath before," she said, "but I promise, it won't kill you."

Chapter 36

"Get this disgusting thing off yourself," Agnes said, her rough fingers wrenching my dress down to my waist. I tried to cover my breasts as she nearly pushed me out of the skirt. Then I watched in alarm as she hurried into the other room and threw it into the fire.

"That's my only dress! My mother made it for me!"

"It *was* your only dress," Agnes said grimly. "Now it's cinders."

"We'll find you a new one," Margery said. "Get in, if you please."

I balked—what if this was the torture the baron talked about?—so Agnes picked me up and dumped me into the water.

I shrieked. It was *warm*.

Margery laughed again at my shock. "Nice, isn't it?"

Mutely I nodded. I'd never felt anything like it—I'd bathed in the river since I was old enough not to drown.

The tub's clear water had turned muddy already, and a wound on my hip that I hadn't even noticed before opened up. Narrow streams of blood floated into the bath, and I stared, dazed, at the strangely beautiful swirls.

Margery held out a small white cake of soap. "Scrub every single part of yourself."

I washed slowly, numbly, as the two watchful sisters stood over me. As I soaped my feet, my legs and in between them, then my stomach and chest, an old memory came back to me. I was tiny, and my mother was bathing me with a bucket of river water and singing.

> *A little bath at the end of the day*
> *To wash the mud and cares away*

The recollection was so strong I could almost feel her tender fingers combing through my hair right now. The soap slipped from my fingers. *Mother, did you know how many of your babies would die?*

"I'm done," I said abruptly. I stood up, water streaming down me.

Margery led me over to the fire, where I dried myself with a square of linen. I'd stopped caring about my nakedness in front of her. I only wanted to crawl into that enormous bed and fall asleep again. When I slept, I didn't feel.

But now Agnes was walking toward me with a magnificent dress in her arms. It was green and gold brocade, with a scooped neck and a long train, and there was a pair of velvet slippers to go with it.

"I can't—" I said, shaking my head and stepping back as if the gown would bite. It was forbidden for people like me to wear clothing as fine as that.

"You can and will," Agnes said curtly.

They pulled the dress up and over my shoulders and fastened it behind me. It was so tight that I struggled to breathe.

"You look beautiful," said Margery. "Though you could use a comb." Then she and her sister turned to leave.

"What now?" I said as they walked toward the hall.

But neither of them answered, and the door shut behind them with a heavy thud.

Alone again, I blinked at the fire, watching the flames flicker and dance. And though I tried to keep my mind blank, I thought of Otto hanging in the courtyard, his death a baron's justice and a crowd's entertainment. I thought of Mary, and how her life had slipped away as I held her in my arms.

What now? What now? What now?

The words beat against the inside of my head. I felt as if invisible hands were circling my throat, strangling me. I opened my mouth as wide as it would go, but I still couldn't get enough air. I started shaking all over. My vision narrowed to a pulsing tunnel, and all I could see was the fire and the flickering red stones around it.

My hands and feet were icy-cold now, as if I'd come out of the winter river instead of a warm bath. My fingers curled in on themselves, and it felt as if my skin everywhere was being poked by a million tiny thorns. My ears were ringing. I gave a choking cry. Pain filled me, inside and out.

What now? What now? What now?

Suddenly, I knew the answer. I was dying, too.

CHAPTER **37**

A re you okay, Hannah-Lily?"
Belman Psych's newest patient was looming above me, her face round as a moon and her red hair brushing against my cheek. "Do you have, like, absence seizures or whatever those things are called?"

"What?" I managed. My breath was coming too fast, and my heartbeat fluttered and skipped.

"One minute we were talking, and then the next minute it was like you weren't even here," Sophie said. "Your eyes were open, but you couldn't see me. Then I started calling your name, but you didn't answer."

"I'm okay now," I said, willing my pulse to slow. "I'm okay."

"It was so weird," Sophie went on. "You were, like, *gone.*"

I know I was.

"You were like this." Sophie opened her eyes really wide and stared dead ahead. She looked catatonic.

"I get it," I said, feeling shaky and embarrassed. "You don't have to keep talking about it."

She moved back to her side of the room. "Okay, sorry. But I was worried."

I rubbed my face with my hands, hard. Sometimes it took a

long and disorienting amount of time to come back to the present day, and sometimes it was more like being slapped in the face. This was one of the second instances.

As my breathing calmed, Sophie just kept glancing over at me like there was something wrong with me.

Of course there's something wrong with me! There's something wrong with all of us in here.

Sophie said, "You did yell a bit, too."

"I really, truly don't want to know," I said.

"Sorry. Just trying to be nice."

"I know," I said. "It's just…well, sometimes it's hard to wake up here, you know?"

I meant wake up *in this century*, but of course Sophie didn't know that. I learned a long time ago not to bother telling roommates about my other life. I wondered, not for the first time, what it was about Jordan that made me think he'd be the one to believe me.

"I know what you mean," Sophie said. She jabbed at the wall with a pink manicured fingernail. "There's a bunch of marks here. Someone counting the days they were inside, I bet."

"I think that was me," I said.

"Oh," she said. Sophie's voice was suddenly quiet and serious. "I've been here before, too," she said. "It was the summer I was twelve."

"Twelve?" I said incredulously. "You rich kids are supposed to be going to *camp* then. Getting Girl Scout badges or whatever."

"If I hadn't tried to kill myself, I guess I would've gone to summer camp," Sophie said.

She looked away from me and gazed pensively out the window.

She seemed different than she'd been before I . . . well, before I went to the castle. She was quieter. Sadder.

"Are *you* doing okay?" I asked.

She turned to look at me, and it seemed like she was trying to decide how truthfully to answer the question. But then there was a knock on the door.

"Enter," said Sophie flatly. "If you dare."

Jordan poked his head in. "Safety check," he said.

Sophie's mood brightened a little. "Bullshit," she said. "Mitch just made the rounds."

"Oh," he said.

"Busted," Sophie mouthed to me.

Jordan's agate eyes met mine, and I tried to hide my smile.

"I have something for you, Hannah," he said. He held out a book, but Sophie grabbed it before I could take it.

"*Reasons to Live?*" she read, practically howling. "God, that's a little on the nose for a psych patient, don't you think?" She turned the cover over. "Though I should probably read it, if I'm being honest with myself."

"It's a book of short stories," Jordan said, sounding pained. He took it back and handed it to me. "They're fiction."

It was a thin blue book, and I could tell the copy was used. I opened the front cover. Sure enough, it said *Jordan Hassan* in neat script.

"I read it in a seminar last year and I thought it was really good," he said earnestly. "It's got nothing to do with psychiatry. It's just these really great stories." He shuffled from foot to foot in his dumb khakis and his hospital-issue scrub shirt. "They're, like, funny and sad at the same time. I know you read a lot, so…" And then the rest of the sentence got strangled in his throat.

"Thanks," I said, placing the book next to me on the bed. "That was really sweet of you."

"Sure, yeah, no problem," he said. "Anyway…"

"Buh-bye!" Sophie chirped, and Jordan Hassan gave me one last indecipherable look before turning around and vanishing into the hall.

Then Sophie clapped her hands together in delight. "He's in love with you, it's so obvious. He's read all the nurse's notes, he has a savior complex, and now he's made you his pet project. He's going to make you better or die trying!"

A gorgeous, ambitious Columbia student in love with a girl he believes is probably a schizo but maybe possibly a time traveler? The idea was so ridiculous that I started laughing. A minute later, Sophie joined me. We were both cackling like a couple of crazies, which, of course, the world thought we were.

Maybe she and I would be friends after all.

CHAPTER **38**

Suddenly, though, Sophie wasn't laughing anymore. "The thing is," she said, "ever since I was twelve, what I've thought about the most is dying." Her voice was blunt, and her face deadly serious.

I felt like I'd been punched. How had we gone from giggling about Jordan to a confession like that in a span of fifteen seconds? And how was I supposed to respond? Believe it or not, people didn't share their darkest secrets all that often at Belman. Most of us tried to keep our problems as private as we could, guarding those scary parts of ourselves like they were a treasure instead of a curse.

"The first time I tried to commit suicide, I took a bunch of pills," Sophie went on. She tucked her legs under her and pulled a hospital pillow to her chest. "I counted them out into these neat little groups of five, and I just worked my way through the piles. Then my dad walked in and saw what I was doing. He was so pissed—like, 'What are you trying to do, kill yourself?' And I'm like, '*Duh!* Is that not obvious?'" She clutched the pillow tighter. "They made me start seeing a therapist three times a week, but it didn't change anything."

"Oh, Sophie," I began, but she kept talking without seeming to hear me.

"The next time I tried, I took my dad's gun from the garage. It turned out he'd hidden all the bullets, but I put the muzzle in my mouth anyway, to see what it felt like, and then I held it to my temple. I was trying to decide where the best place was. This time my mom found me, and she brought me straight to Belman. And that's the story of how I got here the first time." Sophie shook her head. "It would've been better if she would've just brought me the goddamn bullets. And by now, she probably thinks that, too."

Then I did something that surprised me. I got up and went to sit beside her, and I took her hand in mine. "I know that's not true," I said. "Your parents love you. They want you here, where you're safe." I squeezed her warm fingers. "I'm sorry, Sophie."

She shrugged and squeezed back. "What can you do? I was born like this. Just like I have red hair and big feet, and like you can't help looking like Lily Collins, I have this thing that comes over me—like this awful black fog or something—and when I'm inside it, there's no light or happiness or meaning. I can't describe how awful it is, because the words don't exist. When I'm in the fog, I just need to get out of it again. And dying feels like the fastest way."

"But it's the worst way," I said. "You know that, right? You can't get better if you're dead."

"When I'm inside that fog I don't believe there's any way to get better."

"But there is," I said. "I have to believe that, and you should, too. So maybe coming to Belman is a good thing."

"Oh, sure," Sophie said. "Belman is super great, super historical, and it's got gobs of famous alumni. It's basically the Harvard of psych wards."

I laughed. "On the adult wing, maybe. Here we're just a bunch of messed-up teenagers. Then again, who knows what we might accomplish someday? Our potential is still untapped."

"Exactly. Maybe someday I'll actually manage to kill myself," Sophie said. But then she smiled, and I realized that she was trying to be funny.

"Or maybe you'll manage to get well," I said.

Sophie nodded thoughtfully. "Could happen. All I know is, if I was, like, riddled with cancer, I could be cured tomorrow. My parents would pay all the money in the world for the greatest doctors in the history of mankind, and *snap*, I'd be healed." She slipped her hand out of mine and slapped it against her forehead. "How come they can take out tumors, but they can't take out thoughts?"

I didn't know what to say. It was a question that all of us had asked at one point or another. But no one had ever come up with an answer.

Date: 1/23/23
Name: Hannah Doe

PROGRESS REPORT: Hannah became agitated
during group therapy. She accused fellow
patients of being helpless, lazy, and
overfed. She called them "pig people"
and said that the only thing wrong with
them was that their lives were too easy.
She was removed from group.

She subsequently informed staff that
they were also pig people, slavishly
working for a corrupt system and failing
to understand "anything about anything,"
including grief, legacies of deprivation,
and the realities of time travel.

After that she wouldn't speak at all.
She ate dinner in her room and refused
all medication with the exception of
5 mg zolpidem for sleep.

CHAPTER 39

I just wanted to sleep, but sleep wouldn't come. Maybe that was because it never actually got dark on the Belman ward, and it definitely never got quiet. People cried and moaned at night. They talked to themselves or to phantoms. Nurses chatted through their shifts, their words muffled by the fan they kept near their station. I'd learned to make these sounds fade into a kind of white noise. It wasn't comforting, but it was familiar. The lullaby of the psych hospital.

Sophie breathed quietly beside me, sleeping. I wondered if she'd wake screaming like Indy sometimes did, or if she'd sleepwalk the way Michaela used to. Before she started gaining weight, Michaela would sneak into the kitchenette and sleep-eat. This was her body, in its animal will to live, grasping at the chance to feed itself.

For now, though, everything was peaceful. I lay on my back, looking up at the ugly ceiling. The dots on the tiles were like constellations of tiny black stars. If I stared long enough, I thought I could find the Big Dipper, or Orion's Belt.

I looked for a long, long time. But instead of constellations, I saw blackness curling into the room, seeping up from the floor and down from the ceiling. It was like the fog Sophie talked about, but it wasn't coming for her. It was coming for me.

Chapter 40

I stood at the castle window, icy night air stinging my cheeks. Along the battlements, the shadows of guards passed back and forth beneath a half-moon. I watched them at their dreary duty until dawn, when I could smell smoke from the kitchens and hear the neighing of horses and the shouts of men beginning their work.

"—and now Lord Sicard says he awaits word of Baron Joachim's surrender."

The voice was coming from right outside my door. I flung myself onto the giant bed and pulled the curtains tight around it as the door opened and two people came into the room. I could hear one of them poking around in the hearth. I smelled bread, hot from the ovens.

"He says Baron Joachim's too green to rule." This was Margery's voice. "Sicard always held it was his banners that should fly on the ramparts, and now he sees his chance. He has twice the army, if not more. If Baron Joachim doesn't bend, we'll see the bloodshed."

"A curse on men, all of them," said the other voice—Agnes's. "They play at feuds and warfare, and the rest of us suffer." She cursed. "We need more logs. Where's that stupid Paul when you need him?"

"The baron won't yield," Margery went on. "He'd never. But we'll be safe in the keep."

"Safe? Joachim would launch us over the wall on a trebuchet if he thought it'd help his cause," Agnes said darkly.

"You're unfair to him," her sister said. "His father was the cruel one."

"The apple doesn't fall far—"

"Oh, this wine is sour," Margery suddenly exclaimed. "It needs honey and spice. Why didn't you taste it before bringing it up?"

"I did taste it. It's plenty good enough for the peasant," Agnes replied.

"Oh, go get a touch of honey at least."

I could imagine Agnes's glare, but after a moment she left, grumbling as she went. When she was gone, I pushed my face through the curtain and said, "Who's Lord Sicard?"

"Oh!" cried Margery, jumping back and clutching at her chest. "I thought you were sleeping." She quickly composed herself. "I've brought you breakfast," she said. "There's bread and cheese and—"

"Sour wine."

A flicker of a smile appeared on her lips. "Exactly."

I looked straight into her pale eyes. "Why am I here, and will I be let go? Or am I to be killed by an enemy I've never heard of, or else starve in a siege with the rest of you?"

"That'll not happen, I can *assure* you," Margery said.

I was almost touched by her certainty. I'd been confident like her once, and look where it'd gotten me. "Are you a fortune-teller?" I asked. "Can you see into the future?"

Margery began to slice the bread with a large, bone-handled knife. "No. I'm blind as a newborn babe when it comes to such a thing. But I have faith in the baron."

"As my friends and family had faith in me," I said, climbing out of bed, still wearing my beautiful, absurd dress. "And now my sister is a corpse and the man who was going to be my husband hangs from a rope in the courtyard. Faith doesn't mean safety. It means death." I laughed bitterly. "And you all think *I'm* the idiot."

If I'd expected Margery to take offense, I was wrong. She merely shrugged. "The baron certainly doesn't think you're an idiot," she said. "I hear he finds you—oh, what was the word? Intriguing, I think it was."

I eyed the knife, which she had set down on the table. "I would relish the chance to show him just how intriguing I can be," I said.

Following my gaze, Margery quickly tucked the weapon into her skirts and then turned on her heel. "Agnes may or may not be back with honey," she said. "In the meantime, I'll let you sup in peace."

"Don't leave me," I cried, suddenly desperate. "Please, I—"

But the door had already shut behind her.

Chapter 41

*F*or the next two days, people streamed across the drawbridge. Men, women, and children from Dunwall, the large town nearest the castle, came seeking protection and bearing everything they could carry. Once through the gatehouse, they set up temporary camp in the outer baileys. So, too, did inhabitants from the little hill hamlets that lay in the path of Lord Sicard's army. Anyone with grain or livestock brought it to sell to a castellan suddenly eager to purchase supplies at a premium.

All this I learned from Margery, who brought me news along with my humble meals, and who—unlike her sister—seemed to enjoy my company. She said the mood inside the walls was almost festive.

"It's like they're preparing for a feast instead of a battle," she said.

"The fools don't know what to expect," Agnes replied, straightening the blankets on my bed and frowning furiously as she did so.

"And how many attacks have you lived through, sister?" Margery asked. She turned to me. "The answer is none, of course."

"Because the old baron knew how to keep his enemies in line," Agnes said. "He kept a larger force—he wasn't afraid to show his strength."

"Until he died with an arrow through his neck," Margery reminded her.

"Such's the perils of lordship," Agnes said. "He was serving his king, as he should. I don't miss him, God knows. But he'd have kept us from being killed or raped or starved, unlike the stripling we serve now."

"The walls will protect us," Margery said firmly.

I thought of the people gathered in the courtyards. "Did anyone come from my village?" It was so small that it had never been given a real name, but it was where the Vernet River turned and curved south. "The Bend, they call it."

"We don't go asking where the stinking lot comes from," Agnes said.

I didn't think anyone from home would have sought protection in the castle—not after Maraulf, Merrick, and Vazi returned to The Bend wounded, with news of my failed plan and its deadly consequences. But I told myself that distance would keep them safe from enemy swords.

Opening a locked trunk, Margery reached in and drew out a woolen cloak. "Here," she said, "put this on. You're coming with me."

I stared at her in surprise—I was going to be allowed out? I took the heavy garment and draped it around my shoulders. "Where are we going?" I asked.

"Baron Joachim is on the wall—"

"Is he going to have his ogre hang another starving commoner?" I interrupted. "Or will he behead someone, just for the novelty? Must get all the *justice* done before Sicard comes!"

Margery fastened the cloak at my neck with a silver clasp.

"Enough, child. He's going to speak—to prepare us for what's to come."

I hardly cared about anything the baron had to say unless it was about letting me go back to my village, but Margery hustled me out the door and down a series of long hallways until we came out onto a narrow tower balcony.

The baron stood a stone's throw away on top of the gateway to the middle bailey. His cheeks were flushed in the sharp wind, and his dark brows were furrowed. "—and so Sicard comes, leading five hundred men, to try to take what is ours. There are some on my council who say I should meet him on the battlefield. *Make a show of force*, they say, though we have less than two hundred swords at hand. *Our men are better fighters*, they say. Does that mean I should set them riding toward a foe twice their number? I don't think so. To the men who itch for battle, I ask this: What sword can pierce stone? The castle is our shield—our best defense and our greatest weapon." He looked at the crowd of knights and villagers. "We cannot stop them from coming," he said. "But when they get here, we will drive them back."

And what if you don't? I wanted to call out. But I knew the answer to the question already. Sicard's army would make camp outside the walls and wait until we were starved into surrender.

And then, when the baron and his men finally understood what it felt like to be truly, horribly, and achingly hungry, I would stand there with my hollow cheeks and my empty belly, and I would laugh.

Chapter 42

L ord Sicard's army charged over the hill before dawn on Sunday, the Lord's day. The horses' hooves sounded like thunder as they churned the winter fields, and behind them, the night sky roiled with smoke and flames.

The guard on the watch turret frantically blew his trumpet, and the baron's men woke and scrambled to arm themselves. The castle and its courtyards exploded with the clatter of swords and armor; commanders shouted orders as the knights raced to the wall. Soon every arrow slit in the castle walls had a man and a bow behind it, and in the hoardings, squires and stable boys readied stones and firepots to drop onto the attackers below.

Roused by the terrifying clamor, I watched from my window as Sicard's men began their assault on the castle. They moved quickly and lethally. In a darkness lit by torches and burning brush, I could see soldiers trying to lay a temporary bridge across the moat, while others drove a team of armored oxen to pull a catapult within range.

The baron's archers fired on them, volley after volley, and their arrows streamed down like hail. When they found their marks, men shouted and horses screamed.

If I'd thought the baron might stay safe in his chambers and let his men take the arrows for him, I was wrong. The baron stood on the wall-walk, armed in iron and girded with steel.

"Aim for the oxen!" he shouted.

Knights on either side of him obeyed, and I watched as two of the creatures pulling the catapult stumbled and fell, arrows sticking out of their necks. But Sicard's men cut them from their harnesses and the weapon jerked forward again. Soon the catapult was close enough to fire. Soldiers packed the bucket with flaming pitch. With a shout, they let it fly.

The fireball hurtled toward us, crashing against the side of the curtain wall. Flames streamed down into the dry moat, even as soldiers tried to cross it to scale the walls and the baron's men flung rocks down through the hoardings. Sicard's men fell shrieking from the walls, but more kept coming. Five hundred men? It seemed more like a thousand.

The sun rose higher and the fighting went on. Sicard's men had partially filled in a section of the moat with earth and logs so that they could roll a siege tower close to the castle. It was covered with wet animal hide to protect it from flames, and inside there were dozens of swordsmen, ready to charge over the wall. As the baron's knights fired upon the tower, more of Sicard's men braved the dry moat and rushed to climb the walls. It was impossible to shoot them from directly above, so the squires took aim with rocks and dropped them down through holes in the hoardings.

Everything was chaos, but the baron's men were holding off the attackers. Then a volley of burning arrows from the ground set one of the hoardings on fire, and fighters scrambled out of it, retreating to the safety of the wall-walk. Meanwhile, the siege tower was moving closer. Any moment now, the two sides would be fighting hand-to-hand high on the walls.

I ran to my door, but of course it was still locked.

Dear God, my name is Hannah Dory, and this is not how I want to die.

Returning to the window, I watched the siege tower make its final lurch toward the castle wall. Two of the baron's commanders were trying to push him toward safety, but the baron shook them off. He drew his crossbow, the arrow's tip already alight, and shot it into the siege tower. It hit in a corner not covered by rawhide, and the flames caught the wood and the tower began to burn. More burning arrows followed, and soon the tower blazed like a torch.

Smoke filled the air and stung my eyes. It seemed like everything in the world was burning. Even on the far-off horizon, I could see black clouds of smoke curling miles into the sky.

Margery came in, her face even paler than usual. She poured me a cup of ale and we sat in silence, listening to the sounds of battle. It raged into the evening and then, as the sun went down, it suddenly quieted. We could hear nothing but the wind, crying through the ramparts.

"What's happening?" she whispered.

"Men have to rest at the end of a day, I suppose," I said, "whether they're farmers or fighters."

The lines of my song came back to me, and I sang them for Margery.

Now's the time to be at peace, our day's long work is done
And mothers are calling their children in, one by one by one.

"Mothers, call your soldiers home," Margery said. "Before they kill us all."

The door swung open and Agnes stalked in. "They burned all the towns on the way," she spat. She flung a tray with bread and sausage onto the table in the corner. "Sicard's army. That's how they rode through the night, you know—they lit their way with burning houses."

My stomach clenched. So *that* was the black smoke I'd seen in the distance. But I shouldn't have been surprised: the great men fight, and the poor men pay the price.

"What quarrel did he have with them?" Margery asked.

"None," Agnes said. "But they were a fine source of light, weren't they?" Her voice was choked and furious. "We came from one of those, you and I!"

Sicard burned farmers, sheepherders, and children asleep in their beds, I thought, feeling sick. I had no love for Baron Joachim, but I was sure he would never do such a thing. He'd shown me mercy, hadn't he, in his own strange way? And he'd proven his bravery on the wall today.

"The baron must summon all who are left," I said.

Margery leaned toward me. "What are you talking about?"

I walked to the window and looked out. All was peaceful darkness. But it was a false peace, and it could be broken at any moment. "The farmers and weavers and ploughboys," I said. "They'll come."

"To fight?" Margery asked. "With what weapons?"

"With whatever they can find," I answered. "They can attack at night, the way Sicard did. Let them pay back treachery with treachery." I turned back to the sisters. "A sleeping man is easy enough to kill."

"Do you have many strong men in The Bend?" Margery asked.

I paused. "We did," I said. "But you'll find little help there now." *And that is all my fault.* "I need paper and a quill."

Margery stared at me. "Whatever for?"

"To write with," I said, exasperated.

Her eyes grew even wider. "You can do that?"

"A little, thanks to a priest. Now bring me—"

Agnes thrust a scrap of wrinkled parchment into my hands. "No quill," she said.

And so I used charcoal from the fire to scratch out my idea.

Chapter 43

*M*argery placed the scrap of paper on a table in the baron's chambers, but if he saw it, no one ever told me. What I did know was that after another day of bloodshed, of men on both sides killing and dying, Sicard's men withdrew for the night. And in the winter darkness, every farmer and peasant for miles tiptoed through the woods, the blades they used for slaughtering pigs and butchering rabbits clutched in their work-roughened hands.

They'd cut the throats of a hundred men before the rest could draw a sword or notch an arrow. By the time Sicard's soldiers had armed themselves, the baron and his knights were waiting, having crept out through the secret sally port armed with spears and battle axes and maces.

It was a rout. By the time the sun was an inch into the sky, Sicard had surrendered.

The baron rode back into the castle across the lowered drawbridge and entered the outer bailey to the sound of deafening cheers. He didn't take off his helmet or acknowledge the people reaching up to him in gratitude.

"He just went into his chambers," Margery said, pouring me wine she swore wasn't sour, "and then summoned the doctors. He was cut by Sicard's own blade." She smiled. "But he was brave,

Hannah. He had two mounts die beneath him and he never turned away—"

"I should hope not," I said, taking a sip from the silver cup. It tasted thick and sweet. "A man who orders others onto the battlefield belongs in the midst of it himself. Is his wound fatal, I hope?"

"You say the most terrible things!"

"I'm only being honest."

"Just keep your mouth shut when you leave this room," she said. "Otherwise you'll be sent to the stocks, and they won't let me wait on you there."

"Are you taking me to hear another of the baron's pretty speeches?" I asked sharply. "Or is he still in his feather bed, nursing his scratch?"

"He's in the great hall," she said, "and you're to dress and see him there."

Chapter 44

After Agnes combed my hair so hard that I thought my scalp would bleed, Margery twisted it into a series of low, dark whorls at my neck. Then she pulled a pale-blue gown edged with white lace from the locked trunk. "This will do, I think," she said.

"Whose dress was this?" I asked as she tugged the satin sleeves up my arms.

"Does it matter?" Margery stepped back to admire it. "It's lovely."

The satin was cool and smooth under my fingertips, and the lace was so delicate I was almost afraid to touch it. I'd never seen anything so beautiful in my life. Had it belonged to the old baron's wife? Or was it made for a daughter she hoped she'd have? All I knew was that it belonged on the shoulders of a lady, not a peasant, and I felt like an utter fool in it.

"Why does the baron mock me?" I asked as Margery slipped fine leather boots on my feet. "Does he give his pigs pearl necklaces?"

Agnes snickered, but Margery looked at me with great offense. "You're a beautiful girl," she said.

"I'm a commoner," I said. "I'm not even supposed to look a noble in the eye."

"I don't pretend to know what the baron wants or thinks," Margery said. "I just do as I'm told."

"And so will you, if you know what's good for you," Agnes added. And she gave my arm a hard pinch as she shoved me out the door.

Two waiting guards—not the hard ones who had brought me here, though I felt sure these would be no better than the others—took their places on either side of me and led me away down the passage.

The great hall, which occupied the second floor of the keep, was warmed by a huge fire and lit by countless candles. The smell of charred meat made my mouth water. At the long wooden tables, there must have been a hundred men at least, and by the look of them, they'd been eating and drinking for hours already. Their faces were wine-flushed and their voices rang out as they bragged of their roles in the fight.

At the far end of the hall, on a raised platform, the baron sat at a table draped in rich velvet. He seemed freshly scrubbed, but there was a gash across his brow that looked red and angry. He raised a goblet to me, as if in a toast.

"Go and join him," the first guard said.

I shook my head and remained where I stood.

"Tebben was right about her," he said to the other. "Doesn't do as she's told."

"There's a remedy for that," said the other one. He took a step toward me, and the next thing I knew he'd hit me across the face so hard that I saw stars floating in blackness. My knees buckled, and I grabbed on to the table to stay upright.

"Now go and present yourself to Baron Joachim," he said.

I put my hand to my stinging cheek. "I won't," I whispered.

"You damn well will." He raised his hand to strike me again.

But he couldn't see what I could, or else he would've run. The baron had left his table, and his face was full of rage as he came toward us, his hand on the hilt of his sword.

"I don't have to go to him," I said. "Because he's right there behind you."

T he guard's eyes widened as I began to back away, uncertain as to which of us had drawn the baron's anger. Before the guard could turn around, the baron struck him with the flat of his sword and he stumbled sideways, nearly falling into the fire. After catching himself against the stones of the hearth, he stood up as straight as he could. Then he bowed his head and bent his knee.

"Forgive me, your lordship," he gasped. His left cheek was already swelling and turning purple.

The baron's green-gold eyes shone with anger. "We do not strike those smaller and weaker than we are," he said. Then he turned to me and his expression softened. "Well, we do, of course, when they require it. But during a celebration, *never*."

With a flick of his wrist he dismissed the guard, who slunk away into the corner, where someone handed him a mug of wine, which he downed in one gulp, staring blackly at me.

The baron held out his arm—I supposed I was meant to take it—but I looked at it as if it were a snake. "I have nothing to celebrate."

He raised an eyebrow. "How about your life?" he asked. "It was nearly lost on more than one occasion, including the very attack we just repelled. As far as I can tell, it is thanks to me that you are still in possession of it, however miserable it seems to have been for you so far."

"And is it not thanks to me that a legion of farmers and swine-herds helped you repel the attack? It was certainly thanks to you that my life was in danger in the first place," I said. "Or have you forgotten that you nearly had me hanged, and then you threw me in a dungeon?"

His expression clouded for a moment, but then he offered me the smallest of smiles. "Let's talk of happier things," he said. He had dropped his arm, seeing that I wouldn't take it, but I felt his fingers close about my elbow. Slowly but forcefully, he steered me toward his table at the head of the great hall. I was still dizzy from the guard's blow, and the sea of men blurred and swam as we moved.

"Here," he said, pulling out a carved and painted chair right next to his. "Sit."

I sank into it—not because I wanted to, but because I needed to. I could taste blood in my mouth and my right ear was ringing.

A servingman placed a goblet of wine in front of me, while another set down meat and potatoes on a trencher of thick-sliced bread. I stared mutely down at the fatty, glistening meat. There was more of it right now, for me alone, than my whole family had had in our lives.

The baron held out a gilded bowl, intricately fashioned in the shape of a boat. It was full of a fine, crystalline powder. "Salt," he said.

It didn't look anything like the hard gray blocks of it we got in our village. Again my mouth watered. But I declined the salt and pushed the trencher away. "I'm not hungry," I said.

The baron withdrew the golden boat with a shrug. "Well, have a little wine," he said. "And then perhaps you will sing a song for us. I'm told you have a beautiful voice."

"I won't sing," I said.

"You're very impertinent," he said, looking at me with surprise.

I was pleased to confound him like that. "A fine dress doesn't give me fine manners," I said.

"Obviously not," he said.

I picked up the glass of wine, sniffed it, and put it down again, just to aggravate him.

"Sing," he said. "The men would like to hear it."

"The men are drunk, and they're telling tales of fighting and wenching," I said. "I wouldn't presume to interrupt them."

I could see his hands tightening on the arms of his chair.

No doubt he's beginning to question his rule about hitting someone smaller and weaker than he is.

"You've been struck by my guard, and you're not yourself," he said.

"On the contrary," I said. "I am exactly myself, which is why I won't sing for you."

His eyes were cold again—colder than they were when he stood on a wall above Otto's swinging corpse.

"Then go," he whispered furiously.

CHAPTER **46**

Buzzed on coffee and mildly hungover from celebrating the A on his Organic Chem exam, Jordan Hassan thumbs through the *Diagnostic and Statistical Manual of Mental Disorders, Fifth Edition*, a.k.a. the *DSM-5*, while he waits for the morning staff meeting to start. Excited to have been invited to observe the meeting, he showed up ten minutes early. Trichotillomania: when someone can't stop pulling out their own hair. Frotteuristic disorder: when someone gets off on rubbing themselves against strangers.

Creepy, he thinks, before he reminds himself not to judge. No one wakes up and chooses to like that sort of thing, any more than they would choose to suffer from kleptomania.

Or, of course, schizophrenia.

Although schizophrenia affects only about 1 percent of the population, it's one of the most disabling diseases known to humankind. Jordan can still remember writing that sentence in his Psych 101 notebook.

For his current class, Abnormal Psychology—an unfortunate name, he now realizes—his notebook is full of observations about life on a locked psychiatric ward. He's written about Brandon's seizures, Sean's violent outbursts, and Indy's portfolio of intricate, astonishing drawings. He's noted mealtime habits, med pass routines, and the weird popularity of old John Hughes movies: the minute an aide puts on *The Breakfast Club*, the whole ward shows up in the TV lounge.

But mostly he's written about Hannah. Her intelligence, her love of books, her beautiful singing voice—and her unshakable belief that she travels hundreds of years back in time.

He drains the last of his coffee and turns to the schizophrenia page. Hannah's page.

Delusions, it says. *Hallucinations. Disorganized speech.*

He's never heard Hannah using so-called disorganized speech, but others on the ward use it. *See the moon. Rune. Tune. I used to sing opera because God told me to. Toodle-loo!* That's how Brian H., in Room 19, sounds. *There's a ledge. It's alleged that I'm dead. I'm dead twice over, it's all part of the plan. I know they're watching. They've infiltrated the ceilings. They want to kill me again and again.*

Jordan never quite knows how to respond to it—to what the staff call "word salad."

"Learning anything new?"

Dr. Klein has just entered the staff room, with Amy, Mitch, and the rest of the morning shift behind her. Jordan snaps the book shut.

"Yes and no," he says. "I mean, it's just symptom after symptom. Where's the part about how you're supposed to help deal with them?"

Dr. Klein sinks heavily into a chair. "You'll note that the title says 'diagnostic manual,' not 'treatment protocol.'"

Mitch snickers. Feeling stupid, Jordan puts the book back onto the shelf. "Right," he says. "Of course."

They roll through the meeting, going down the list of patients and how they're doing. Jordan's scrambling to keep up, but he snaps to attention when he hears Hannah's name.

"—and Ian said that Hannah did agree to an increase in medication," Mitch is saying, "so we'll see how that goes."

"So she's back from the castle?" Amy asks.

That's how they refer to Hannah's episodes: *going to the castle.*

Mitch nods. "I wonder how long we can keep her here."

What Jordan can sense—but which no one has said out loud—is that Hannah is getting worse. It seems like every time she comes to the hospital, she spends more and more time caught inside her fantasy, oblivious to anyone's attempts to help her. But there's something about that fact that perplexes him. He raises his hand. Mitch snickers again, but Dr. Klein nods at Jordan to speak.

"I was wondering…is it common for a patient's hallucinations to be so consistent?" Jordan asks. "I mean, sometimes Andy thinks his hand doesn't belong to him, and other times he insists he doesn't have a face. Sean saw giant bugs crawling all over his dinner the other day, but now they're gone and the TV's talking to him. Whereas Hannah—all she ever talks about is that one world."

"There probably *were* bugs on his dinner," Mitch mumbles, clearly hoping for a laugh.

"It's extremely unusual," Dr. Klein says, ignoring him. "Coherence is not a hallmark of the schizophrenic mind, and I've never seen a patient with hallucinations so consistent, as you say."

"That's kind of what I thought," he says. "So—do you think there's a chance that this castle is a real place?"

Mitch shoots him a *What the hell?* look, and Amy says, "Oh, boy, here we go," like Jordan's gone off the deep end or something.

He feels his cheeks go hot. "What I mean is," he says, "could there be some truth to it in the here and now?"

Dr. Klein doesn't laugh at him the way he was afraid she might.

"It could be real in some sense, in that its image has something to do with Hannah's past. But is it the hospital? Or is it something she saw in a horror movie? We don't know." She runs her hand through her silvery hair. "There are genetic *and* environmental components to schizophrenia, but we know nothing about Hannah's background or family. Whether she's unwilling to tell us, or frankly incapable of it, I'm not sure. I can't emphasize this enough, though: whatever we do, we must not reinforce her belief that she time-travels to an actual medieval castle."

"She has to understand that it's *completely impossible*," Amy agrees. "That's the only hope she has of getting better. She accepts that we're right, and she takes her damn medicines."

"Which she's never really liked to do," Mitch says.

For understandable reasons, Jordan thinks. *They make her feel like a zombie.*

"How old was she when she first came here?" he asks.

"Thirteen."

"And her parents didn't bring her?"

"An ambulance did," Amy says. She sighs. "An ambulance always does."

"And lucky for her, there's always been room here," Mitch adds.

"How does *that* work?" Jordan asks. It's notoriously difficult to find beds in psychiatric wards—everyone knows that.

"When Hannah was first admitted," Dr. Klein says, "the granddaughter of Delia Belman, the hospital's namesake, was visiting. She saw Hannah—a helpless, scrawny, dark-haired child, stuck in an agonizing delusion—and she said to me, 'I want you to do whatever it takes to care for her.' So we have."

"Hannah's very lucky, like Mitch said," Amy says resolutely.

Jordan's mouth almost falls open. By all accounts, Hannah suffers from a brain disease that torments her, that's capable of completely disconnecting her from reality. She's spent a good portion of her teenage years in a locked hospital ward. How the hell is that lucky?

CHAPTER 47

On Friday, Jordan gets permission to take Hannah outside. It's not on her list of ward privileges—she hasn't earned any this time around—but Dr. Klein thinks that going for a walk could be good for her. "Maybe it will remind her of the real world," she says, "in which she is a present-day psychiatric patient whose sole job it is to get better."

After lunch (eggplant parmesan), Jordan gets Hannah a spare coat (a bright red parka three sizes too big for her) and signs her out. Hannah's friend Michaela and her roommate, Sophie, who aren't supposed to have outside privileges, either, grumble about how no one takes *them* anywhere, but Nurse Amy guides them away to the TV room before they can get too worked up about it.

Hannah doesn't say anything as she and Jordan go through the double set of locked doors, walk down the long hall, and take the elevator to the ground level. He has no idea what she's thinking and it makes him nervous.

What if this is a terrible idea? What if she tries to run?

And also: *What if I say something stupid? What if she doesn't want to talk to me?*

Those are questions he might wonder about with any girl he's just getting to know.

Which makes it weird when he thinks them about Hannah, because he's a college student, and she's a psychiatric patient, and though they've spent a lot of time together lately, their lives could hardly be more different.

But is it okay that they might be becoming something like friends?

They pass through the lobby, with its watercolor posters and its fake potted ficus trees: Hannah walks through it like she's in a dream. Then they step outside, and the winter sunlight dazzles them. Hannah blinks in surprise.

"When was the last time I felt so many gorgeous UV rays?" she says, tipping her face to the sun. Her skin is alabaster-pale, and her dark hair's tangled and unwashed. Still.

"Well, it's been a minute," Jordan says evasively.

Tears sparkle in her eyes, and she wipes at them with the corner of her borrowed coat.

"I'm not crying," she says, answering before he can ask. "It's just really goddamn bright."

He digs into the pocket of his coat and pulls out a pair of cheap plastic sunglasses. She puts them on and purses her lips like she's posing for a picture. "How do I look?" she says, and then she flashes him a quick and sudden grin, looking for a split second like any other smiling, goofy, neurotypical girl on the street.

Albeit one who could use some help with personal hygiene.

"You look great." He pulls his cap down over his ears. It's goddamn bright, but it's also goddamn cold. "Come on, let's walk," he says. Maybe walking he'll be less nervous.

The hospital grounds are beautiful. On the other side of the tall, wrought-iron fence, there's the crowded, loud, gritty world of

New York City. But on the Belman side, it's like they're taking a stroll in a private park. Compared to state-run psychiatric institutions, Belman is a country club. A palatial estate.

"So," Hannah says, tossing one of the fat squirrels a bit of a croissant, "do you like working in the loony bin?"

"That's not what—"

"Oh, God," she interrupts. "If *I'm* not allowed to talk shit about it, who is? But, fine, whatever." When she speaks again, she sounds stiffly officious. "Tell me, Mr. Hassan, have you been enjoying your experience at Delia F. Belman Psychiatric Hospital, the preeminent institution of its kind on the North American continent?"

Jordan hesitates. Can you *enjoy* being on a psychiatric ward, caring for people living through the worst moments of their lives? Unless your empathy button's broken, he's not sure you can. You can love it, maybe, but you're not going to find it *fun.*

He says, "Well, I'm learning a lot. And I think it's really important work."

Hannah tosses another crumb to the squirrel, which is now following them. "That's kind of a bullshit answer, but I guess I'll take it."

They go a little ways in silence. Hannah's walk is shuffling and slow—the exact opposite of Jordan's thoughts. Should he try to find out more about the castle? Should he ask her about her family? Might she be willing to talk to him the way she wouldn't to a therapist? Could she climb the fence if she tried?

He's trying to figure out how to break the silence when Hannah does it for him.

"I read that book you gave me," she says. "*Reasons to Live?* I liked it. It was...short."

He laughs. "Yeah, it's definitely not *Moby Dick*."

"*Moby Dick* was pretty good," Hannah says. "I mean, when it's Ishmael and Queequeg hanging out on land, it's great. But once they go to sea, there's just too much ship's rigging and psychological torment."

"I'm impressed by your literary analysis," he says.

What he's really impressed by is how good she seems. If he was meeting her for the first time right now, he'd never guess there was anything wrong with—correction, *different about*—her. Anything *neurodivergent*.

"What's your favorite book?" he asks.

"John Steinbeck, *East of Eden*," she says without hesitation. "Also *Brideshead Revisited* by Evelyn Waugh, *Love in the Time of Cholera* by Gabriel García Márquez, and *The Woman in White* by Wilkie Collins."

"I'm even more impressed now. Did you read those in school? All I remember from high school was *Animal Farm* and *The Great Gatsby*."

"School? Please," Hannah says, scoffing. "Try the New York Public Library system." She pushes the sunglasses up on her head. "It's the fourth biggest in the entire world, for your information. What books do you like, Jordan Hassan?"

Jordan gives a half shrug. Did he like *Foundations of Psychology, Eighth Edition*? Or *Cell and Molecular Biology*? *Modern Physical Organic Chemistry*? The truth is, he can barely remember reading the book he gave to Hannah. It was from a class he took his freshman year, and now that he's a sophomore, every book he reads is aimed solely at getting him into med school.

"I read the *New Yorker* on the subway," he offers, but this isn't even true. He brings the *New Yorker* on his commute, and then he sticks his face into his phone. What did people do before there was Wi-Fi in the subways? His score on Mario Kart Tour is sick.

"Haven't you read all the studies about how being a good reader makes you a better person?" Hannah asks him.

"I've only read the headlines," he says.

She laughs. "Pitiful."

"I think I'm doing okay, though," he protests. "I work all the time, I study, I—"

"Does that make you a good person?" Her gaze is piercing.

Jordan thinks about his dad, the guy who treated everyone but his own son with kindness and respect. Ali Hassan was a champion in the Little League dugout, the life of the neighborhood barbecue, and a goddamn disaster when it came to keeping his anger in check. Does Jordan have that same kind of darkness inside him? When he looks at the hole he punched in his dorm room wall last October, he wonders.

"Do you think you're a good person?" Hannah says again.

Jordan looks down at her and sees once again the terrified girl he trapped like a deer. *I did the right thing, didn't I?*

"I really try to be," he says.

She throws one last crumb to the squirrel. "I think you are," she says.

And his heart lifts.

CHAPTER **48**

They've come to the pond on the hospital's west side, where dozens of koi fish glide through the cold, black water. According to Mitch, Delia Belman was "an undiagnosed manic depressive who spent all her money on funding a psychiatric hospital and breeding exotic Japanese carp." One of the pond's fish, Mitch claimed, had been worth twenty thousand dollars. "But then," he said, "it got eaten by a hawk."

Hannah's gone quiet, despite Jordan's attempts to draw her back into a conversation. Her hands are shoved into her pockets and her shoulders are hunched protectively up to her ears. He doesn't know what happened: one minute they were talking about the soul-sucking hellhole of chain restaurants, street performers, and tourists that is Times Square, and the next minute she was staring mutely down at her shuffling feet.

Then he remembers: that's where Hannah had been found on January 17th, half naked and fully psychotic.

Shit, he thinks, *and I just made her go back there*.

She'd last left Belman, against medical advice, in November. Where had she spent the two months before being admitted again? No one had any idea. Maybe she'd left town, or maybe she'd lived under a bridge—all they knew was that she broke down in front of a Gap, and then the police were called.

"I wanted to ask you something," he says.

At first he thinks she hasn't heard him. Or that she's just done talking for the day. But then she says, "Everyone always does. Lulu, Amy, Dr. Nicholas... The phrasing varies, but it all boils down to 'what the hell is wrong with you, and why won't you get *better*?'"

"My question isn't one they like to ask you."

This seems to spark her interest. "What is it?"

"I want to know more about the castle," he says. "Can you just... describe it to me?"

She sighs. "You think you can help me. You think you *need* to help me. But I don't need to be helped—I need to be *believed*."

"Just tell me what it's like," he urges.

She doesn't say anything for a whole circuit of the pond. And then she says, "It's made of black stone, with a gatehouse in the south wall and towers at all the corners. It's not like a Disney castle, with turrets and fluttering flags and whatever. It's a fortress. A place that doesn't like to let people in or out." She looks up at him. "You with me still?"

He nods. "Do you live in it?"

She gives a short, sharp laugh. "I'm a peasant, remember? I live in a one-room, wattle-and-daub hut with my family and some goats—before we had to eat them, anyway."

He decides not to ask what wattle-and-daub means, or what it was like to share a room with livestock. "Right," he says. "But you get to visit the castle?"

"Well, first I tried to rob it," she says matter-of-factly. "And then I got locked inside it. There are two women who take care of me, and one's nice and one's not, and they give me beautiful dresses that are literally against the law for a person like me to wear."

From the depths of Jordan's mind, an AP history note swims up: medieval sumptuary laws forbade people from "dressing above their station."

"Do you read nonfiction?" he blurts.

She turns to him in confusion. "What?"

"All your favorite books are novels—I...I just wondered." *I'm wondering if you've just read a million books about the Middle Ages.*

"Novels," she says firmly. "Are you trying to change the subject?"

"No, no, sorry." He pulls his hat farther down onto his head. Her past world is so detailed...so *tangible*. When she talks about it, he almost feels his own grip on reality fading.

"Have you ever tried to find it? Like, have you googled the castle to find out what happened?" Jordan is surprised by the questions tumbling out of his mouth.

She raised an eyebrow. "Of course I've tried to find it. And sometimes I've thought that I have, but they didn't exactly keep stellar records back then. Now that we've established that there wasn't Zillow in the Middle Ages, can we get back to where I left things?"

Jordan flushes a little with embarrassment. "Yes, of course. I'm listening."

"Good, because this is the scary part. Before I...*left*, I guess, there were people attacking the castle."

"Who were they?"

She shrugs. "I don't know—some other noble who wanted the

castle for himself, plus a couple hundred of his men." She pulls her sunglasses back down over her eyes. "I was locked in one of the rooms, and I was terrified. I'm used to people dying, but not in *battle*. You can't imagine the noise—all the screaming of men, of horses. Have you ever heard a horse scream? If not, then that's just another reason you can count yourself lucky, besides winning the genetic lottery by being smart, hot, and sane."

She thinks I'm hot?! he thinks. But he says, "I guess I don't understand why you would want to . . . to keep going back there."

"Because my family is there!" she cries. "Do you think I could just *leave* them?"

"No, I guess not," he admits.

When Hannah goes on, her voice is calm again. "Anyway, at night, when everything was quiet, you could hear the wounded men lying in the field. They were calling for their wives and their mothers. But they weren't ever going to see them again." She shudders and shoves her hands even deeper into her pockets. "There were so many of them, and they were in so much pain."

"Did you want to help them?" Jordan asks.

"No, I didn't," she says bluntly. "They were the enemy, and I just wanted them to hurry up and die."

CHAPTER **49**

Jordan stared at me in surprise. But I didn't have the energy to explain it. Life in the fourteenth century was not a goddamn picnic, which he should definitely know by now.

"Maybe we should head back," he said quietly.

I nodded, though my heart felt like it was sinking all the way down to my knees. *You freaked him out, Hannah. Why'd you have to do that?*

But then another little voice piped up. *What if you freaked him out because he* believes *you?*

We walked back toward the hospital. When we got close to the doors, he said, "Hannah?"

"What?" My voice came out sharper than I meant it to.

He scuffed his toe into some dirty slush near the curb. "I liked walking with you," he said.

I felt the sunshine get a little brighter right then.

"I liked it, too," I said. And then the doors slid open with a rush of hot air, and after that we didn't say anything else.

As soon as I'd signed myself into the ward, Michaela and Indy pounced. Michaela was crabbing about not being invited, and Indy looked me up and down and demanded, "Did you kiss?"

I took off the borrowed coat and draped it over my arm. It was warm and puffy, and I was hoping I could keep it forever. "That's so incredibly inappropriate."

"Do you mean the question—or the deep tongue kiss?" Indy asked.

"Indy, please shut up." I tried to walk past him but he stepped in front of me, grinning.

"You know I can't do that," he said.

"Of course he didn't kiss her, idiot. He'd get metoo'ed," Michaela said.

"He'd get *fired*," I said. "He's trying to do a good job here, in case you haven't noticed. Have some respect."

"Some what?" Indy said, blinking at us. "I'm not familiar with the term."

He was joking, but Michaela and I knew what he was talking about. We didn't necessarily feel *respected* as patients at Belman. Cared for, yes. Occasionally fussed over, too. But respected as functioning humans capable of decision-making and self-direction? Not so much. We were subject to the Almighty Schedule; we were given drugs we didn't always want by people who weren't necessarily sure that they would work; we were locked up like convicts and watched over twenty-four hours a day. And as nice as everyone on staff was, they still looked at us like we were flawed. Like we were broken.

And maybe some of us felt like we were. But we were still people who wanted to be treated with dignity, and there's *nothing* dignified about being strapped down to a bed when you're in the midst of a psychotic episode, which had happened to both me and Indy on more than one occasion.

Michaela held my hand as they walked me down the hall to my room. "Was it nice out there in the real world?" she asked.

"It was until it wasn't," I said.

"I guess that's true about a lot of things," she said. "Do you want to go do a word search with me? Mitch brought in a whole new book of them."

I shook my head. "Thanks, but I think I need to lie down."

I was relieved when I saw that my room was empty. I liked Sophie, but I just wanted to be alone.

I lay down on the bed and closed my eyes. I was thinking about my mother and Conn. I ached to see them again. I needed to make sure they were okay.

Jordan wondered how I could ever want to go back to that world, with all its hunger and darkness and death. I couldn't make him understand that those people were as real to me as he was.

And in that world, I was only myself: Hannah Dory. Here, I was *us*.

I am a me who doesn't know me, and I am a me who knows both of us.

Can you make sense of that? No?

Welcome to the club.

I was resting, breathing deeply, trying to call up the other world, when the air was split by screams.

CHAPTER **50**

The lounge was mayhem. An episode of *America's Got Talent* was playing at near-full volume on the giant TV, and Michaela was freaking out. Andy was rocking by the window with his hands over his ears, and "I don't belong here" Sean was standing there with his mouth hanging open, an expression of shock on his face.

At first I had no idea what was going on. Then I saw what Sean was staring at.

In a corner of the room lay Sophie. She was curled in a ball on the floor, clutching at her wrist, and kicking Nurse Amy away from her. "No!" she was crying. "Don't touch me! No no no!"

"Sophie, let me help," Amy yelled, but Sophie wasn't listening. Blood seeped through her fingers. Blood was on Amy's shoes, and it was smearing across the shiny white floor.

"Sophie!" I screamed.

My roommate looked up at me from where she lay, and her eyes were huge and scared. She said, "Oh, it's my friend! Hannah, I'm sorry—I didn't mean—Oh, *shit*—"

She couldn't get a full sentence out. She was scared by the blood, I could see that, and so was I.

I tried to run to her, but suddenly it seemed like the entire staff of Ward 6 had appeared out of nowhere, and they got in between me and my roommate. They surrounded her, making a wall of hospital scrubs that blocked my view. I could feel waves of panic building in my chest as I tried to see through them. I dropped down low, trying to get a better look at what was going on.

"Sophie!" I kept yelling. "Sophie!"

I was crawling toward her on my hands and knees when someone grabbed me by my shoulders and started pulling me back. I fought against whoever it was, but then I heard Indy's voice in my ear.

"Let them do their thing, babe," he said. "They're trying to help her."

I tried to push him away, but he was too strong. When I gave up, Indy half dragged me toward the edge of the room, propped me against the wall, and smoothed the hair from my forehead.

"It's okay," he was saying soothingly, "it's going to be okay."

I was shaking, my teeth chattering, adrenaline coursing through me. I could hear Michaela's screams fade as someone hurried her away down the hall.

"What'd Sophie do," I said to Indy. "What'd she *do*?"

Indy grabbed my hand and squeezed it between his—no one was going to tell us not to touch each other right now. "She hurt herself, but she's going to be fine."

His voice trembled as he spoke. How did he know? Did he have any idea what he was talking about? Or was he just telling me what we both wanted to hear?

The knot of aides around Sophie finally broke up, and I saw Mitch and Amy lifting her from the floor. She wasn't fighting them anymore. They were carrying her away, her body limp and helpless.

"Sophie!" I yelled again, but she didn't acknowledge me at all.

Then they were gone, and there were half a dozen stunned patients alone in the lounge, and there was blood smeared all over the floor.

Beatrix and Jade were standing side by side, just staring at where Sophie had been. Sean had started scratching at his cheeks, which he did when he was upset, but there was no one to tell him not to, and Andy was still rocking back and forth by the window and moaning.

Then our group therapist, Lulu, came rushing in, followed by a couple of aides, and they started tending to everyone like we were victims of a train derailment or something. Their voices were calm but urgent. "Let's go back to your rooms," I heard Lulu saying to Beatrix and Jade. People took Sean and Andy away, but no one came for us.

A shocked silence had descended. I couldn't stop staring at the blood. It was drying. Darkening.

Indy was still holding on to my hand. "I remember the day I broke," he said. "I was in my basement—just a regular guy playing a video game. And then, I don't know, it was like I'd been shot with a poisoned arrow. I was *in* the video game, and the game was controlling me. I suddenly realized that all that time, the game had been trying to send me messages, and the messages were telling me that I needed to die. I hadn't been able to hear them before, but now I could. The game wanted me to kill myself."

Indy's hand was growing sweaty in mine. "What did you do?" I whispered.

"I ran upstairs to the second floor of my house and I jumped out the window," he said.

"I'm so sorry," I whispered.

"I wasn't hurt," he said.

"But you were," I said.

He smiled grimly. "Right. Just not physically."

I thought about meeting Sophie for the first time, and how she hadn't been able to stop talking. She hadn't needed any sleep, and she said that food tasted like ashes in her mouth. That was mania. But how had it shifted so quickly? One day she was talking about how amazing she was—and the next thing we knew, she'd sliced her own perfect, God-given wrists.

A custodian wheeled his cart into the room, and he started mopping while some little kid on the TV was singing Frank Sinatra at the top of his lungs.

I said, "Maybe Sophie wasn't really trying to kill herself. Maybe that was just the cry for help."

Indy pulled his hand away and wiped it on his pants. "I think the cry for help was coming here. This—*this* might be a cry that says I don't think I can be helped."

DELIA F. BELMAN MEMORIAL PSYCHIATRIC HOSPITAL
INCIDENT REPORT

Patient Name: Sophie Forrester

Date of Birth: 9/12/2006

Date and time of incident: 1/27/23 1:49 p.m.

Type of Incident: Self-injury

RESTRAINTS USED?

- ☐ None
- ☐ Chemical
- ☑ Seclusion
- ☐ Mechanical
- ☑ Physical

INCIDENT REPORT: Pt cut herself repeatedly on wrists and arms with a spoon. Utensil was taken from cafeteria service and sharpened against a table leg. Event occurred in the lounge, in view of other residents. Pt was restrained and isolated while staff administered first aid. Transfer to Acute Ward recommended if bed available.

RECOMMENDED:

- ☐ Internal investigation
- ☑ Policy and procedure review
- ☐ Staff training
- ☐ Disciplinary action to staff

CHAPTER **51**

Lulu called a special group therapy meeting that afternoon. When she took her usual chair, I saw that there was a faint rust-colored stain on her white shoes.

Sophie's blood.

I felt bile rising in my throat, but I swallowed it back down. *Don't look at the blood.*

Lulu took a deep breath and looked at all twelve of us in turn before she spoke. *I see you*, she was trying to say. *I'm here for each of you.*

But a lot of us couldn't return her gaze. A lot of us stared at our hands lying there helplessly in our laps. A lot of us were terrified.

If Sophie could do something like that, what was stopping any of the rest of us?

"What happened today is a very, very difficult thing to deal with," Lulu said gently. "Belman is supposed to be a safe space, a place where you're cared for and protected and healed. And when it isn't—" Her voice caught. She blinked rapidly, almost like she was trying to keep back tears. "When it isn't," she went on, "that can be really scary."

I'd never heard Lulu rattled like this before, and I didn't like it. I was still shivering, my teeth still chattering. *Breathe in, breathe out, just like that. Don't look at the blood.*

"Is she going to be okay?" Michaela asked. She was hugging her old one-armed teddy bear tightly to her chest.

Milton—his name came to me in a flash. She used to carry him everywhere.

Lulu nodded. "Yes, she is."

"But how'd she do it?" Sean wanted to know.

"What we should focus on right now is that she's getting the help she needs," Lulu said.

She wasn't offering specifics because she didn't want to give us any ideas. But somehow Indy had found out the details and reported them to me: how Sophie had taken one of the cafeteria's plastic spoons, sharpened it against a table leg, and then started sawing it along her wrists.

I couldn't stop wondering if I'd missed some sign. Did she try to tell me what she was planning? What if she was talking to me, confessing to me, and I wasn't even there because I was in my other world? What if she'd thought I was listening, but instead I was standing in front of some damn fourteenth-century fire trying to get warm? What if she was really hurt? What if it was my fault? What if my other world prevented me from seeing *this* world, right when it was the most important that I pay attention?

"Does anyone want to share what they're feeling right now?" Lulu asked.

No thank you. I wanted to keep everything closed up tight inside me where it was safe.

For a long time nobody spoke, and Lulu let the silence settle around us. My eyes kept going back to the stain on her shoes. It was so small that Lulu probably hadn't even noticed it. I felt nauseous looking at it, but I couldn't stop.

Across the circle, Michaela had started to cry. Sean reached out and patted her shoulder. It was the only nice thing I'd ever seen him do, and Lulu saw it, too, and let it happen.

After a while, Lulu leaned forward and said, "I just want you all to know, this is really hard for me, too."

I looked over at Indy. Staff at Belman never said things like that.

"Fuck," Indy shouted suddenly. "Fuck!"

"Adam," Lulu said, and we all looked at her like *who's Adam?* But of course it was Indy's real name—the one we never used.

"Maybe Sophie's just another goddamn Upper East Side self-slasher, but I was in the *room*, I was literally watching her! And I was so stuck inside my own head that I didn't even notice what she was doing." He punched at the air. "Fuck!"

Lulu's voice was full of emotion when she spoke. "It isn't your job to monitor other patients," she said. "It's ours. And today, we didn't do our job." She shook her head and squeezed her eyes shut. "We don't want bad things to happen to any of you, ever. We've dedicated our lives to trying to help people like you. But none of us are perfect, and a psychiatric hospital isn't an easy place to be, and I know that, and I'm so sorry for the pain that you are in."

Indy slumped forward in his chair and put his face in his hands. Even Lulu seemed like she was moments away from bawling, and she was the one who was supposed to keep us together, cheer us on, prod us into talking about our problems.

I looked at Lulu's shoe again, and I thought about the blood on the lounge floor—and the blood that poured from Mary's side.

Suddenly, anger surged through me. It wasn't fair that some-one like Sophie could try to take her own life when someone like my sister had had hers taken from her.

"Do you know how easy it was to die in the Middle Ages?" I heard myself yell. "Starvation, fever, torture, the bloody flux." I took a deep breath. "You can cut your leg on something and die of an infection. Then there's war, childbirth—"

"Hannah," Lulu said, "if I could ask you to calm down a little—"

"—poisoning, burns, plague, pox—"

"Be quiet, Hannah!" Michaela hissed.

"You can be hanged for stealing bread!" I shouted.

"Enough!" Lulu said sharply.

But I didn't care. My voice rose to a scream and I was still calling out all the ways to die when Lulu pressed the button on her lanyard for support, and Mitch came and escorted me from the room.

CHAPTER 52

I took my pills that night, just like I was supposed to, and I saw my appointed therapist Monday. Dr. Nicholas's office was very small and windowless, and filled with the chemically sweet scent of air freshener.

"Tell me what's new with you, Hannah," he said. He steepled his fingers under his chin while he gazed at me thoughtfully through smudged bifocals.

Sometimes I wondered if Dr. Nicholas had studied how psychologists were supposed to look by watching movies. That didn't mean I didn't like him, I did. I just didn't always like talking to him. Like today, when I had to work so hard to keep my worries about Sophie in check.

"I've noticed they started serving curry in the cafeteria," I said. "That's new." I paused. "It's not disgusting, either, if you can believe it."

Dr. Nicholas nodded. He'd let me stall for a little while before he started to force the issue. I wondered how many inanities I could come up with before he cut me off with a pointed question.

"I think they painted the visitors' bathroom, too," I said.

I'd thought that was a meaningless observation, but Dr.

Nicholas pounced on it. "What do visiting hours make you feel like?" he asked.

Shit, I walked right into that one.

The unavoidable fact was that pretty much everyone else on Ward 6 had regular visitors. Michaela's parents came every week, bearing bags from Shake Shack or Sweetgreen. They always brought extra food, too, which Michaela handed out to people like candy canes at Christmas.

Indy's parents lived upstate, so they only came every other week, but they called him on the ward phone every other day.

People's boyfriends and girlfriends came, and sometimes shuffling old grandparents, and once in a blue moon you even saw someone's kid sister with her thumb in her mouth and her eyes wide at the epic levels of dysfunction surrounding her.

Even the patients who weren't here for long, who came in, got stuffed full of pills, and left three days later, good as new (maybe)—they had visitors, too.

I never did.

Not once.

Dr. Nicholas was waiting for me to answer.

I shrugged. "I like it fine. After the nurses check through all the bags, there's some pretty good loot."

"Do you ever wish you had visitors, Hannah?"

"No," I said. The only people I really wanted to see didn't live here. Or maybe I should say they didn't live *now*.

Dr. Nicholas took a deep breath—he was doing an excellent job of maintaining his patience—and tried his first question again, this time with slightly different phrasing. "Tell me how you think you're doing these days."

"I'm doing fine," I said. *I'm not thinking about Sophie. I'm not thinking about Jordan. I'm not thinking about Mary. I'm not thinking about Otto. I'm not thinking about anything anything anything....*

"Have you been experiencing hallucinations?"

I smiled. "No shadow people, no voices telling me to throw myself out the window. Doing great!"

"But...your other life," he said. "You're still experiencing that?"

I supposed I owed it to Dr. Nicholas to be honest. "Yes," I said. "Because it's *real.*" I was so sick of explaining this to him. "You can't make something real go away. Like, if you have a dog but you don't like it, and you wish it would vanish, it doesn't actually go anywhere. It's still your dog."

"Do you want it to go away?" Dr. Nicholas asked.

"I don't have a dog."

At this point, I could see I'd gotten to him. He rubbed his temples and sighed. *Sorry, Dr. N, I couldn't help it.*

"Do you wish you didn't go to the castle?" he said.

"No. I don't. Because they need me there."

"Hannah—"

"It's *real,*" I said. "Just because you can't see it doesn't mean it isn't. I've never met your dog, but I know he's real. I've heard you complaining about vet bills."

Dr. Nicholas took off his glasses and set them carefully on the desk. "It's been a while since we've talked," he said, "and I was hoping we could have a good session today. But I'm not sensing the level of cooperation I'd like—and that frankly would benefit *you.*"

I leaned back in his squeaky chair. There wasn't one comfortable piece of furniture on the entire ward. "I'm sorry," I said, which I both meant and didn't mean.

"We can talk about something else," he said.

"Like what?"

"Your childhood."

That was an instant "Nope."

"Hannah—"

"I don't remember it. You can ask me all you like, but that will always be my answer."

And it was mostly true. There was a door in my mind that was shut tight and locked hard.

All the memories I had of my childhood—of the family I couldn't save, our little hovel, the stench of death—would've made his hair turn white. I figured that if I could recall that kind of thing, then what I didn't remember must be a whole lot worse.

"Your parents—"

"What parents?"

Never taking his eyes off me, he reached for his water bottle, unscrewed the cap, took a long drink, and then said, "Right. You're a legal adult. You don't have to acknowledge them, I suppose. But—"

"I think what would help me is town privileges," I interrupted. I was surprised to hear myself say it. For one thing, I'd barely managed to walk around the hospital grounds with Jordan, and for another, there was no way Dr. N would agree.

"Really." Dr. Nicholas sounded so tired right then that I almost felt sorry for him. Dealing with me was probably a thankless job.

"I'm not a danger to myself or to others," I said. "And maybe I won't go to the castle as often if I'm exposed to more stimulation from the world outside." *What everyone keeps on calling "the real world.*" "Maybe it's so boring in here that my mind can't help constructing elaborate fantasies."

Dr. Nicholas put his glasses back on. "That's an interesting theory," he said.

I knew he'd love it that I said *fantasies*. I decided to push it a bit further. "I think the new intern could take me," I said. "I...trust him."

I feel better when I'm with him. I see that the world here and now might have its bright spots.

I could see Dr. Nicholas actually considering it, which was shocking.

"Maybe it'd help me remember where I came from," I added.

He probably didn't believe me, but he'd known me for years and he'd still never gotten what he wanted out of me.

"I'll speak to Dr. Klein," he said.

CHAPTER 53

J ordan is in the break room, choking down a sawdusty nutrition bar, when one of the Belman therapists comes in looking
for him. The man, who is soft and gray-looking, sits down at the
table across from Jordan. Jordan quickly turns his phone facedown.
He'd been reading about an asteroid due to pass by close to Earth;
the first link he clicked said it would provide a fascinating chance
to observe an interstellar phenomenon, and the second said it was
going to do to human life what the Cenozoic asteroid did to the
dinosaurs. *Kaboom!*

"I'm Dr. Nicholas," the man says. "Staff psychologist." He
doesn't hold out his hand.

"I'm Jordan," he says. "Columbia student."

"I know." He pushes his glasses farther up on his nose. "I spoke
with Hannah this morning. And Dr. Klein."

Jordan breaks off a piece of the nutrition bar but doesn't put it
in his mouth. "Okay," he says neutrally.

"We think it could be beneficial if you took Hannah outside,"
Dr. Nicholas says.

"I actually did that," Jordan says. "We took a walk around the
grounds." *It was kind of awkward.*

"I'm talking about going into the city," Dr. Nicholas says.

"Oh," says Jordan. "Wow." It's hardly an eloquent response, but to call the prospect nerve-racking is an understatement. Jordan can already picture it: Hannah, suddenly overcome by one of her episodes, sprints away from him, he loses her in the crowd, and then after hours of searching he has to go back to the hospital without its favorite patient. *"Yeah, sorry, you guys, she slipped her leash."* Say good-bye to the internship, to the scholarship he's applying for, to the résumé he's been trying to build since age sixteen.

"I've been through sessions with her countless times," Dr. Nicholas goes on, "and we can't seem to break new ground. Frankly, I've never met anyone who seems to want my help less. We're not making progress here, and a big part of your program is for interns to engage with the patients in constructive ways. It doesn't get more constructive than this."

"Why do you think going into the city would be a good idea?" Jordan asks.

"I think she grew up here," Dr. Nicholas says. "I think if she were from anywhere else, some geographical point would have come up in conversation—even if it was by mistake. But it's nothing but Manhattan and some goddamn castle. I can't send you to Europe or wherever the hell she thinks she lives, but I can send you into the city." Dr. Nicholas watches Jordan crumble his bite of nutrition bar into chalky dust. "Walking helps people talk, did you know that? Sometimes when people aren't looking at each other, they find it easier to share things."

Jordan nods. Probably the deepest conversations he ever had with his mother were when they were driving in the car together. Not that they'd been that deep, but at least they'd gotten past questions about his weekend plans or his SAT scores. "What do you think Hannah might share with me?" Jordan asks.

"If she shares anything at all, then that's more than what I'm getting from her in our sessions." Dr. Nicholas sighs. He looks exhausted. "Most patients diagnosed with schizophrenia hear voices, you know, and these voices tell them the most terrible things. They might come from passersby, or cars, or radios, and the person who hears them can't tell what's real and what's not. And this confusion persists for weeks or months. Whereas Hannah cycles in and out of lucidity extremely quickly."

"And when she's with us, she's not delusional at all."

"Exactly. She doesn't think people are whispering about her, or that she's being controlled by microchips the government planted in her brain. She seems perfectly fine."

"It's just like she goes into this awful fairy tale sometimes," Jordan says. "As if this other life is a book she's reading."

"But it's a book that doesn't exist," Dr. Nicholas says.

"I know." Jordan has looked up those barons Hannah talks about, and he hasn't found any historical record. It doesn't mean that they never existed, but it does make them seem extra imaginary.

Sometimes he wonders if it'd be easier if she just thought the CIA was spying on her. After all, it was a delusion that everyone was familiar with.

But what if, by taking her outside of the hospital, he could find out something about her past? Something that would give them a clue about her other, nonhallucinatory life?

"Is there any place I should take her?" Jordan says.

Dr. Nicholas smiles. "No. But whatever you do, don't take her to Times Square. And Jordan? Don't pretend that you know anything about her illness, because you don't. You're a sophomore in college, and you know nothing at all. You're just someone she seems to trust."

Jordan says, "Right. Thanks." He hopes he managed to keep the sarcasm out of his voice.

"I'm sorry that I'm not here to tell you that you have any special talents. But Hannah likes you, and Hannah needs an ally." Dr. Nicholas stands up. "I apologize for interrupting your...lunch," he says, looking with mild disgust at Jordan's bar.

Jordan covers it with his hand. Dr. Nicholas is right: the bar *is* disgusting. But it's cheap, and student loans are no joke. "Thanks for trusting me," Jordan says.

"I don't know that I do," Dr. Nicholas says. "But I have run out of other options."

CHAPTER **54**

Michaela and I were in the lounge working on a puzzle, since neither of us wanted to do art therapy with the Bob Ross knockoff who came on Mondays. We'd covered half the table's surface with tiny colorful pieces—one thousand of them, to be exact—and so far we had most of the border and a little kitten with half a face.

"I need to find its other eyeball," Michaela said, pushing pieces around. "Have you seen a cute little green eyeball?"

We were actively not talking about Sophie, or about the new kid who'd been admitted and had gone running up and down the hall last night, screaming. His name, Nurse Amy told us, was Caleb, and he would probably be staying with us for a while.

I picked up a border piece and fitted it next to its neighbor. We were doing the puzzle on the Ping-Pong table because it was big, and because no one knew where the paddles or balls had gone.

"I think there's a tiny chance they'll let me *outside* outside," I said.

Michaela didn't respond, and I wasn't sure if she'd heard me. Then she picked up a puzzle piece, looked down at the fragmented picture we'd started to assemble, and then threw the piece across the room. It hit the corner of Sean's chair, and he looked up at us with a snarl.

"It's not fair," Michaela said. "They took that pimply kid to the electric chair this morning, and *you* get treated like a princess."

"His name is Peter, and he's severely depressed," I said. "That's not actually my particular problem. And, as you know perfectly well, it's called electroconvulsive therapy."

ECT meant that you were given muscle relaxants, put under general anesthesia, and then basically your brain was electrocuted. But the thing was, it helped. By some mysterious process it changed people's brain chemistry. I knew two people from Belman who said in group that it had saved their lives. Where were they now? I didn't know. But they weren't in *here*.

"Whatever," Michaela huffed. She called over her shoulder, "Indy! Come help Hannah. I don't want to anymore."

I knew Indy wouldn't answer. He was halfway down the hall at one of the nurses' stations, pestering them about one thing or another. Anyway, he hated puzzles. He said they were nothing but mutilated pictures.

"Michaela," I said, "please stay." But she went and flopped down in a chair by the window and closed her eyes.

I'd managed to put together a good portion of another kitten when Jordan came into the lounge. I didn't look up when he said my name. I'd found another piece of my kitten, and when I put it in place, its face went from messed up to sweet, just like that.

It suddenly occurred to me that encouraging psychiatric patients to complete puzzles was an embarrassingly obvious metaphor. It was like, *Let's put the broken things back together! With patience, we can make anything whole!*

"That's a really good point," Jordan said.

I lifted my head. "Did I say that out loud?"

"No," he said. "I just took a wild guess." A smile flickered at the corner of his mouth—he was obviously joking.

"I guess you'd better add 'talking to self' on my list of oddities," I said.

"Definitely," he said. But it seemed like he was kidding again.

He pulled an edge piece from over by the Ping-Pong net and snapped it into place. Then he looked at the picture on the top of the puzzle box and frowned. "What genius said to himself, 'Gee, I think a drawing of a bunch of kittens on a yacht would make a great puzzle?'"

I picked up a piece and tried it in a spot it didn't fit. "All I know is that I asked for a Brueghel reproduction, but no one listened."

Jordan's smile grew wider. "Brueghel, huh? I'll bring that up in the staff meeting. I mean, they could at *least* get you a Monet."

"Exactly. His colors are very soothing."

"Hey, I have good news," Jordan said. "You're getting out of here for the afternoon."

I couldn't quite believe my ploy had worked. Michaela glared at me from her chair.

"*East of Eden* is playing at an art house downtown."

"There's a *movie*?" I said.

"From 1955, starring James Dean. We should leave in about an hour if we're going to get good seats."

"Okay," I said, nodding. "Okay." An event like this was *unprecedented*, and I felt a dizzying surge of nerves.

"I'll come get you in your room," Jordan said.

"It's a date," I said, trying to be flip. "I mean—not really. Obviously."

He blinked at me. "Right," he said.

My cheeks flushed scarlet; I could feel them. The world in which a person like me could go on a date with a person like him was *definitely* a fantasy world.

I ducked my head and all but ran back to my room.

CHAPTER **55**

I ripped off my shapeless, oversized clothes and threw them at the foot of my bed. In the bathroom I turned the shower on so hot that clouds of steam billowed out. When I stepped under the stream, I gasped—first at the heat, and then at the almost unbearable pleasure of all that water pouring over my skin. I closed my eyes.

I dimly remembered being bathed after my admission to Belman, but I couldn't name the last time I'd run a bar of soap down my own arms. It was such a basic, human act of self-care, and I hadn't done it. Hadn't even *thought* about it.

That's because you're just trying to keep it together, I told myself. *Because you have bigger problems than how messed up your hair looks.*

When I came out of the shower, my skin bright pink and cleaner than it had been in days, I found a gray sweatshirt and a pair of black pants in my drawer, plus a pair of socks that seemed to match as long as you didn't look at them too closely. I'd definitely worn better outfits in my life. But then again, I'd also been stark raving mad and half naked on a street corner, so this hand-me-down comfort wear was…okay. I wondered if Amy would let me put laces into my shoes before I went out.

I used a hospital-issue comb to brush through my knotted hair, and then, in front of the unbreakable mirror, I smiled at myself for the first time in weeks.

I'd been pretty once, I knew that. But if I had to pick an adjective to describe myself now, it wouldn't be pretty. It would be haunted. My eyes were huge in my too-thin face and my skin was pale as milk.

I pinched my cheeks until they grew rosy, and that helped a little. Belman staff confiscated patients' makeup, so there was no mascara to borrow from anyone. I thought about the time when Michaela, furious at having to give up her Stila liner, took a Sharpie from the nurse's station and used it to draw a thick black line around her eyes, with Cleopatra wings in the corners and everything.

"That looks…deranged," Indy had said to me as we watched her parade up and down the lounge.

I thought it looked defiant and glamorous. It took days to fade.

"Hello, Lily-Hannah, I'm back."

I whirled around. Sophie stood in the doorway, accompanied by a mental health tech I didn't recognize. Her wrist was taped, and she was struggling to hold a tiny, lopsided smile on her face.

I ran over and hugged her, holding tight for a split second before the tech moved us apart. "I was so worried." I looked over at the tech. "She's okay. I've got her."

"No, you don't, sweetheart," said the tech flatly.

"That's Bella," Sophie said. "She's my one-to-one."

When a patient had a one-to-one, that meant that a staff member was assigned to watch them all hours of the day.

"Oh," I said. "Hi."

Bella grunted what I took to be a hello as Sophie came into the room and flopped down onto her bed.

"Don't ever go to the Acute Ward," she said. "It's terrifying. I spent the whole time crying and saying how sorry I was—I had to get out of there." She pulled the thin blanket over her legs. "I don't know if they believed me or if they needed the bed for someone worse off than I was."

I glanced over at Bella.

"Just try to ignore her," Sophie said, following my gaze.

"But are you...okay?" I asked.

She put that little smile back on her face—I could tell that it took an effort. "I didn't even need stitches. They used tape." She held up her wrist.

"No, I mean how are you feeling?"

"I'm on so many pills I don't even know. It feels like someone wrapped my head in a bunch of towels." She picked at the hem of the blanket. Her voice got smaller. "But I know I'm embarrassed," she said, "for causing all that fuss. I'm sorry, Hannah."

My heart ached for this girl I barely knew, this girl who swung so quickly from giddy mania to soul-crushing despair. "I'm sorry you were in so much pain," I said. "I'm so glad you're back. I missed you."

"Thanks," she said softly. Then she turned to me, and her face brightened a little. "You look nice," she said. "What do you look so nice for?"

It was an innocent question—a compliment even. But it struck me like a hand across the face.

Was I trying to make myself look good for Jordan Hassan? Did I think that if I combed my hair for once, he'd forget that he was my chaperone and think we were just hanging out for fun?

What stupidity—what embarrassing, awful stupidity.

I sank down to the floor. "I'm ridiculous," I said.

I could feel my heart beginning to pound. I wrapped my arms around my knees and squeezed.

"What's the matter, Hannah?" Sophie asked. "Did I say something wrong?"

Her voice sounded far away and hollow.

I didn't have to stay here. I could go.

Not with Jordan to a movie.

Farther away.

"Hannah?" Sophie said.

"Knock, knock—"

Jordan was standing in the doorway. He was already in his coat, a big blue puffer with a big North Face logo on it and yellow duct tape on the arm.

"Ready, Hannah?" he asked. His smile was electric.

I shook my head. I wasn't ready. I would never be ready.

"No," I said. "I've got somewhere else I need to be."

Chapter 56

I walked the long road back to my village in a brown kirtle stained with grease. The freckled scullery maid had jumped at the chance to trade my gown for her rough-spun wool. That she'd never be allowed to wear such finery didn't matter: once she'd smuggled it out of the castle, she'd trade it or sell it. A dress like that would be worth more than a few sheep.

My feet were blistered and my cheeks wind-chapped by the time I got to the outskirts of the village. Still, I started to run.

Mother, I'm coming!

But when I turned down the lane to my cottage, I faltered. What could I possibly say to her? Mary was our light, the best of us, and now she was gone. My mother should turn me away. Disown me. Say she never had a raven-haired daughter they called Blackbird.

I forced myself to start walking again, as a bitter wind swirled up the lane, cutting through the dirty wool of my bartered dress. Too soon, I was outside my cottage. And there was no smoke rising from the roof.

Panic rose in my chest. *Is the rest of my family gone, too?*

I slammed through the door. It was so dark and so cold inside that I was sure it was abandoned. And then, from the corner of the room, I heard a faint rustling.

"Mother," I cried. "Conn!"

A shape no more substantial than a shadow rose from a pile of blankets. "Hannah?" came the whisper.

I ran forward and threw myself down, reaching for my mother. I pulled her against me. Her ribs were sharp against my fingers.

"I'm so sorry," I cried. "I am so sorry." The tears I'd held inside spilled hot down my cheeks, wetting her tangled hair.

"Hannah," Conn said, and I felt his thin arms wrap around my waist. "You came home. I missed you so much."

I held all that was left of my family and cried.

When there were no tears left to shed, I stood up and wiped my cheeks. It was time to take care of my mother and brother. We needed light. Warmth. Food. I felt around the edges of the dark cabin, my fingers scraping the empty shelves and the bare table.

"Do we have no candle?" I asked.

Conn, who had followed me, knotted his hands together. "I ate it," he whispered.

How could a broken heart break yet again? I took his face in my hands and I kissed him on each cold cheek. "Don't worry," I said. "We'll get another one."

My mother was still wrapped in blankets. "I can't seem to—" Her voice faded as she waved a hand around the frigid room. She sighed heavily. "Can't seem to manage it..."

"Conn," I said, "go ask Zenna for some kindling, and a candle if she has one she can spare."

I opened the shutters. The wind came in, but so did a little light. My mother blinked silently in the corner, her hands picking fitfully at the blankets.

Oh, Mother, what have I done to you?

I found an old linen rag and started ripping it into pieces to help start the fire.

"Hannah, Hannah, here, look what I have!"

Conn was already back, bearing a sack full of sticks, two candles, and a loaf of hard black bread. God bless Zenna. I would never speak ill of her again. If anyone called her crazy, I'd tell them how she'd saved us.

As quickly as I could, I made a little fire. I'd save the candles for when darkness fell.

I cut the loaf into five pieces, one for me and two each for my mother and my brother. "Come," I said to my mother, "it's time to eat. Time to get warm."

She finally rose from the bed, and as she approached the light of the growing fire, I could see how much she had changed in only a matter of days. The skin on her cheeks sagged, and her eyes were sunk deep under her brows. She looked ten years older.

She looked like she was dying.

And I knew it was my fault.

I took her hand. "I'm going to take care of you," I said.

"I love you, Hannah," she said quietly, removing her hand from mine and sinking down onto the bench. "I love you more than my life, and I always will. But I will not forgive you."

Chapter 57

*M*y name is Hannah Dory, and I have never been good enough. Not faithful enough, or meek enough.

I have made horrible mistakes. Fatal ones.

Frozen grasses crunched beneath my feet as I walked along the edge of the forest. The sun was barely up, and mist rolled toward me over the barren fields.

I don't deserve it, but I ask for Your help anyway. Not for me, but for what's left of my family.

My fingers were blue with cold and clouds of my breath floated in the air before me. But I'd found a tiny clutch of waxcap mushrooms a ways back, and this had given me hope.

I'd gathered enough sticks and deadfall to last a few days—the trees weren't ours to cut down, even if I'd had an axe or the strength—and I'd taught Conn how to mind the fire, to keep it burning when our mother lost herself in sadness.

If only I'd brought a blanket from the castle, a slab of pork, or even a handful of turnips. If only I hadn't run away as fast as I could once the baron offered me my freedom.

My name is Hannah Dory, and I am—

A piercing scream split the air. I froze, but only for an instant. Then I began to sprint. I knew that sound! My heart was in my throat as I crashed through the underbrush. Briars snagged my skirt and tore at my hands, but I kept going. After a few breathless minutes I came out into a small clearing. I stopped, gasping, and looked around, and I saw a giant hawk struggling to free something from a thorny vine.

Then I saw what had screamed: a rabbit, its back broken, still caught in the bird's grip.

I ran toward the hawk, waving my arms and yelling. "Go! Go!" The panicked bird flapped its great wings wildly, and a moment later, it was aloft, leaving its still-living prey behind.

I fell to my knees in gratitude. And then I crawled forward, lifted a rock, and smashed the rabbit's skull.

It had been a long time since I'd been lucky enough to have a rabbit to skin, but I hadn't forgotten how it was done. Making little cuts in the skin just above the rabbit's knees, I stuck two fingers into the slits and pulled the skin down from the legs as if I were taking off a pair of stockings. Then I lay the rabbit on its back and cut through the skin of its belly from its tail to its neck. I was careful not to cut too deep, because if I pierced the stomach or the intestines, I'd ruin the meat. Then I stepped on the rabbit's back feet to hold it in place, and yanked the skin up toward the rabbit's head. It was grisly work, but it was over quickly.

At home, I put the carcass into the pot over the fire, along with water, a few shreds of old cabbage, and the crust of Zenna's bread that I had not eaten. The fire crackled, and soon the smell—rich, meaty, wonderful—filled the cottage.

Then I took my little brother aside. "You must take care of Mother," I said. "She'll forget to eat. She might forget to feed you.

So you must do all the work. You have to make sure that the two of you survive."

His lower lip trembled. "Why? Why can't you do it?"

"I have to go," I said. "I failed to save us once. But I'm not going to fail again."

Chapter 58

There was no farmer or merchant to hide behind as I crossed the drawbridge to stand before the guards at the castle gatehouse. But it didn't matter. I was done pretending to be anything but who and what I was.

The guard named Finnet greeted me with a glob of phlegm he spat to the ground. "I know *you*," he said. "And you can turn around and go back to the shithole you came from."

"Don't send her away yet," said Gorn, the bearded one. "We have unfinished business, she and I. Come closer, thief. You wouldn't take a kiss from me, no—and you spit in my face. I should cut you in two right now. But I'm a merciful man. A generous man, too, and so I've got something else to give you. It'll fill you right up." Leering horribly, he grabbed his crotch as he lurched toward me.

"Fill me?" I said, curling my lip at him. "I doubt it."

His face darkened and his hand went to the knife at his belt. "Then I'll give you this instead." The next thing I knew, his blade was at my throat.

I didn't flinch. "Certainly *this* is harder," I said through gritted teeth.

I felt a bright flash of pain as the blade punctured my skin. A warm trickle of blood ran down my neck.

Gorn snarled. He put his other hand between my legs and squeezed. "So soft," he whispered. "So lovely. But now you're about to get your dress all bloody."

"Get away from her!"

I gasped and put my hand over my bleeding throat as the guard stepped back. We both knew that cold voice well.

Baron Joachim stood just inside the raised portcullis, the reins of a great black horse held loosely in his hand. The guards melted away to either side of the gatehouse opening. I could see Gorn trembling. But the baron didn't even glance at him. Instead he was staring at me.

"You've come back," he said. He stroked his mount's velvet nose. "I can't imagine why."

"For the same reason as the first time," I said. "Desperation." I took my sticky fingers away from my neck. Looking at them, I felt suddenly dizzy, and there was a low roaring in my ears. Was the cut deeper than I thought? Or was I just weak with hunger and fatigue? My voice cracked as I spoke. "I didn't know what else to do. Where else to go."

The baron's eyes were fixed on my neck. "You're hurt," he said.

I held up red-smeared fingers. "This is nothing," I said, with far more certainty than I felt.

"I will have it tended to," he said.

I shook my head and the world blurred. "I don't need any such thing. I only need to speak with you."

"His time's worth more than your life," hissed Gorn.

"I'll decide what you need and what you don't," said the baron, ignoring Gorn's words. "In the meantime—" He turned and called out to a passing figure. "Take this girl to the keep."

"My name is Hannah Dory—not *girl*," I said as loudly as I could.

I took a stumbling step sideways; I was having trouble keeping my balance.

"I know who you are," Baron Joachim said. "You're a thief and a fool."

His words stung for their truth. They echoed in my ears.

But no. Not anymore.

"I was those things once," I said. "But now I am only a beggar."

My knees buckled and I dropped to the ground. "Please," I begged, as darkness came down over me like a cloak. "Please help."

FIELD OBSERVATION
REPORT INTRODUCTION

by Jordan Hassan, CC'25

The purpose of this assignment is to record
observational data via close attention to the operations
of a psychiatric hospital, with a particular focus on
patient care. I have been able to shadow numerous
RNs at Belman Psych, as well as interact regularly
with patients via recreation time. I hope to be able
to make connections between class content and
real-world experience.

Delia F. Belman Psychiatric Hospital was founded in
1901 with a bequest from its namesake, Delia Belman,
with the goal of providing compassionate, specialized
care to improve the lives of people and families
affected by psychiatric illness.

Ward 6, where I have engaged in my observations,
is an adolescent and young adult unit, serving
approximately two dozen patients ranging in age
from fourteen to twenty-two. The days on Ward 6 are
carefully organized, with a typical schedule looking
something like this:

8:00	Breakfast
9:15–9:45	Room cleanup, personal care time

9:30–11:00	(varies by patient) Individual therapy meetings
11:00–12:00	Group cognitive behavioral therapy
12:15–1:00	Lunch
1:15–3:15	Small group work (art therapy, yoga, guided meditations, creative writing, etc.)
3:30–4:00	Communication skills
4:00–5:00	Lounge activities
5:15–6:00	Dinner
6:30–8:30	Group movie time
9:00	Lights out

As noted by the *American Journal of Psychiatric Nursing*, "When wards offer a wide range of activities, including art, meditation, organized games, and exercise opportunities, service users reported better moods and decreased levels of boredom."

CHAPTER **59**

It's been a quiet morning on Ward 6, as far as these things go. Breakfast went smoothly, and later, during free time, one of the doctors brought in doughnuts for the patients and staff. A radio plays softly in the nurses' station, and Andy lurches up and down the hall, humming tunelessly to a Bruno Mars song.

There are two new names on the hall whiteboard that lists the ward's residents, and three old ones have been recently erased: Sean L., Jade P., and Cora S. They've gone back to their homes and families, armed with prescriptions, reassurances, and outpatient therapy appointments. With any luck, these will be enough to keep them safe in the world. If they aren't, Belman will welcome them back.

Jordan Hassan walks down the hall, peering in through doorways. "Safety check. Safety check. Safety check." Most of the rooms are empty, since patients are supposed to be in one kind of therapy or another, or at least hanging out in the lounge with everyone else.

Then he comes to Room 5A. The door's shut, so he knocks and opens it. Hannah crouches in the corner near the bed, shivering. Her lips move quickly but silently, and her hands flap and circle the air around her head like birds.

"Shit," he breathes.

He looks up and down the hallway. He knows that Sophie, Hannah's roommate, has gone to a meditation circle, where she's listening to New Age music and the low, soothing voice of Harold Wong, Belman's part-time yoga and breathwork instructor. Sophie's struggling, but she's doing her best to get better.

Meanwhile Hannah is here, alone and lost. Not getting better.

Jordan says her name, and she looks up at him. Her dark eyes don't focus on his face.

"Help me," she whispers. "Help me."

"Oh, Hannah, I want to," he says, moving toward her. If he could take her into his arms, he would. He *hates* seeing her like this.

She shrinks farther into the corner, and Jordan can tell that she doesn't know who he is. Her body's in a psychiatric ward, and her mind's four thousand miles and seven centuries away.

Chapter 60

*A*t first I thought I was back in my cottage—that all of this was a dream. But it wasn't. I was alone in a vast, high-ceilinged hall. Gray sky was visible through slitted windows, and a fire flickered in the enormous hearth. I was cold, though a heavy fur cloak had been draped across my shoulders. Underneath it, I still wore a scullery maid's dress and a lady's fine, soft boots, their leather the color of dried blood.

A feast had been laid out before me: meat, bread, and wine on a linen-covered table. A single candle burned in its polished brass holder.

I looked around in confusion, but there were no clues to how I'd arrived here, or who had brought me. My last memory was seeing the baron when I stood on the drawbridge, a guard's knife poised at my throat.

I put my fingers to my neck. The blood was gone, a salve had been applied, and the cut was already healing.

A sudden commotion sounded in the corner, and I jumped, crashing my knee hard into a bench. But it was only a crow who'd found its way into the hall. I watched it circle near the rafters, black feathers flapping, before making its escape out the narrow window.

I turned back to the food. Mouth watering, I took a few hesitant steps toward the table. Could it really be just for me?

I meant to be cautious, but my hand shot out and grabbed a handful of roasted nuts. I shoved them into my mouth, barely chewing them before I swallowed. They were crunchy, salty, and flavored with spices I'd never tasted before. I scooped up another handful.

Then I stopped and listened. Looked all around, peering into every dim corner.

Nothing happened. No one called out for me to stop.

Then the hunger in my belly woke all the way, uncurling like an animal coming out of hiding. I forgot to be worried about why I was here or what would come next. I ate and ate and ate: pigeon pie, braised leeks, jellied fish, baked apples. It seemed as if I would never be full. What I couldn't put in my mouth I shoved into the big greasy pocket of my apron.

I was putting rolls into my pocket with one hand and raising the roasted lamb to my lips with the other when I heard a low, haughty laugh.

"It can't run away from you, you know."

I turned and saw Baron Joachim's chiseled face, his green-gold eyes blazing at me from the shadows. I felt my cheeks flush in shame. If I'd known he was watching, my pride would've conquered my hunger. I set the meat down and wiped my hands on my dress. I turned away from the table.

A smile played in the corner of his mouth. "Chagrined, are you? How surprising, considering that you stole from me shamelessly under the cover of night. Why do you balk now at eating what is freely offered—is it because I am here to see you chew?" His smile grew wider. "You are a very peculiar girl indeed."

My cheeks still burned, but I kept my mouth in a hard line. Yes, I was embarrassed to have been caught shoving food everywhere I could get it. I didn't want to accept kindness from the baron.

But I'm so hungry.

"Well?" he said.

I swallowed the last bit of meat. "It is fine food," I allowed.

"You are unaccustomed to such fare, I suppose, living on gruel and potage. It's an ugly life for a beautiful girl, isn't it?" Baron Joachim picked up an apple and tossed it into the air, catching it without looking. "It hardly seems fair."

An ugly life. A beautiful girl. That he could compliment me and mock me in the same breath filled me with anger. But I said nothing.

And wasn't the baron right, anyway? Our lives weren't fair, and I'd always known it. Nobles deserved their power and riches, while people like us deserved our toil and our poverty, and that was how God and everyone else wanted it.

Such was the claim, anyway. I had no use for it.

The baron threw me the apple, and I caught it without thinking. He laughed. "So you *are* paying attention," he said.

I set the apple on the table. I'd eat no more, not with him watching.

"You're trembling. Are you frightened?" he asked, moving another touch closer.

"No." There, I'd spoken. But it was a lie. I *was* frightened. Not because I thought he was going to hurt me, but because I couldn't understand what was happening. Why had I been brought here? Why did this nobleman even notice me at all? I was no better than an animal to him—he'd made that very clear.

"Have a drink," he said, picking up a gilded cup and holding it out to me. "It will soothe your nerves."

"I'm not thirsty," I said. "And I shouldn't have eaten. It was a mistake." I'd come to the castle to ask for help, and then, when faced with platters of food, I'd devoured them like a mindless glutton. "I was weak."

"Drink," Baron Joachim said again.

The sudden threat in his voice was subtle but real. He'd spared me on the gallows, but there'd be nothing to stop him from gutting me like a rabbit if the fancy took him. What was a peasant's life when held up against a nobleman's pleasure?

I accepted the cup and drank. The wine was rich and sweet. It warmed my throat.

"There now," he said. "That's a good girl."

"My name," I said, "is—"

"Hannah. I know it." With his thumb he reached out and wiped a red drop of wine from my lip. My heart clanged in my chest. "Are you done?" he asked softly.

"I am." I wouldn't touch anything else. Not when he was watching. Not when everyone I loved was starving.

"Then come with me," he said.

Chapter 61

Mutely I followed Baron Joachim down one long stone hall-way after another. He walked quickly and never looked back, his shoulders broad and his spine ramrod straight. It was the posture of a man who'd never bent under a plough. Who'd never known a single day of hunger, not in his whole life.

I tried to stand taller myself as we passed servants and men-at-arms, each going about their business. Some looked at me strangely but said nothing. Others never raised their eyes to see whom they passed.

The castle streamed with life, and everyone's spirits but mine seemed high: after Lord Sicard's defeat, no one needed to wonder if Baron Joachim was up to the task of ruling his lands. He'd been tested, and he'd proven himself.

And if he'd done so thanks to help he hadn't expected, did it matter? Surely his knights would happily forget how farmers and tanners from the surrounding villages had brought their crude weapons to the fight.

And no one—not even I—would know if my hastily scrawled letter had had anything to do with the baron's victory.

"Hurry along now!"

I jumped. Suddenly Baron Joachim was at my side.

"There's a long walk to make still."

I turned away; I didn't want him to see the confusion on my face. He'd only taunt me more. "Are you sending me home?"

He didn't answer.

"I came, as your subject, to ask for help," I said. "I beg you, don't make me leave without it. You're capable of mercy—I myself am proof of it."

"Yes, and you're not hungry anymore, are you?" he said lightly.

"I didn't come for myself. I came for everyone else."

"That certainly isn't how it looked."

But before I could respond, a man in velvet robes swept up, pulling the baron aside and speaking in hushed tones. I hung back, hoping not to be noticed. The man's eyes shifted to me anyway, and as they did, his expression darkened.

"*Why*, my lord—" he began.

Baron Joachim cut him off with a flick of his hand. "She amuses me," he said.

The man visibly shuddered. More conversation followed, too low for me to hear. And then the velvet-robed man glided toward me, smelling of wine and incense. "I have encouraged my lord to find a more suitable whore," he whispered as he passed.

I froze where I stood. *How dare he, that vile, oily—*

"Come now," the baron said, returning to my side. "Don't mind Lord Ashling."

"That's easy for you to say. He bows to you and spits on me."

"As he believes he should. But no matter, I will show you something that will make you forget your wounded dignity."

He thrust open a heavy wooden door, and when we passed through it, we were in the muted gray light of the outer bailey, where two wagons, heavily laden with supplies, stood waiting. The baron walked up to one of the mules resting in its harness and gave its neck a gentle slap. "See?" he said.

I didn't understand at first what he meant.

"Are you being stupid on purpose? Lead the way to your village," he said. He gestured to the two drivers. "They will follow. Surely you can manage this?"

Without answering I ran to the nearest wagon and peered inside. There were wheels of cheese, crocks of butter, sacks of barley. Hay for our livestock. Smoked fish and goose eggs packed in straw. Toward the back of the wagon was a wooden chest held closed by leather straps.

"What's in there?" I whispered.

"Medicine," he said. "Salt. Spices."

I held on to the wagon to steady myself as relief and gratitude flooded my body.

We would live!

Chapter 62

I ran all the way to my village without stopping, five miles' journey as if it were an inch. By the time I arrived at the lopsided, abandoned huts that marked the village edge, I was sweating and breathless. Lungs aching, I flung myself down the narrow lane to our cottage.

Relief flooded through me when I saw the smoke from our fire curling up through the thatched roof. Conn had made good on his promise: he'd kept himself and our mother alive.

"Mother! Conn!" I shouted. "I've come back! With supply carts! Meet me at the church!"

My brother came stumbling out, barefoot and blinking his eyes against the weak sunlight. "Hurry," I cried, blowing him a kiss as I went on down the lane, pounding on Zenna's door first, and then on Ryia's and the weaver's. "Come out," I shouted. "Follow me!"

None of the doors opened. "Hello?" I called.

Where was everyone?

Finally I saw Zenna's skeletal face peering out from the dark interior of her cottage. Her rheumy old eye slowly focused on me, and her expression brightened ever so slightly. "Blackbird," she rasped. "Do you have a song for me?"

"I have something better," I said. "Food."

She clucked her tongue. "Don't tease an old woman."

"I'm not. It's coming from the castle—two whole wagons of food."

"It can't be," she said.

"It can." I shouted, "Everyone, we'll eat tonight!"

"Well, Death, you'll have to wait a bit longer for us," Zenna cackled.

Slowly, other doors began to open. But I wasn't prepared for the sight of my friends and neighbors as they came lurching out of their huts. Their eyes were dull, their skin yellow. They looked half dead, like skeletons somehow still breathing. Only pretty Ryia had any color in her cheeks. She walked toward me with a ragged bundle in her arms. Shyly, she held it out to me, her eyes shining. "Born yesterday," she whispered.

I looked down and saw a tiny pink, pinched face and a shock of red hair, and then I looked back up at Ryia. "She's beautiful."

Ryia nodded, her expression full of pride, love, and fear. "I know. She's perfect."

"Send your husband to the church," I said. "We're going to distribute everything there."

She shook her head. "He's in bed, burning up," she said. She squeezed the baby tight to her chest. "But the baby and I can make it. Can't we, little one?" She smiled at me. "She's so new I haven't even named her yet."

"You should rest," I said. "We'll find someone to bring you your share." I turned to everyone else. "Grab empty sacks or baskets—anything you've got."

But they didn't move, and they were staring at me like I'd gone mad. Only then did I realize that the carts were still nowhere in sight. I'd run my legs off, but the drivers were stuck navigating the frozen, rutted road into the village. "The food is on its way," I promised. "It'll be here soon."

I saw their mistrust. Fine, I'd earned it.

Soon enough they'd know that I was telling the truth.

I began walking toward the church, Conn trotting along at my heels, a rough sack slung over his shoulder.

"Really, Hannah? Real food?"

I'd described so many rich feasts to him and the twins, filling their minds with words when I couldn't fill their bellies with meat, that he had reason to wonder.

I ruffled his golden hair. "More than you've ever seen at once."

As I pulled open the churchyard gate, shouts rose up behind us. The carts had made it.

The scene outside the church was one of stunned happiness. After nearly crushing me to his chest in a hug, Vazi lifted all the heavy sacks out of the carts while Maraulf helped count and divide everything fairly. Merrick, his left arm ending in a bandaged stump, watched from a short distance.

I walked over to him, my heart in my throat. I bent my head. "I'm so sorry," I said.

I waited for him to yell—to strike me, even. But he only shrugged his good shoulder. "I don't blame you, Blackbird," he said gruffly. "We took the chance we needed to take. Fed or dead, right? Well, I'm not the latter, and by the looks of it, I'll be eating well very soon." He reached out and touched my cheek. "It's you who blames yourself."

As I should. I cost us Otto, and Mary, and—

"Hannah," Merrick said, turning me around so that I faced the carts. "Guilt didn't make you give up, see? I don't think anything will. And we all thank you, whether we say it out loud or not."

I tried to let his words comfort me.

In the end, every family in the village got three pounds each of barley and rye; a sack of soft white flour; ten pounds of turnips, parsnips, and cabbage; a slab of fatty pork; and a gallon of ale. Some people cried. Others took their shares in mute disbelief.

To Otto's younger brother I gave all the medicines in the chest, as well as a jar of golden honey. But I couldn't look him in the eye.

Herbs and sweetness, in exchange for a brother and son.

For the man who was supposed to be my husband.

I felt dizzy and steadied myself against the wall. *Breath in, breath out. Breathe in, breathe out.*

Someone was tugging on my skirt. I looked down. Conn's eager little face peered up at me.

"May I ring the bell?" he pleaded.

"What for?"

"Because today is like Christmas," he said.

I smiled at him. "Today is a good day indeed," I agreed. "Yes, ring the bell all you want."

CHAPTER 63

U p the elevator to the sixth floor, down the hall, key card pressed tight against the lock. Jordan's done this dozens of times now, but the buzzing of the first door as it opens still makes him jump.

Two more locked doors to get through and then he's on the ward itself, with its bright lights and security cameras. He greets the day's charge nurse, a big, patient woman named Renée, and puts his backpack in the staff lockers.

"I need you to help Nyla with the collaging project in G," Renée says when he comes out again. She reaches into her desk and hands Jordan a pair of hot-pink safety scissors. "Here. An extra pair so you can make a collage, too." She grins like she's daring him. Then she glances down at the white paper bag he's carrying. "What's in there? Not contraband, is it?"

Inside the bag is a beautiful eight-dollar chocolate eclair that Jordan impulse-bought for Hannah at the fancy French bakery on Broadway. "My lunch," he says.

"Huh. Be careful Amelia doesn't steal it," Renée says, dismissing him.

Amelia is relatively new to the floor, a food hoarder with kleptomaniacal tendencies. The other day, a search of her room revealed enough packets of Chips Ahoy!, Cheez-Its, and Oreos to fill an entire vending machine.

"You bet," he calls over his shoulder as he heads down the hall.

Room G is small, windowless, and easily the most depressing room on the ward. Nyla, one of the art therapists, is passing out piles of donated magazines, glue sticks, and more brightly colored safety scissors. There are eight patients in the room, and none of them is Hannah.

Jordan moves as if in a dream toward the table.

Where is she, where is she?

"Everything you cut out should represent something you hope for," Nyla is saying. She holds up a finished collage. "I made this last night while I was watching *Real Housewives*," she says. "See? I hope to swim in a lake this summer, and I want to get a dog someday, and I want to learn how to knit."

Andy, who isn't dead today, reaches for a *Smithsonian* magazine and starts cutting out a picture of a fighter jet.

Beatrix mutters, not very quietly, "I fucking hate crafts."

Since Beatrix almost never curses, Jordan assumes that one of her alters has stepped forward. Beatrix has been diagnosed with dissociative identity disorder, and different people speak through her mouth.

He sits down next to Sophie. "Good morning," he says.

Don't ask "Where's Hannah?" Just leave it at that.

Sophie doesn't answer, but she's smearing a glue stick all over her construction paper, which he takes as a decent sign.

Jordan looks at all the magazines fanned out on the table. *Golf Digest*s from two years ago. *Dwell*. *Vanity Fair*. A few *Cat Fancy* magazines older than he is. He sure as hell isn't going to make a collage, but if he did, what would it show?

A man in a doctor's coat. A two-bedroom apartment south of 14th Street. A blue sky.

A dark-haired, dark-eyed girl, reading a book in a cozy window seat overlooking a garden.

He stands up again. Jesus, what's wrong with him? "I'll be right back," he says to Nyla. He gives Andy's arm a quick pat. "You're doing great."

"Piss off," says Andy.

Jordan jogs down the hall to Room 5A. It's empty.

Mitch passes by with a clipboard. "Your girlfriend's with Dr. N."

"She's *not* my—"

"Yeah, yeah, whatever." Mitch pokes his head into Room 5B—"Safety check!"—then pokes it back out.

"So does that mean Hannah's back...from the castle?" Jordan's embarrassed by the hope he can hear in his voice.

"What makes you think that?"

Jordan's heart thuds heavy in his chest. *Shit, shit, shit.*

At noon, he eats the stupidly expensive eclair he bought for Hannah.

See, Renée, I wasn't lying. It's my lunch.

It's not even that good.

DELIA F. BELMAN MEMORIAL PSYCHIATRIC HOSPITAL

Patient Name: Hannah D

Date: 2/1/23

Therapist: Dr. Nicholas

OBSERVATIONS

APPEARANCE:
- ☐ Neat
- ☑ Disheveled
- ☐ Inappropriate
- ☐ Bizarre
- ☐ Other

SPEECH:
- ☐ Normal
- ☐ Pressured
- ☐ Disorganized
- ☐ Impoverished
- ☑ Other

EYE CONTACT:
- ☐ Normal
- ☐ Intense
- ☑ Avoidant
- ☐ Other

MOTOR ACTIVITY:

☐ Normal   ☑ Restless

☐ Tics   ☐ Slowed

☐ Other

AFFECT:

☐ Full   ☐ Contracted

☐ Flat   ☑ Labile

☐ Other

COMMENTS: Hannah could not identify correct date or her location; she did not respond to most questions. She denied experiencing any hallucinations and was insistent that she needed to "get back to cooking." Said she was making potage. That everyone was very hungry, and Zenna (?) was coming for dinner.

CHAPTER **64**

The next day, riding the subway back to Belman Psych for an evening shift, Jordan Hassan reminds himself not to expect any changes in Hannah's condition.

Fine. But he can't help *hoping* for one, even though it seems like she's spending more and more time in her other world, and less and less time in his.

Did she want it that way? Was it something she could somehow control? Or was she as trapped and terrified as she seemed?

A panhandler makes his way down the train car, holding out a filthy baseball cap. Automatically Jordan reaches into his back pocket and fishes out a dollar.

He can hear his father's voice: *What if he uses that money for drugs?*

What Jordan never had the guts to say back was: *So what if he does?*

"God bless," says the man. "Don't let the spiders get you. There's too many spiders and they all got a lot of eyes."

Mental illnesses are some of the most common health conditions in the United States. That was what Dr. Čtvrtník had said the first day of class, before she even told the students how to pronounce her name.

As the subway hurtles Jordan toward Queens, the same unanswerable question swirls around in his mind: Why is it that hearts know how to beat, and lungs unfailingly take in oxygen, while the brain, which is supposedly in charge of everything, sits up there in its bone case and screws everything up?

Jordan thinks about the girl in his dorm who studies physics all the time, and the all-American bros who go drinking on upper Broadway every night, and the shiny-haired girls who party in Soho and show up late to classes, and he wonders how many of them privately suffer.

More than half the US population will be diagnosed with a mental illness or disorder during their lifetime.

Jordan's had a few panic attacks himself. And sometimes, when he imagines the future—with its diseases, wars, droughts, and famines—he wonders if it wouldn't be easier to simply stop existing.

This isn't the same as wanting to die. It's more like a nagging fear that what you have to face is more than you think you're capable of facing.

Maybe Hannah deals with those feelings, too, but in a manner so extreme that she keeps having breakdowns. And Jordan understands now that Nurse Amy was right: Hannah *is* lucky, always having a bed at Belman. She's not screaming on a street corner all the time. Just some of the time.

Four percent of Americans live with serious mental illness, such as schizophrenia, bipolar disorder, or major depression.

It is thought that only half of people with mental illnesses receive treatment.

Forty-five minutes later, Jordan walks into Hannah's room, his heart pounding. He can't stand to see her lost and hurting. He can't stand that it feels like he's failed her.

Please let her be lucid. Let her be here.

She's lying on her bed, wearing a shirt so big she's almost lost inside of it.

He goes up to her bed, barely breathing.

Suddenly she sits up. And her dark eyes brighten when she sees him, and she smiles.

"Hello there, Jordan Hassan," she says.

He's so relieved that he feels his knees almost buckle. If he could pull her into his arms, he would.

"You're okay," he whispers. "You're here."

CHAPTER 65

Y ou're here," Jordan said for the third time at least, and I could hear the warmth in his voice.

"*Tada!*" I said, like I'd just completed a magic trick.

He laughed. "I'm so happy you're back."

Was *I* happy to be back, though? That was harder to say.

I was tired of being locked up. Tired of my shapeless clothing and laceless shoes and the Almighty Schedule and the chemistry experiments of my medications. *Oh, Seroquel makes your tongue twist around inside your mouth? Let's try Latuda for a while!*

And this world just felt so much dimmer, so much more muted than the other one. Like all the life and color had been drained out of it. Jordan Hassan was the one ray of brightness.

I didn't mind coming back to *him*.

"I was sorry we didn't get to see the movie the other day," he said.

I remembered trying to make myself look pretty—or at least bordering on *normal*—and felt a cold shiver of embarrassment. Why had I bothered to pretend? What was the point?

At least Indy hadn't seen me. He always shouted "Sanity drag!" whenever he caught anyone trying to dress like they cared about themselves or their lives. "Why shower *today*," he'd say, "when you're just going to have to do it again tomorrow?"

"Yeah, I was bummed, too," I said. "But I was, um, called away."

Jordan sat down on Sophie's bed, which was empty because she was getting ECT.

He smoothed her blanket and frowned, and then his mouth opened and closed a few times. Either he was doing an imitation of a fish underwater or else he was trying to decide whether or not to say something.

"What?" I said.

"Can you go to the castle on purpose?"

Maybe the question shouldn't have surprised me, but it did. "No," I said.

But recently, I'd noticed, when I felt the first tugs of that other world pulling at my mind, I could sort of... *lean into it*. It was hard to describe, but sometimes if I breathed right, the spiral could suck me down faster.

Away, away from all of this.

"Because sometimes," Jordan says, "it seems like when you're threatened, or scared, you sort of go—"

I cut him off. "Do me a favor, and don't pretend you're a shrink. You're a college student. A psych major." I didn't mean to be harsh, but it was true.

"Sorry." He jiggled his legs a little. Ran his fingers through his dark hair. He seemed almost nervous.

"Do you have another question for me?" I asked.

He was quiet for a minute, and then he said, "Yeah, I do." He smiled. "What's got five toes but isn't your foot?"

What?

"I have absolutely no idea."

"*My* foot," he said, suddenly looking utterly gleeful.

I almost fell backward onto my bed. "Oh, my god," I said. "That's the stupidest joke I've ever heard."

"But you're laughing," he said. "And be careful, because I've got more where that came from."

"Please, no more," I said, trying to look serious and failing.

"Fine, if my awesome dad jokes are too much for you right now. But it isn't bedtime yet, and so you need to get *out* of bed. We have to find something to do. Do you want to play Ping-Pong? Mitch said he ordered a new set of paddles."

He was waiting for me to say yes, but how could I? I'd come from a world of hunger and guilt and sorrow into one of jokes and roommates and sweatpants and Ping-Pong and a cute college boy who seemed to actually enjoy spending time with me, even if he *was* getting college credit for it. And it honestly just felt like too much right now.

"It's too late for Ping-Pong," I said.

"That's your excuse, but the truth is you don't want to suffer humiliating defeat," Jordan said.

I couldn't help smiling. "You can't goad me into it."

He shrugged. "It was worth a try. We could do a puzzle?"

"I brought enough food to feed everyone, you know," I said.

Jordan leaned toward me. "What?"

"Grains and butter and beans and bread... Everyone was so happy to see me. And Ryia—she had a baby girl. But I'm really worried about her husband."

Jordan said abruptly, "How about we take a walk? Just around the ward." He stood and held out his hand, but I didn't take it.

"What for?"

"Well, everyone here will be happy to see you, too. You were kind of out of it for a while."

"Out of it—is that the technical term?" I said dryly. But I got out of bed and stretched my stiff limbs. I felt heavy and slow. I couldn't hit a Ping-Pong ball if someone begged me, bribed me, or threatened my life. Shuffling down the hall, though, I could probably manage.

Jordan tossed my shoes to me, and I slipped them on over my mismatched socks. "I like the leather boots I got at the castle better," I said.

"Living one life is hard enough," Jordan said quietly. "Isn't living two of them exhausting?"

His tone was gentle, but for some reason I bristled. Did he think I wanted to give one up? Did he think I *could*?

"Well, we all have our probs, don't we," I said.

He paused. "Yeah, I guess we do."

We walked into the glaringly bright hall. Andy was pacing up and down as usual, and he turned to me as we passed, his eyes wide and spooked.

"Get them off me," he said.

I didn't know what he was talking about. "Get what?"

"The bugs! I can feel them on the back of my neck."

"Oh," I said. I stepped closer and stood on my tiptoes so that I could see the back of Andy's long, hairy neck. He'd never believe me if I told him he was bug-free, so I picked up an imaginary critter. "There! Got one. It's tiny—totally harmless."

"Get the other ones!"

"Sure, sure." I removed two more invisible bugs and pretended to flick them away down the hall. "All done! We'll tell Mitch to clean those up," I said, smiling.

"Okay," Andy said.

Jordan and I kept on walking toward the lounge, and I thought he might say something about Andy. But instead he said, "What do you do when you slap Dwayne Johnson's ass?"

I said, "I really don't know."

"You hit The Rock bottom," he said.

"I hate you," I said. But I was laughing again, and it felt good.

And I thought to myself: If only we were just two regular people walking down a hall together—in a school, maybe, instead of a psychiatric ward. It didn't seem like too much to ask. And yet I might as well ask for the moon on a string.

January I-have-no-fucking clue,
maybe it's February, 2023

Dear no one,

When I look out the window, nothing looks real to me at all. Buildings, stoplights, pigeons, streets, trees: everything is a ghost of itself.

I am a ghost of myself.

An hour ago I called my boyfriend. I begged him to visit me, but he didn't want to. I told him I need him to come to the hospital and bring a knife. I want you to murder me. *That's what I told him.*

He hung up.

Mom, you were right. Fuck that guy.

I'm crying again. I'm always crying. My nose burns from cheap hospital tissues. And I'm just sitting here. Taking my last few breaths.

I've never been able to explain it to anyone. How the despair is like a black hole. It sucks everything into it, even the words I need to describe it.

I don't want to go on. I can't go on. I'm broken and I can't be fixed.

There's nothing to look forward to, not now, not ever. Even if I feel better for an hour, or a day, the dead, dark feeling always comes back. The despair aches. I'm actually in pain.

The doctors gave me a new medication and it makes everything worse. I want blackness. Oblivion. Nothingness. Forever.

This is the best thing I can do.

It isn't a cry for help.

It is a choice to leave.

I'm done. It's too hard.

I don't expect you to understand.

This is what I want.

I've got a pair of bandage scissors. If I weren't supposed to die, they wouldn't have been so easy to steal from the drawer.

I know how it's done. Cut vertical, not horizontal. Don't hesitate. Breathe slowly. Focus.

The blood'll come slowly at first, and then much faster. It'll hurt. But then it'll be over.

Love,
Sophie

PS. I'm sorry about the mess.

CHAPTER 66

A piercing cry comes from down the hall. But it stops, mid-scream—like in a horror movie, when the killer sneaks up from behind and slashes the screamer's throat.

Jordan sprints down the hall. Other people are sprinting, too.

The patients stay where they are, shock on their faces. Terror.

Not again.

Not this again.

Beatrix pulls at her hair. "Who is it, who is it, who is it?" she yells.

Indy says, "I think that was the safety check on Sophie." He leans hard against the wall and then slides down it. Grief twists his face into something strange and terrible. "And I think that was Amy finding out that Sophie wasn't safe."

Hannah overhears him, and her face goes utterly white. Her legs give out.

She's down. Out.

Gone.

Chapter 67

I don't remember him at all," Conn said, wiping up the last drops of his stew with a heel of soft bread. "I try and try, but it doesn't matter."

"Father left when you were three," I said quietly. "How could you remember him?"

He'd joined Baron Jorian's army when it left to fight in one of the king's foreign campaigns, and half a dozen other men from our village had gone with him. They had no weapons or training; they were porters, cooks, and diggers of trenches.

My mother had begged him not to go, but he wouldn't listen. "I'll come home with pockets full of silver," he'd said.

But what happened instead was that he never came home at all.

"What was he like?" Conn asked.

My mother abruptly got up from the table and went to stand by the fire. She twisted her hands in her apron and her eyes shone with unshed tears. She'd never stopped missing him, and I knew that part of her believed he was still alive. That he was lost some-how, somewhere, and he didn't know how to get back home to us—but that someday he would.

I couldn't have convinced her otherwise, even if I'd tried.

If we'd had a body to bury, maybe that would've brought her

some peace. If she could lay her hands on him one final time before committing him to the earth.

I remembered him perfectly, and I missed him horribly. But not as much as I missed Mary, buried in an unmarked grave outside the castle walls. Buried next to Otto, my would-be husband.

"Was he very big and very brave?" Conn asked. "Was he ugly like Vincy's pa?"

I took his hand in mine. "He was very brave indeed," I said. "He was tall and thin, with a long, black beard. He had a big, deep voice, and he used to sing us songs. Would you like to hear one?"

Conn nodded eagerly. My mother turned her back to us, and I could see her shoulders shaking.

I took a sip of ale and sang.

> Fair was the evening time and still the sun shone bright
> Upon the wood, upon the field, upon the brave young
> knight
> His sword gleamed silver and his horse was fleet, no
> worry creased his brow
> He thought not of war but of the sweet maid free and
> the love she did avow—

I stopped. "I've forgotten what comes next," I said. "But it's about a noble knight who loves a girl from a nearby village." A girl who's beneath him, I didn't say. A peasant.

"She dies," my mother blurted.

"Right," I said. "I guess that's what happens."

"They meet again in heaven, though," Conn said, insistent.

"Yes, you must be right," I said. "Anyway, it's time for bed. You'll sleep well tonight, won't you, with your full, fat belly?"

Conn nodded. His eyes were heavy already. "But where's my soldier?"

"Your what?"

"My wooden soldier! Merrick found him in the cart—there was a whole pile of them. Vincy got one, too." Conn began to paw frantically among the tattered blankets. A moment later, he pulled out a small, intricately carved knight. When he held it up and gazed at it, his face shone with delight. "There you are," he said, and he hugged it to his chest.

The baron had thought to include *toys* for the village children? I wouldn't have believed it if I hadn't seen it with my own eyes.

I went to bed not long after Conn. Sometime in the middle of the night, I woke to the sound of fists on the door. Rising from the rough mattress, I walked past the dead fire as fear trailed icy fingers down my spine. "Who is it?"

There was no answer. Grabbing the knife from the table, I opened the door. It was Ryia. She was bathed in cold moonlight, and she was holding her little baby in ragged blankets.

"She's gone," she screamed, thrusting the bundle toward me.

I didn't understand what she was talking about. Then I looked down and saw the baby's lifeless face.

"John's fever—choking—gone—" Ryia was crying so hard she could barely speak. I pulled her into my arms. I felt her dead baby against my chest. Grief and horror pierced my heart.

"I loved her so," Ryia wept. "My Sophie, my little Sophie."

CHAPTER **68**

After Sophie Forrester's suicide, sadness hangs over the ward like a fog. *Or maybe it's guilt*, Jordan thinks. When he makes his way through the locked doors in the morning, he can feel its invisible weight pressing down on him. It almost makes it hard to breathe.

I am a ghost of myself, Sophie's note had said. *I'm sorry about the mess.*

The words might as well be burned across Jordan's retinas. Along with every other Belman employee, he feels like he failed Sophie Forrester. Because they did. They were supposed to take care of her, but she died on their watch.

Two of the ward nurses have asked for a leave of absence, and Dr. Klein is resigning. Jordan will miss the doctor's frankness, her quiet, chilly competence. But he won't miss Mitch, who's being transferred to a different ward on a different floor. Was Mitch the last person to see Sophie alive? Is Mitch any more or less to blame than anyone else? Jordan has no idea, and he's not about to ask.

There's no farewell party for Dr. Francine Klein. On Friday she's in the office, and on Monday she isn't. An interim medical director takes over her office, a lithe, dark-eyed woman named Dr. Ager. When she calls her first staff meeting, she doesn't invite Jordan.

All that week, Jordan makes his observations, tries to engage patients in board games in the lounge, and performs his duties as stunned as the rest of the staff. He walks the halls with Andy, talks to Beatrix about the dissociative identity disorder community on TikTok, and helps Sam, a new patient, write a letter to his parents: *I forgive you for putting me here, but don't come visit.* He makes Sam cross out *or else.*

Meanwhile Hannah wanders the halls, talking to herself. Singing to herself. Oblivious to him and everyone else. Not even Michaela or Indy can bring her back.

But then on Friday morning, when Jordan walks into the lounge, still shaking the rain from his hair, she's eating a breakfast sandwich and calmly talking with Indy.

Jordan hides his surprise—his nearly giddy relief—as he sits down at the table with them. "Good morning, team," he says, like there's nothing different at all. As if Hannah isn't just back from some incomprehensible and indescribable internal journey. "It's a beautiful day out there."

"Liar," Indy says, sounding bored, and Hannah smiles faintly at him. Her hair's still uncombed and she looks beautiful and feral.

"Belman Psych has the shittiest coffee in the world," she says. "Have you tried it? It tastes like boiled cardboard."

"With a dash of vinegar," Indy says.

"You could microwave the East River and it would taste better."

"Not the Hudson, though," Indy says, picking at a hangnail. "*That* thing rubs up against Jersey for miles. It's got nasty New Jersey germs." He shudders dramatically.

Hannah giggles, and Jordan says absolutely nothing about growing up in New Jersey, less than thirty miles from said river. He also says nothing about Sophie. Let them have their banter.

Then Indy looks up at him and says, "Can we help you with something?"

Jordan starts, momentarily taken aback. Then he says, "No, no, I'm just checking in with everyone."

"You miss us when you're not here, I know," Indy says.

Some of you, Jordan thinks. *One of you*. He pushes back his chair and gets up. "Sure. See you later."

Hannah finds him after lunch, when he's coming out of Kevin's room, having helped him wash off the knives he'd drawn on the door with a Sharpie.

Hannah tugs urgently on his sleeve. "Listen, I have to go back," she says.

Jordan doesn't understand. "Back where? To the lounge?"

"To my village," she says, exasperated.

He clenches his fists, stifling a horrifying urge to take her by the shoulders and shake her. "Why do you need to do that?" *You were gone for so long.*

"The help I got from the baron wasn't enough. We need more food. More medicine. The baby died!"

With effort, Jordan unclenches his hands. He says, "Whose baby?"

Hannah looks like she's about to cry. "Ryia's. A newborn. She was so perfect, so tiny, with her blue eyes and her red hair...."

A chill runs north along Jordan's spine, because he can think of someone else with blue eyes and red hair. Someone else who's dead. Again he has to resist the urge to grasp Hannah by the shoulders. "What was the baby's name?" he asks, as gently as he can. Already knowing the answer.

Hannah blinks, and a tear slides down her cheek. "Sophie."

Frustration and anger well up in him. It's time to put an end to this goddamn fantasy. "This isn't about a dead baby from the fourteenth century, Hannah," he says. "This is about Sophie from the hospital. Sophie Forrester, who was your roommate."

But it's like Hannah doesn't even hear him. Is it that she can't understand, or that she won't?

He tells himself that he just has to keep talking. He's got to make her deal with the present moment. "Sophie killed herself, Hannah. There's going to be an investigation. Dr. Klein's gone, and Mitch is, too. The hospital might get sued. And you feel scared and sad. You're grieving. We all are. But we're dealing with it, okay? We're dealing with it here and now."

But her eyes show zero comprehension. "Sophie caught a fever from her father," she says. "She died before she even lived."

So did Sophie Forrester! She was sixteen!

"I'm not saying that your other life isn't real, but you're acting like this one *isn't*, when it *is*," Jordan practically shouts. "*I* live in it, okay? I'm telling you, it's real! And someone you cared about *here*, in this world, felt so hopeless that being dead seemed better to her than living! Can you imagine that pain?"

Hannah sets her jaw in a stubborn line. She turns away, so he's looking at her in profile. Her high forehead. Her tiny ears, pierced in half a dozen places but without any earrings.

"I don't want to," she says. "I won't."

He waits a few beats. Then something occurs to him. He says, "Have you ever known someone who killed themselves?"

His voice is much quieter now, but Hannah's eyes go wide, as if he's just screamed at her, and her body gives a lurching shudder.

He reaches out to touch her shoulder, gentle now, then stops himself. "Hannah?" he says.

She doesn't answer him. She seems to collapse into herself, almost like she's expecting a blow. "Stop," she whispers. *"Stop."*

And in that instant, Jordan understands that Hannah is keeping an awful secret. It's part of why she's locked up in Belman. She's never told anyone, and she never, ever wants to. But suddenly, suddenly he knows what it is.

"Hannah?" he says again. "Has anyone you know—"

"Go away," she gasps. "Just leave me alone."

Then she runs down the hall and hangs a right into the quiet room. Slams the door behind her.

CHAPTER 69

At the morning meeting on Monday, Jordan eats his sawdusty nutrition bar while the staff discusses which patients require more medication, who might next try ECT, and who might be ready to go home someday soon.

Everyone's still reeling from Sophie's death. And they must be extra vigilant, Dr. Ager reminds them, and be on the lookout for any new signs of suicidal ideation.

"Research shows that exposure to suicide can increase suicidal behavior in others—what some call 'suicide contagion,'" she says.

Jordan represses a shudder at the thought of self-harm catching like a cold. Everyone on the ward is already struggling. Some are getting better. But some seem to be getting worse.

Like Hannah.

When it's time to talk about how she's doing, Jordan decides to tell them what he knows: that someone close to Hannah died by suicide, he's sure of it. And whatever the story of that death is, it's so painful that Hannah can't speak it out loud. She's walled it up inside.

Locked it in a castle, you might say.

But when he's done talking, he sees Nurse Amy staring at him and Lulu frowns over her mug of tea.

"How do you know that?" Amy asks.

When Jordan describes his interaction with Hannah, Amy crosses her arms over her chest. "So basically you're telling us that you have a *hunch*," she says. "A feeling that's completely unconfirmed. Well, I hate to break it to you, but this isn't a crime show, Jordan. You're not a detective about to solve a cold case."

Who are you, anyway? Dr. Ager's expression seems to say. *Are you supposed to be in this meeting?*

Jordan feels his heartbeat accelerate. "I just feel like we might be asking the wrong questions about Hannah," he says. "Like instead of always talking about what's *wrong* with her, and what drugs we can give her, we should be asking about what *happened* to her."

Renée nods curtly. "Thank you for assuming that you know more than we do, Mr. Hassan. The fact is, we have tried to find out about Hannah's past for years, and she has systematically blocked us."

But there's a chance that she won't block me, he thinks. He crumples the nutrition bar wrapper in his fist and pitches it into the trash can. *And maybe she won't be my only source of information, either.*

CHAPTER 70

After work, Jordan takes the subway to Times Square. Instead of transferring to the 1, he gets off and emerges into the midtown evening. The weather has turned misty, and the streets seem quieter than usual. He heads north along Seventh Avenue, his hands shoved deep in his pockets and his ratty old parka zipped up tight around his neck.

Hannah had been questioned by police, then picked up by an ambulance, on 44th Street between Seventh and Eighth. Considering she has no known address listed, he figures that's as good a place to start looking for more information as any.

It's not really a residential neighborhood, but there are a handful of apartment buildings around. Might one of those windows be hers? Might there be neighbors who know something about her?

He stands near the corner where she broke down, squinting through the gray drizzle. Who should he talk to first? The angry-looking guy behind the bodega counter? The three men he sees crouched under the scaffolding on 44th, openly shooting up as pedestrians pass by? The kids working at the Gap?

As he's debating, a woman comes toward him, weaving along the sidewalk. She wears a huge pink scarf and bright purple leggings. As she passes him, he hears her say, "I knew all the ingredients and all the right spells. Those Wall Street motherfuck-ers took the money. But I invented ice cream!" And she goes on making the argument to the uncaring world.

Four blocks away, Jordan could buy a four-hundred-dollar pair of socks, a two-thousand-dollar tie; where he stands now, he sees commut-ers, pigeons, and homeless people. Poverty and misery and addiction.

And, of course, he sees that there's a sale at the Gap. When is there not a sale at the Gap?

Then through the mist he spies a fruit vendor, staying mostly dry under a battered red umbrella, and he suddenly remembers one of the first things Hannah ever said to him. *What if we'd met because we wanted the same apple from the fruit cart on 45th?*

Jordan dashes down the block, pulling out the picture of Han-nah he'd taken and printed out on his crappy printer.

"Excuse me, sorry," he says, thrusting it toward the man, "do you know this girl?"

The man peers closely at it. Turns it over as if there might be some secret message written on the back. Scratches at his eyebrow. Hands it back.

"Well?" Jordan asks impatiently.

"Yes, I think so," he says. "I give her apples. Sweet, sweet girl." Then he twirls a finger around his ear. "But she was too crazy."

We don't use that word, Jordan thinks but doesn't say. "Did you ever talk to her? Like, do you know anything about her? Where she lives or—"

"Sure, sure," he says. "I talk to her. But only when her eyes were…" He pauses, trying to think of how to say it. "Only when her eyes could see me," he finishes.

"Right," Jordan says. "So you don't know where she lives, or—"

"Sorry."

"Did you ever see her with friends? Family?"

The man shakes his head. "No." He blows on his hands to warm them. "Maybe once she told me of a sister. Young."

A sister here and now? Jordan wonders. *Or a sister hundreds of years ago?* But this doesn't seem like the kind of question he can ask.

"Did you ever see the sister?"

"No, never."

"Okay." Jordan picks up an apple so green and bright it hardly looks real. "I'll take this," he says. "And two bananas."

"Two dollars."

Jordan pays him in quarters: his laundry money. "Thanks for your help."

"I hope she's okay," the man calls after him.

Me too.

Jordan steels himself and walks over to the drug trio sitting on the stoop of a former bank. Only one of them appears to be conscious now. His face is scabbed and filthy. Looking down at him, Jordan feels a mix of pity and terror.

"I'm looking for someone," he says.

"Fuck you."

Jordan holds out the photo, which is getting water-streaked and wrinkled. "Do you—"

"Never seen her." He leans back against the wall. "Don't want to see you, neither."

Jordan hesitates. "Do you need any help?" he hears himself ask. Not that he has any idea what he could do. But this man might be sick or hurt, or maybe he wants a hamburger—

"I need you to get your candy-ass the fuck out of here."

CHAPTER 71

That night I lay on my thin mattress with my hands folded over my chest like a corpse. Breathing. Waiting. Trying not to feel anything at all.

I didn't belong here. Not in this hospital, not in this time.

"I'm not tired!" Andy shouted from somewhere down the hall. "You can't make me sleep! I have rights!"

I closed my eyes. Breathed more. Waited longer. Counted the slow beats of my heart. And finally, when I was on the edge of sleep, it happened. I saw myself standing at the lip of a great precipice. Below me was a swirling, cloudy blackness, and I knew that if I could get through it, I'd be on the other side. Back in the world full of people I had to save. Back to where I was supposed to be.

My breathing became shallow and my eyelids fluttered like I was already dreaming. Tingling waves passed over and through me. It felt like my cells were vibrating. Shimmering.

I almost laughed, because it was working. I'd made it happen. I could feel myself start to dissolve. And then—

Chapter 72

I t seems we'll never be rid of you," Agnes said, snapping a blanket into shape over the huge canopied bed. "Proves what they say, don't it? A stray dog lingers where it last got scraps."

Margery, passing by with a mug of wine, swatted Agnes on the shoulder. "Bite your tongue, sister." To me, she said, "I'm glad to see you back, Hannah. It's lonely here. There are never any visitors."

"Only beggars and thieves," Agnes muttered.

The ornate castle bedroom looked different than I remembered it. Brighter somehow, as if the stone walls had been scrubbed. Gone were the lacy cobwebs, the pale dust on the tapestries. The fire in the hearth was almost cheerful.

Had they been expecting me?

"That's for you," Margery said, nodding to a dress draped over the back of a chair. "I think it will fit, don't you?"

I touched the deep purple velvet, the golden vines embroidered around the neckline. My rough fingertip snagged a gold thread, pulling it loose. Whoever this gown belonged to first had been tall and slender. I was tall but half to skin and bones. "Why do you give me this to wear?"

"As I've told you before, I do as I'm directed," Margery said lightly. She gave the wine a sniff and seemed satisfied.

"By whom?"

"Oh, you're a dumb one. I surely don't know what he sees in you," Agnes whispered, pretending she didn't want me to hear.

"But I don't understand why I'm given dresses for a woman far above my station," I said stubbornly.

"The baron prefers pretty things," Margery said. "Your face is perfectly good, but your clothes won't do. He wouldn't like to look at them."

"And how fine for the baron, to see only what pleases him!"

"It's his right, isn't it?" Margery asked innocently.

"His *right*," I nearly spat. "Did God decree that he should live in luxury while my family starves? Or that when his feet are dirty, *you* should wash them? The baron's shit smells like everyone else's, and when he dies, he'll be judged no more kindly than the lowest thief. The worms will eat his carcass, same as they eat a dog's."

Agnes gaped at me in horror at my outburst, but I didn't care. Who was to speak the truth if I wouldn't?

"I just meant that he tries to see what he wants to see. Don't we all do that, if we can, milady?" asked Margery.

"I'm not a lady. And I've only seen hunger and death and misery."

"Not *only* that, child. You've seen a touch of kindness from the baron, haven't you?" Margery asked gently. "And from us?"

I turned away from her, because she was right. She'd always been good to me. And the baron was not proving to be the monster I'd assumed he was. Unaware and ignorant, maybe. But once I opened his eyes, he'd fed my family, my neighbors. He was brave in battle, protecting his people and refusing to cower in safety.

And—he found me *amusing*.

"Well, anyway, come, let's bathe you," Margery said. "Let's comb your hair."

I knew that I should resist, but I wanted to be clean. To be cared for. Was that so wrong?

An hour or three later, I was perfumed, brushed, and fastened into the purple gown, with a gold chain and a jeweled brooch at my throat. A velvet sash pulled the dress, which was indeed too big, more tightly around my waist. Instead of boots, I wore velvet slippers encrusted with pearls.

"You look like a lady *now*," Margery said.

She held up a piece of polished silver so I could see for myself. She was right. But why me? Why wasn't Margery ever asked to put on something so fine? She was pretty and soft, with hair the palest gold. If the baron wanted a girl to amuse him, he had one right here under his own towering roof.

"Have you ever been asked to—" I began, and then I gestured mutely to my dress.

Margery's eyes widened. "Never."

Agnes said, "The baron's had his pleasures, but not with the likes of us."

I knew she referred to all three of us. Village-born. Hunger-carved.

"Not yet, anyway," she added darkly.

"To the hall, then," Margery said quickly. She took the key from her waist and unlocked the door, opening it into the narrow passageway. "Follow me."

Our steps echoed along the dark hall. I trembled with cold. With anticipation.

Margery led us quickly through the maze of the keep. But as

we neared the great hall, I found that I couldn't keep up with her. My limbs grew heavier and heavier, until it seemed like my legs were made of wood. I put my palm out to the wall and felt the scrape of stone on my skin.

"Come now," Margery said briskly as she pushed me into the vast hall.

Something's wrong.

"Hannah?" Margery's voice seemed ever so faint.

My vision narrowed into a tunnel. I felt her hands on my arms, helping me forward. But I was falling down, down, into blackness.

"Come, come," she was saying in her soft voice. "There's no need to be afraid."

But I heard another voice, and this one told me that she was lying.

Something's wrong, something's wrong.

My fingers tore at my dress. From somewhere inside the darkness I heard a rising wail. A high, terrible shrieking.

Chapter 73

*I*n the flickering torchlight of a great stone hall stands a girl, half naked and screaming.

She's ripped off her dress, and now she's wearing nothing but a sleeveless woolen shift and velvet slippers. Goose bumps prickle her pale skin. Her hair, which had been combed and plaited into elaborate coils, spills down dark across her shoulders.

The baron, in his doublet of black wool and his fine black breeches, stands up so abruptly that his chair falls over with a crash. He looks over to the chambermaid. "What's going on?"

The chambermaid is stricken, white as snow. "Hannah," she says, fluttering in front of her, waving her hand in front of the girl's face, "Hannah, what is wrong?"

The lute player by the hearth stares open-mouthed at this howling, half-clothed banshee. Automatically he crosses himself. The girl must be demon-struck.

The baron pulls off his cloak and hurries to try to put it around Hannah's shoulders. The words that come out of her mouth are jumbled and nonsensical. Something about *scissors*. Something about *safety check*.

"Bring the physician," the baron shouts.

The chambermaid scurries off. The lute player stands, grabs

a goblet full of wine, and throws all of it down his throat in three enormous gulps.

"I'm supposed to be in the hospital," Hannah shouts. "Where is the hospital?"

The baron doesn't understand what she's talking about—he doesn't even know what *hospital* means. He clenches his teeth as he tries to grab her arms, trying to stop her from tearing at her hair and her cheeks. "Hannah, calm down," he urges uselessly. He looks toward the door. "Where is Goriot, that old bastard?"

The lute player shrugs, then belches, all the while staring at her full lips, her long, nearly naked limbs.

"I need the quiet room!" Hannah screams.

Finally, footsteps sound in the hallway. In comes a rush of black cloaks, the physician and his assistants arrive with their elixirs and leeches. They swarm around Hannah, black as ravens, hushing her, catching her flailing arms.

"Drink this, child, drink this."

"Hold her down!"

"There, there—hush…"

CHAPTER 74

Hannah, can you hear me?" The voice came from very far away. So far away it sounded like an echo.

I don't know where I am.

"If you can hear me, move your right hand."

I can't move my hand. I can't open my eyes.

"We want to give you something to calm you down."

The voice was floating in the air somewhere. Maybe it came from a bird in the rafters. Maybe it came from the walls. Maybe it came from inside my head.

"You're safe. The doctor is here."

Is the doctor a dream? A delusion?

There's only darkness.

"Poor thing, you're shivering."

There's a weight pressing down on me.

"This will help."

A blanket, just a blanket.

"You'll feel better soon, Hannah."

If I could've laughed, I would've.

I might be crazy, but I know a lie when I hear one.

CHAPTER 75

J ordan sits in the Columbia cafeteria, eating a soggy grain bowl topped with a rubbery fried egg. In front of him is a large black binder that he carries with him all the time these days. *HD*, it says in tiny letters on the spine, and inside the binder is everything he knows about Hannah Doe. He flips it open.

She doesn't know anything about this. The voice of Jordan's conscience is quiet but insistent. *You say you want to help her, but you're really just helping yourself.*

The rational part of him understands that the situation is more complicated than that. He's desperately trying to find out what happened to Hannah before she came to Belman. He's certain it will help her. Then, if she can get out, maybe she'll be able to *stay* out. But the voice doesn't go away.

She doesn't have any idea what you're doing.

There it is: his weak spot. The one sentence he can't argue with. *You're using her.*

He glances down. The first page lists all the medications Hannah has taken at one point or another, sometimes multiple at once:

Wellbutrin SR 100 mg PO
Geodon 200 mg PO QHS
Trazodone 150 mg PO QHS

```
Risperdal 2 mg BID
Depakote ER 1500 mg PO QPM
Zyprexa 10 mg PO QAM
Ativan 3 mg PRN
```

The list of medications goes on and on, Seroquel, Latuda, Invega...PO means by mouth, QHS is at bedtime, BID means twice a day.

He flips to his notes on her behavior.

> **1/19/23:** RNs took Hannah to the quiet room at 10:43 a.m. It took ninety-plus minutes for her to calm down. I didn't see anyone give her meds but I think they must have. Maybe she took them willingly.

> **1/24/23:** Hannah shared a poem in group therapy. She said it was a sestina about time, but no one knew what a sestina was. Then she yelled that everyone was "a bunch of cretins." Lulu scolded her.

> **1/26/23:** Hannah didn't recognize me. Or she didn't seem to. Maybe she was pretending. Which would be worse—her not recognizing me, or her acting like she didn't?

The binder began innocently enough—a class assignment on what life in a psychiatric hospital was like. But he quickly had to admit that he primarily cared about *Hannah's* life in a psychiatric hospital, and soon after that, he had to acknowledge that he was writing down everything about her because he was hoping that this would actually help him think about her *less*. He wanted Hannah to live on paper instead of inside his head.

It didn't work. He keeps thinking that he sees her in the common room of his dorm. Or in a big lecture hall, headphones over her ears, waiting for class to begin. Or once, standing outside a bubble tea place with a boy with locs and a girl wearing a panda backpack. Laughing. Posing for a picture.

It feels a lot like being haunted.

She comes to him in dreams, too. In the one he has most often, Hannah visits his dorm room. She's dressed in regular clothes—clothes that fit, and shoes with actual laces—and she's carrying a fat binder and a heavy backpack. She tells him that he missed class that morning, that there was a huge test, and that because he wasn't there to take it, he'll fail the whole semester.

It's a nightmare on the one hand, and wishful thinking on the other. Because in the dream, Hannah's better. And Dream Jordan knows that it's all because of him.

So he wakes up in the middle of the night and stares at the ceiling and wonders if he's a good person—or the worst person he knows.

Because his notes are becoming a case study. In this fat, black binder is the raw material for his Ab Psych thesis, which is turning out to be all about Hannah Doe.

Every interaction with her has become research. Information. A data point. He isn't just a hospital intern anymore. And he isn't just Hannah's friend.

He's a sleuth and a spy.

Chapter 76

R ouse yourself, Hannah. You have a visitor." Margery's voice was quiet but urgent.

Blearily I sat up, pushing off the heavy layers of velvet blankets. I rubbed my eyes until the chambermaid came into focus. *What happened? What am I doing in this bed?*

Margery held out a silver cup. "Drink."

Obediently I took a sip. The wine filled my mouth with a terrible, cloying sweetness. I could barely swallow it. I pressed the cup back into her hands. "Margery," I said, "What happened? What day is it?" My throat was raw, and it hurt to speak.

She pressed her finger to her lips, silencing me. "She's awake now," she said over her shoulder, turning and curtsying. "My lord."

She pulled aside the heavy drapes that surrounded the bed. The baron himself was standing, tall and stiff, in the muted light of the narrow window. He wore a deep red doublet and a matching tunic, and a ruby ring flashed on the long third finger of his right hand.

When he stepped toward me, I shrank back against the pillows. He stopped, frowning in confusion. "Why do you flinch?"

"I don't know," I whispered.

You killed Otto. You killed Mary.

But here you are, taking care of me.

"You have nothing to be afraid of." Baron Joachim narrowed his cool eyes at me. "You were the frightening one, shrieking like you were blind and mad."

"I've come back to my senses now," I said. *I think.*

The baron turned away and paced back and forth in front of the hearth. "You were beyond reason, and you spoke words no one understood. There were some who believed you demon-possessed." He looked back at me sharply. "What do you have to say to that?"

My heart lurched in my chest. "I was not, and I am not, I promise," I said. "Though I confess I don't remember—"

I stopped, because suddenly I *did* remember. My legs had turned to stone, the world had gone black, and there was nothing to do but tear at my own flesh and scream.

"Never mind," I whispered. "I do recall it."

"My physician had never seen such a fit." The baron stopped his pacing in front of the nearest tapestry, the one with the white-horned horse tied to a flowering tree. He stared at it while he spoke. "It seems that I have been under some misunderstanding. Or perhaps some…ignorance," he said haltingly. "I did not understand the desperate nature of your situation until"—and here he turned to gesture toward my half-prone body—"this."

"Desperate how?" I whispered. What if *he* was one of the people who thought me possessed? Would he summon priests to pray the devil out? If that didn't work, would they hang me—or burn me?

"Goriot believes that grief and hardship have weakened you in body and spirit. You are neither mad nor in thrall to the devil. You are simply wretched."

Wretched. I bristled to hear him say such a thing, but it was true. I pulled the thin chemise tighter around my neck. "Yes, I am," I said, "and I come from a wretched place, where we watch our brothers and our neighbors and our babies die, and there's nothing we can do about it." My voice dissolved into a sob. I didn't know how to hold in all the pain.

"But you will do something about it," he said.

"I have tried," I said, "and I have failed." *At a cost so great I can't think of it.*

"On the contrary," Baron Joachim said, "you have shown me the truth. I've ordered more provisions to be gathered. Your village will have as much as it needs, for as long as it needs it."

"Truly?" I was afraid to believe his words. I'd thought he didn't care about us in The Bend—but maybe it was just that he didn't *know.*

"You should not doubt me."

I bowed my head as tears of relief rolled down my cheeks and landed on the silken coverlet. I had *hated* this man—and part of me still did—but here he was, opening his hand to us, giving us back our lives. "My lord," I said, "I will be forever grateful for your generosity."

The baron looked at me strangely. After a moment, he said, "But perhaps you are possessed after all. The Hannah I know is not capable of such politeness."

The smile on his lips was so faint it was almost invisible.

"I have suffered a terrible shock to my system," I said gravely. "Perhaps I am not myself."

"Most likely that is the case."

The next thing I knew, he'd sat down on the edge of the bed. Something shifted in the air, and it did so as quickly and absolutely as the sun coming out from behind a cloud. I could feel the heat of his body through the covers. Hear the beating of my heart in my ears. He was so near that I could slide my leg over and touch his thigh if I dared. Or if he reached his hand out, he could cup the curve of my hip—

Hannah, stop. You are a peasant, and he is a lord.

"I saw you years ago, when I was but eight," I whispered. "You came to my village on your fine horse, in your own little shining suit of armor, and you looked down on us like we were no different from the dirt we stood on."

Baron Joachim nodded slowly. "Ah, yes, the tour of my ancestral lands—I remember that day. It wasn't as triumphal as it might've seemed, let me assure you. What I recall most is being petrified of my father. When I told him that I didn't want to ride out that morning—my mother was dying, she'd be dead within a fortnight—he beat me." He gave a hollow laugh. "Well, he had one of his guardsmen do it, so he didn't sully his lordly hands. Twelve lashes of a leather strap right after breakfast. It was a miracle I could sit on that fine horse."

So had it been pain rather than cruelty that I'd seen in his eyes as he rode through our village? It changed that old memory a little, tinging it with sympathy.

"My father never laid a hand on any of us, but he wasn't able to feed us, either," I said. "Had a full meal been promised me at the end of the day, I could've withstood any lashing."

The baron looked at me without replying, and I felt my cheeks flush under his gaze.

"I don't mean to suggest I'm stronger than you are," I added quickly. "Just…more desperate. As we've agreed."

"You don't have to be desperate anymore," the baron said. "You'll have all that you need, today and always."

My hands twisted in my lap. "I don't know why you're being so kind to me," I said.

His cool eyes met mine. He said quietly, "You don't?"

My heartbeat quickened. I couldn't answer him—I was not that brave.

Baron Joachim smoothed the covers of the bed with his hand. "You are unlike anyone I have ever encountered, Hannah. I do not like to see you go, and I hope you will return. Of course, the next time you are invited to dine in the great hall, you must be sure to keep your dress on."

I held my breath as his fingertip traced a light, teasing trail up my leg. When he next spoke, his voice was hardly more than a whisper. "Whether or not the dress stays on elsewhere, however, is a different story."

Desire swelled hot inside me, sudden and unexpected and thrilling. I reached for his hand—

ey, girl. Hey! Hello? Hannnnnnnah!"

No, don't wake me no no no

Joachim! Where did you go?

Take me

Take me

Someone's palm was going *patpatpatpat* on my cheek. I pushed it away. "Stop it!"

"Sorry! But, girl, you've really got to come back to us now."

I dragged my eyes open. Saw white fluorescent light, that hideous tile ceiling, and the looming face of my friend Indy. He was perched on the edge of my bed with his dark hair flopped over one eye, and he was wrinkling his nose at me. "You were moaning," he said. "Hot dreams, babe?"

"Ugh, shut up," I said, feeling my cheeks flush as I pushed myself up to sitting.

It wasn't a dream. It was real.

Indy grabbed my foot and squeezed it. "Come on, upsy-daisy," he said.

I want to go back.

I tried to shake him off. "Leave me alone. You're not supposed to be in my room."

I want to go back. Let me go back.

"I know that," Indy said. "But I don't care. You've been doing that thing too much—you know, where you're here but you're *not* here? And it sucks. It's spooky. But you're really here now, aren't you?" He unfolded a piece of paper and held it out to me. "Look, I made you this."

I stared down at it, waiting for the drawing to come into focus. Waiting to come all the way back into *this* world, even though I didn't want to.

Joachim—

"Hello?" Indy said, stabbing at the page. "I'm awaiting your words of praise, Hannah."

The paper was almost entirely covered with blue ink marking out lines, words, and shapes. I saw two towers, a wide gatehouse. There were staircases and banners and horses. A border of swords and stones.

"It's a castle," I said, wonderingly. I squinted at it, turning it this way and that, as if I'd be able to see the baron in one of the doorways.

"A hundred points for the girl in the hand-me-down sweats," Indy said. "It probably doesn't look anything like where you go, but I thought of you when I was making it."

It was beautiful, and so intricate it made my eyes swim. "It's like a maze," I said.

"Every picture I make is a maze," said Indy matter-of-factly. "I draw what it feels like to be inside my head."

"You want to get out, but you never can," I said. "I know the feeling."

"It's like a funhouse, except that nothing is fun. It's a sadhouse.

A madhouse. A very, very badhouse. God, listen to me, I'm like Dr. Goddamn Seuss over here."

I squinted at the impossibly tiny handwriting. "What does all that say?"

"Oh, just lunatic ravings," Indy said dismissively.

"Is that my name right there?"

"Maybe."

"I can't read anything else," I said.

"You're not supposed to be able to. It's a secret." He was already drawing a new picture in his notebook.

"It's Olivia Rodrigo lyrics," I said, goading him.

"Very funny."

"Is it nice? Or are you cursing me or something?"

"I would never curse you," Indy said, his expression suddenly serious. "You're the best person here. If I liked girls, I would like you so much."

"Thanks," I said. I pushed the thin covers off my legs. One of my socks was missing. "Did breakfast already happen?"

"Lucky for you, it did not, and it's all thanks to me. Are you ready for sausage surprise? The surprise is that nobody knows what the sausage is made of! Personally I think it's horse testi—"

"Stop right there!" I said.

"Sorry. Just hurry up and get dressed."

"Why?" Almost everyone at Belman went to breakfast in their pajamas. Some people never changed out of them.

"I can't escort you to the cafeteria with you looking like that. Not on my last day here."

The words hit me like a sucker punch to the stomach. "You're *leaving*?"

Indy nodded. "I'm sorry," he said. "But I'm totally cured." Then he laughed—but it was a bitter one. "Just kidding. My insurance won't pay anymore."

"Indy, they can't—"

"Of course they can," he said. "Hello, capitalism? But I had a long talk with Dr. Ager yesterday. She thinks that if I keep taking my meds and whatever, I'm going to do okay out there."

My mind struggled to process what Indy was telling me. *He's going home. They say he's going to be all right. Why is this happening so quickly? Why didn't anyone warn me?* "Do you want to go?" I asked. "Are you ready?"

He rubbed his eyebrows. They'd grown almost all the way back in. "You know what Hunter S. Thompson said?"

"I'm sure he said a lot of things," I replied. "He was a *famous writer.*"

"Very funny. He said that the only difference between the sane and the insane was that the sane had the power to lock up the insane. Which means if Dr. Ager doesn't have the power to lock me up, then there's no difference between me and her, which means that if she's sane, *I'm* sane."

"That's some...interesting reasoning."

"Oh, it's all bullshit!" Indy cried. "But I think I'm ready. I mean—I *have* to be, right? So I am. I definitely am."

What am I going to do without you? That was the question I couldn't ask him.

When I looked down at Indy's drawing again, a big, fat tear fell on it. The ink bled, distorting a careful blue line, and a hole bloomed inside the castle wall like a flower.

"I'm so happy for you," I whispered.

CHAPTER 78

Indy hadn't told anyone else that he was leaving. "I'm just gonna French exit the psych ward," he'd said. But everyone found out anyway, because Indy had been at Belman for a month, and suddenly he was packing up his stuff. He was getting out. That kind of thing was big news.

Of course, some people didn't really care—Andy, for one, and a scared-looking new girl who was muttering to herself on the couch—but Beatrix stopped Indy in the hallway and asked if he could smuggle her out. Another newish guy whose name was Stan or Sam wanted Indy to get a message to his dealer. "Tell him ten bars, ten oxys, and an eight ball—I'll be out in forty-eight." Indy nodded at him, like, *Sure, okay, no problem.* He knew not to question someone's delusion.

I moved through the morning in a daze. Whenever someone asked me a question, it took a long time for me to answer. Michaela said that this was probably just a fun new medication side effect, but I knew it was just because I was thinking so much about Indy. He'd helped tether me to this world, and now he was leaving.

What would become of me without him? What would become of *him* without all of us?

"He'll be back," Michaela said flatly. She was watching him packing and repacking his orange JanSport backpack.

"You don't think he's better?" I asked.

"Sure, he's better. But he's not good."

I didn't want to say it out loud, but I felt the same way.

Please take care of yourself, Indy, I prayed. *Please be okay.*

That afternoon, Indy and Michaela and I met in the group therapy room. We pulled up three chairs in such a small, tight circle that our knees were touching.

"No physical contact," Michaela drawled, imitating Mitch (good riddance). Indy gave a halfway laugh.

Indy held out his hands, and we took them. "Okay, girls," he said. "This is it."

Then we sat there quietly. Just being there together for what maybe was the last time.

After a while Indy said, "I just hope that when I'm out, I don't feel like an alien this time. I want to be able to look at people walking down the street and say to myself, 'I'm not so goddamn different from them.'"

He started blinking really rapidly, and I wondered if he was about to cry.

"Is that so much to ask?" he said quietly. "Just to be okay?"

Michaela said, "Keep taking your medications. Make sure you talk to your therapist. And you need to see friends and be social. Don't live on the internet, Adam. Touch grass."

Indy wiped his eyes even as he was rolling them. "I cannot *believe* that you called me my real name, and that you used a prehistoric internet meme as part of your inspirational speech."

Michaela smiled. "Adam's a really nice name."

"Remember when I first got here and you told me I smelled like freedom? Now it's your turn," I said.

Indy nodded. "Okay. Right." He started to look a little happier. "My brother said there's a foot of powder back in Rhinebeck. My freedom's going to smell like snow." Then he let go of our hands and stood up. "I gotta bounce," he said.

I wanted so much to be happy for him, but my heart was as heavy as a stone in my chest. "I'm going to miss you," I said.

"I'll see you again—on the outside," he said.

I nodded. My throat hurt too much to speak.

Michaela walked him to the nurses' station, where I guess his parents were waiting for him. I didn't watch Indy get signed out. Didn't try to furtively hug him good-bye. I just lay on my bed and cried.

Of course we all wanted our friends to get better. To get out. But I didn't think Indy was ready, no matter what anyone else said.

CHAPTER **79**

> **2-15-23** Indy—Adam R.—was released after
> lunch today. Hannah didn't come out of her
> room to see him off. Later, when she got
> her meds, she wouldn't say a word, to me
> or to anyone else. If I had to pick a word
> to describe her, I'd say she looked scared.

Jordan closes his notebook as the train pulls into Times Square. Coming out of the subway, he takes the steps two at a time and emerges into neon-lit midtown. Wind howls through the canyon of the buildings. He takes a second to orient himself and then jaywalks across the street, nearly getting clipped by a taxi.

He shoulders his way past tourists—New Yorkers never walk that slowly—and heads west and north toward the sand-colored stone building that houses the Midtown North Police Precinct headquarters.

Inside the station it's all bright fluorescent light and dull, institutional paint choices. There's the harsh ringing of phones and people shouting to and at one another. In the lobby, two officers are attempting to calm a kid who is screaming about his bike being stolen. He can't be more than twelve, but he's spitting and cursing and trying to fight off the cops.

When Jordan gets to the front desk, the woman doesn't look up from her computer. She offers a noncommittal "Mmm-hmm," which he assumes means that she's ready to assist him.

He explains that he's trying to find an officer who might know something about his friend, who had a breakdown a couple of weeks ago on a nearby street. "A police officer from this precinct... uh, helped her."

"You got a name?"

"Me?" Jordan asks. "I'm Jordan Hass—"

"The officer's name," she says, and Jordan can practically hear her thinking, *you dumbass.*

"No, but if I could find out who was working on January seventeenth at about eight in the morning—"

"You want the time sheets?" she says, then laughs. "No dice, mister. You're going to need a few more specifics. Who do you want to speak to?"

"I don't have the officer's name," he says, and he can feel the people in line behind him getting restless.

"I gotta get my fingerprints done," someone behind him says. "Shit."

"You got a complaint?" the woman asks Jordan, raising an eyebrow. "About the officer?"

"No. I'm just trying to find out some information about my friend."

"If she's your friend, you should probably ask her."

If getting an answer out of Hannah were a realistic option, Jordan would've done it already. Not that he can explain that to this woman. "She's, uh, sick," he says. "Look, I know it's a weird thing to ask, but this is really important."

"I don't know how to help you," the woman says, shaking her head. To her credit, she sounds *almost* sorry about it.

He leans forward, like he's going to tell her a secret. He's never been pushy in his life, but the stakes are too high now. He can't be sent away with nothing. "Listen," he says, "ma'am—please. I don't mean to trouble you, I swear. But my friend is really, really not well, and I'm not sure there's a soul in the world who cares about her as much as I do." He stops. *God*, he doesn't want that to be true. But he's afraid it is. "I need to talk to the officer who found her. I think…" *What* do *I think? How is this going to help?* "I think it's possible that he might have seen her before. And I think he might be able to help me understand what's going on."

The woman looks at him for a long time, her face betraying only the slightest hint of curiosity. Of kindness. She swivels around in her chair, looks back at someone sitting at a desk behind her—her supervisor, maybe?—and then starts tapping something into the computer.

Two minutes later, during which the man behind Jordan complains nonstop about people who take too long in line, the woman hands Jordan a scrap of paper with a name scrawled on it. Officer Brian Dunthorpe.

"He's back on duty next Wednesday," she says.

CHAPTER **80**

At 9:30 a.m. I stumbled into Dr. Nicholas's office for our regularly scheduled appointment.

"Thank you for coming, Hannah," he said, all polite and formal.

Like I had any choice?

I sank into the hard chair on the other side of Dr. N's desk. "I just *miss* him," I said.

Dr. N steepled his fingers and looked over their tips at me and said, very quietly, "I'm listening."

He probably didn't even know who I was talking about—Indy wasn't one of his patients—but I told myself that it didn't matter. Dr. N would pop a bottle of Dom Pérignon if I told him *anything*.

God, he must be so sick of me and my endless refusal to talk.

But if I opened up—if I let myself remember—

What would happen then?

I felt my nails digging into the upholstered arms of the chair. I said, "Maybe I'm jealous of him."

"Go on," he urged.

"He got out of here. He's a civilian again." That was the term Indy always used. I pulled my legs in tighter. I was trying to make myself as small as I possibly could. "Indy says he's ready. But I think he's just saying that because his insurance was kicking him out."

Dr. N leaned back, nodding because he finally knew who I was talking about. "Don't you think he's the best judge of his readiness?"

"Of course not." I waved my hand around the room. "Isn't that why we're all here? Because we *don't* know what's best? We *don't* know how to deal with ourselves? That's why you people have to take care of us."

"Well, at some point, we all have to take responsibility for living our own lives," Dr. N said. "It isn't fair that some of us suffer. That some of us struggle with illness. But we can't just sit back and live in the unfairness. We have to take steps toward recovery."

"We're not talking about Indy right now, are we?" I asked.

Dr. N was silent.

I closed my eyes. I said, "I can't let it go. I can't let it out."

"You're going to have to," he said quietly.

"We'd both been here a lot, me and Indy," I said. "But I always left first."

I put my face down into my hands and cradled it like a baby. It was dark all around me, and Dr. N's smooth, soft voice was rolling over me like waves.

"Indy felt like family, didn't he?" Dr. N said. "And family isn't supposed to leave you."

I don't want to be here anymore.

I wanted to go to the castle. I wanted to see Margery. I wanted her to brush my hair and twist it into gleaming plaits, fussing over me like a mother.

But I couldn't get there.

I shivered in my seat, hunched over, still refusing to open my eyes.

Hannah, you have to hide, said an old, old voice.

Fear shot through me, as sudden and hot as an electrical shock. It was a voice I hadn't heard in over a decade.

I put my hands over my ears, but it didn't help. The words were coming from inside my head. From inside the time I never wanted to remember. And there was nothing I could do to stop them.

Hannah, listen—Hannah, come! Don't cry. We'll be safe in here. Shhhh!!

Hannah, hurry, he's coming.

CHAPTER 81

Checking in that morning, Jordan runs into Brittany, the tech who's on her way out after the night shift.

"Good luck today," she says, loosing her pale blond hair from its ponytail.

Jordan once spent a summer working graveyard at a warehouse, and he knows how much staying up all night sucks. And although the ward's obviously quieter when patients are asleep, there aren't as many RNs on duty if someone wakes up and starts causing problems.

"Rough night?" he asks.

She shrugs. "No more than usual."

"How's everyone this morning?"

Brittany grimaces as she puts on her coat. "Still batshit." Then she flushes. "Sorry—I didn't mean that. Cayden tried to throw a chair and hurt his back. Michaela couldn't sleep and Andy's dead again. I mean, he thinks he is." She waves over her shoulder as she heads out. "Whatever. Nothing a stiff drink won't fix."

"It's not even *nine*," Jordan calls after her.

She turns around and grins. Her eyes, which are an impossibly light blue, are laughing. "Bloody Mary hour! I'll be over at Biddy McBain's, if you want to join me on your break."

Did she just wink at me? Jordan thinks.

But she's already out the door.

After the morning staff meeting, Jordan does a round of safety checks. Most people are with their social workers or therapists. A few pace the hallways, and a handful of others are doing breathwork with Harold Wong in Room G. No one curses at him when he knocks on their door; fortunately he hasn't interrupted anyone's naked burpees since his first day. But TJ in Room 13 is dry humping his pillow.

"Safety—um—sorry—safety check," Jordan mutters. "As you were." TJ is obviously not in danger.

Back in the hall, Jordan sees Hannah come out of Dr. Nicholas's office, her face red and her eyes puffy.

"Hannah?" he says. "Hi! Can you...see me?"

She wipes her nose on her sleeve. "What kind of question is that? I'm not in here for *blindness*."

"Right. Sorry. I just meant—" He falls in step beside her. She knows what he meant. "Want to talk?" he says.

"No," she says.

"How about a puzzle? I brought in a new one. Well, it's vintage. It's called Flat Banana, and it's yellow. The whole thing. Just: yellow."

Michaela drifts down the hallway, and she *definitely* winks at him. "I'll do it," she says.

But Hannah doesn't want anything to do with his stupid puzzle. She looks shaky. Shell-shocked.

"Are you feeling okay?" he asks. Another stupid question. Of course she's not feeling okay. She's been weeping in her therapist's office. "Do you need to lie down?"

Hannah stops in the middle of the hallway. She's cringing like his words hurt her. He bites his tongue. Twists his hands behind his back. *Whatever you need, I want to give it to you, Hannah Doe.*

Finally she says, "I feel like I can't stay."

Instead of asking her what she means, he just waits. His body feels like a string about to be plucked. He's nothing but anticipation. *Just tell me all your secrets*, he thinks. *You can trust me.*

Mostly.

"I can't keep holding up the walls," she says. "There are cracks now. There's daylight."

He tries to get her to meet his eyes, but she won't look up. "Isn't daylight usually a good thing?"

"Some things should be kept in the dark forever." She steps over to the wall, leans against it, then slides down to the floor.

Jordan crouches down in front of her. Michaela makes a huffing sound and stalks off down the hall muttering something about special treatment.

"What sorts of things?" he asks.

"Things that happened. Things I don't want to know."

"Things that happened to *you*?" he says. Maybe they're finally getting somewhere, here in this cold, bright hallway.

Hannah doesn't move or respond.

"You know that everyone here wants to help you. *I* want to help you."

He can hear Andy yelling in the distance: "Why can't you see that I'm a *corpse*?"

Hannah shakes her head vehemently. "Meds and groups and cognitive behavioral therapy and mindfulness and fucking *deep breathing* aren't cutting it. Making collages out of old magazines and writing poems aren't helping. Everyone's always talking about tools to help me get better. Well your tools *suck*."

But Jordan could practically start clapping. Hannah has just admitted that she might have a problem. That the issue isn't that no one believes her, but that she actually needs help.

In other words, she might be beginning to acknowledge that she's not a time traveler. That she's a person with a mental illness.

"Maybe there are things about myself that I just don't want to know," she practically yells. "Don't you ever feel that way?"

"No," he says quietly. "I want to know everything."

"Well I guess that's why you're in college and I'm in a psychiatric institution," she says bitterly. "I can't talk anymore. I have to go."

But she doesn't move from where she's sitting. She wraps her arms around her legs and puts her head down.

Because she doesn't mean she has to leave. She means that she has to go to the castle.

Chapter 82

My name is Hannah Dory, and I have saved us.

Everyone is so happy. Everyone loves me.

I am the one who brought the food. Eight full carts of it, and more whenever there is need.

Mother forgives me for Mary's death. Erik Rast forgives me for Otto's.

Conn laughs and grows fat.

Ryia is pregnant again.

When the baron looks at me, his eyes seem to glow.

CHAPTER **83**

Jordan's been staring at his computer for so long that he can barely read the letters on the screen anymore. The cursor blinks steadily, endlessly. He feels like time could stop, and the cursor would still keep disappearing, reappearing, and then disappearing again forever.

I GO TO THE CASTLE:
A CASE STUDY IN SCHIZOPHRENIA

by Jordan Hassan CC'25

"The barriers to combating schizophrenia include lack of research funding, public disinterest in (or aversion to) the problem, and the nearly infinite complexities of the human brain itself...."
—Dr. Ximena Jones, *The Many Voices of Schizophrenia*

"Go, go, go, said the bird.
Humankind cannot bear very much reality."
—T. S. Eliot, *The Four Quartets*

The first time I saw Hannah D., a patient at Delia F. Belman Memorial Psychiatric Hospital, she was strapped to a gurney in the back of an ambulance.

When hospital staff released her restraints, she made a break for it. And I was the one who caught her.

What follows is her story. And mine.

Jordan rubs his eyes and takes a sip of the instant coffee that he made with warm water from the bathroom tap. If Hannah thinks that Belman coffee's terrible, she should try this brew. It's practically poisonous.

After impulsively deciding to take a break from writing his thesis, Jordan walks down the hall into the common room of his dormitory. A few students are flopped here and there on the overstuffed couches. Jordan can't help but notice the room's sharp-edged tables, breakable glass windows, and regular doorknobs. None of these things would be allowed on the Belman ward. Hell, even a hardcover book or a spiral-bound notebook is considered a potential weapon at Belman.

The girl who reminded him of Hannah is studying at her usual table, her hair twisted into a knot on the top of her head and held in place with a chopstick. Jordan makes another sudden decision and sits down across from her. Her attention doesn't stray from the papers in front of her.

What are you doing, Hassan?

I don't really know.

He finally says, simply, "Hi. I'm Jordan."

She looks up at him. She seems a little confused at first, but a second later she smiles and pushes aside the article she's been reading. He sees, with a start, that it's about muons, the subatomic particles Hannah mentioned when he first met her.

"Do those things really break the laws of physics?" he blurts.

She pulls the chopstick out of her hair, and it spills in dark waves down her back. "I'm Ellie," she says, "and no."

He notices that her eyes are a clear, lovely gray. "They don't?"

Her smile grows wider. "Well, okay, muons appear to violate *known* laws. The currently *accepted* laws. But if it can be broken, then it's not really a law, is it?"

"All kinds of laws get broken," Jordan says. He thinks of Cayden, Belman's resident arsonist, and Amelia, the thief. They were sent to the hospital in lieu of juvenile detention or jail.

"The laws of physics are totally different from human laws, because human laws are *decisions*," Ellie says. "They aren't facts."

Jordan nods. "Okay, so for example, there could be a country where murder was legal—"

"But there couldn't be a country where gravity doesn't exist." Ellie finishes his sentence.

"What about the multiverse?" Jordan asks. "Is that a thing? And does anyone think that time travel's really possible?"

Ellie laughs. "This is absolutely the weirdest first conversation I've ever had with someone. Do you want to go get a drink and see how much weirder it can get?"

Yes. Yes, he definitely would.

CHAPTER 84

D r. Ager has read through everyone's charts and files and records by now, and she's noticed something different about Hannah's treatment.

No one is paying for it.

Health insurance companies pay out big for ICU visits, ER physicians, and surgeries. But they don't like loosening the purse strings for psychological treatments. So every single dollar in revenue matters, even at a private, endowed hospital like Belman.

Dr. Ager pushes her glasses up onto the top of her head and gazes around at the gathered staff.

Why, she wants to know, when there are so many young people in need of care, does one person in particular gobble up so much of Ward 6's resources?

She doesn't even have to say Hannah's name. Everyone knows who she's talking about.

Nurse Amy takes this question, leaning forward with an ingratiating look on her face. She says she knows it's weird—*anomalous*, she corrects herself—but that's how it's been for years. "Delia Belman's granddaughter took a special interest in Hannah," she explains. "She stipulated that care should be extended to her, without expectation of reimbursement."

Jordan looks at Amy like, *Where did all those big words come from?* But the fact is that everyone is trying to impress Dr. Ager, who has been carefully monitoring staff dedication and performance.

"And has she seen the amount of resources that this particular client uses?" Dr. Ager asks. She always says *client* instead of *patient.* That or *service user.*

"I don't imagine she's looked at the numbers," Amy says.

"Well, she will," Dr. Ager replies.

"Hannah has no resources herself."

Dr. Ager nods. "As I assumed. But the majority of people with mental illness get neither treatment nor medication. She isn't the only young woman in New York who needs help. The world is full of Hannahs."

No it isn't, Jordan thinks. *There's never been anyone like her.*

Dr. Nicholas tentatively clears his throat. He didn't use to come to these meetings, but that was before Dr. Ager came on board. "We can't discharge her," he says. "She's too enmeshed in her hallucinatory world."

"No one's talking about discharging her," Dr. Ager says. "Not yet. But I think we should encourage her to leave the ward voluntarily. Just for a few hours. Half a day. Didn't you tell me she suggested that herself recently?"

"She suggested it, yes. But she didn't end up leaving the grounds."

"Hannah has no record of self-harm or suicidal ideation. She's never tried to run away. I believe she can be trusted."

Amy and Jordan look at each other. "It depends on the day," Amy says.

"We'll wait for a day when she's lucid and cooperative."

"Will staff go with her?" Jordan asks.

"We don't have anyone to spare."

And so it's settled. Hannah's going to be sent out into the big wide world. Alone.

CHAPTER **85**

Hannah sure as hell isn't leaving the ward today, Jordan thinks.

She's sitting in a corner of the quiet room, slowly combing her hair with a dreamy, far-off look in her eyes.

"She went in this morning," Michaela tells Jordan. "Voluntarily."

He tries the door. It's not locked. But when it opens and he pokes his head in, Hannah doesn't notice him.

"Mother," she says, "don't let Conn have another piece of cake. He'll be sick. No, just put it where he can't reach. Sorry, love. It's for your own good. I know, I'm cruel, aren't I? Here, have a sip of ale and a bit more bread if you're hungry. Though I can't see how you could be. Are you hollow, my little goose?"

"Creepy, right?" Michaela whispers.

Jordan ignores her. He hasn't been around for med pass lately, and he wonders if Hannah's been refusing her medications.

Michaela steps closer to him, and he smells the bright lemony scent of her shampoo. Unlike Hannah, Michaela always takes care of herself. Brushes her hair. Wears the lipstick that staff finally agreed to let her have. Blush, too, on cheekbones above her hollow cheeks.

She lowers her voice to a whisper. "Sometimes I don't even think she's schizophrenic. It's more like she's a mad genius. Whenever she's stressed out, she just disappears into the Middle Ages."

"I don't think it really works like that," Jordan says.

"It's a killer coping mechanism," Michaela says, unswayed. "Total and complete escape. I don't know why she picked medieval wherever, though. I'd take a yacht in the French Riviera, anytime after 2010. Better drugs, better hygiene. Not nearly as many rats." She glances over at Jordan and smiles. It's a strange, almost mocking look she's giving him. "You think Hannah doesn't have any control over it, don't you? Well, I don't think you give her enough credit. She's not just some fragile, damaged girl, you know. She's a survivor. A freaking *warrior*. Because it's people like us—the ones who people like *you* think are broken—who are fighting for our lives every single day," Michaela says. "And that makes us stronger than you will ever understand." Her finger makes one quick, hard jab into his sternum.

Jordan nods and backs up a little. He knows that Michaela's right. It's plenty easy to paddle downstream.

"Conn," Hannah calls. "Stay close to home!"

"I should go check in with the charge nurse now," Jordan says.

"Remembered you had other patients, did you?" Michaela asks lightly.

He can hear her laughing as he walks down the hall. As he rounds the corner near the nurse's station, his phone buzzes.

It's a text message from Ellie.

what r u doing saturday?

He hesitates only a second.

seeing you

She sends a shooting star emoji.

Jordan tucks the phone back into his pocket before someone yells at him for looking at it. Now he's got a date with a funny and sane girl from North Carolina who's studying how physicists can program particles to assemble themselves, or to have certain physical properties, or something like that—he was a little drunk when she was trying to explain it to him.

Now that he knows Ellie, she doesn't remind him of Hannah so much. But he tells himself that's a good thing.

CHAPTER 86

Jordan spies Officer Brian Dunthorpe coming out of a coffee shop on 49th Street early on Wednesday morning. He's a short, burly man with a splash of freckles across his nose and the cauliflower ears of a former fighter. "Miranda warned me you'd show up," Dunthorpe says.

He starts walking down the street, and Jordan hurries to catch up with him. "And she told me where to find you," Jordan says. "Thanks for talking with me."

"I'm getting paid for it." Dunthorpe throws his head back, drains the rest of his coffee, and pitches the cup into an overflowing trash can. "So what's up, kid?"

Kid. Jordan smiles. Officer Dunthorpe's not that much older than he is. But Dunthorpe has a uniform, a gun, and a bit of a bowlegged swagger. *He walks like his balls are too big for him*, Jordan thinks.

"I was wondering if you could tell me anything about a girl you came across a few weeks ago." He decides not to mention how she'd ripped off her clothes and was screaming about her sister. "She was, uh, having a mental health crisis."

Dunthorpe snorts. "Who isn't these days? We got people robbing stores in broad daylight. Kicking old ladies. Shoving each other in front of trains." He gives an exaggerated shrug of his big shoulders. "Everyone's gone freakin' crazy."

We don't use that word, Jordan thinks for the hundredth time. So, at the risk of sounding like a know-it-all prick, he points out that most people with mental illness are only a danger to themselves. They don't go around pushing people in front of subway trains.

"Oh, you don't gotta lecture me," Dunthorpe says amiably. "I know how it goes. There's a reason I called the ambulance on your friend. There's a reason I didn't let my buddy press charges."

"Press charges?" This is news to Jordan.

"She kicked Haines in the sternum so hard he took two days off from duty. Couldn't play basketball for a month. We got a league, you know." His hand goes up to his cheek. "She punched me good, too. Sharp little knuckles." He gave a half laugh. "Someone oughta teach her to box. Girl's got fight in her."

"Had you seen her before that day?" Jordan asks.

"I never knew her name, but she hung around outside that used bookstore over on Ninth sometimes. I bought her a sandwich once. Egg salad."

"Do you know where she lived?"

Dunthorpe jaywalks across 45th; Jordan follows. "On the street," Dunthorpe says matter-of-factly.

Hannah is homeless? The thought of her sleeping under a tarp or in a cardboard box on the street makes his heart clench up.

"So—like—him?" He points to the sleeping body of a man, curled in a doorway.

"I know that guy, too," Dunthorpe says. "Clay. He's all right when he's not full of meth." His radio crackles, then goes silent again. "I think your friend slept in that tent city south of Javits. You know what I'm talking about? Near Twelfth Avenue?"

"I don't know that one," Jordan says. No wonder Hannah doesn't talk about leaving Belman the way the other patients do. She has nowhere else to go.

"Well, it's gone now. It got swept last week," Dunthorpe says. "But it'll pop up again. We clean the same places over and over and it doesn't matter. Everyone'll be back in a week, with all their trash and their dogs and their drugs."

"Hannah didn't do drugs."

But Dunthorpe isn't listening. "This is New York City! The greatest city in the world! You can't have people shitting on the sidewalks and shooting up in public and passing out in people's doorways. They think some damn Business District Recovery Initiative foot patrol is gonna fix this? We need—"

"Twelfth and what?" Jordan asks.

"Huh? Oh. Yeah. Thirty-third, kid."

"Thanks for your time, officer."

CHAPTER **87**

Where the encampment used to be, Jordan finds a lone guy in a filthy Carhartt jacket sitting on the sidewalk next to a bag of cans and bottles. He's twentysomething, Jordan guesses, with blond locs and a pair of old-school headphones hooked around his neck. The wires dangle down, unconnected to anything.

Nervously, Jordan manages a "Hey," and the guy looks up at him with bloodshot eyes. Instead of saying *"Who the fuck are you,"* which is what Jordan was expecting, he says nothing. He puts the headphones over his ears. Lights a cigarette.

Jordan scuffs a toe against the sidewalk. "There used to be tents here, right?"

At first he thinks the guy can't hear him. Jordan's about to repeat himself when the guy hocks a loogie down between his legs and says, "Yep."

"What happened?" Jordan asks, though he already knows the answer.

The guy takes a long drag on his cigarette. "The NYPD and the mayor and the army. The national guard. The president. I don't know who the fuck they were. They took my tent and my clothes and my radio and put them into a garbage truck. That was *my* shit!" Then he looks up at Jordan again. "You got money?"

Jordan's got twenty bucks in his wallet. But giving it to this guy would feel weird, like he's playing a role in a bad TV movie or something. *I'll give you something to make it worth your while....*

"Well?" the guy says.

"I was hoping you could help me."

"I can," he says. "No doubt."

Jordan almost laughs. "You don't even know what I want," he says.

"Drugs."

"No."

"If you got cash, I can get us some." He scratches the side of his face with a dirty hand.

"I'm trying to find someone who knew a friend of mine. She lived around here. Her name's Hannah. Maybe you know her." *Maybe she lived in the tent next to yours.*

The guy shrugs. "Hmmm," he says.

Jordan figures he'll pretend to think for a few more minutes and then ask for money again. You know, to jog his memory.

But then the guy starts nodding. "Maybe. Yeah."

"Maybe?" Jordan repeats. "Or *yes?*"

"There were like thirty of us, man. I don't know who the hell they all were. But there was a girl named Hannah or Jana or something."

"What did she look like?"

"Black hair. Hot."

Jordan's neck prickles. "Maybe five four? Really dark eyes?" He thinks about the day she showed up at the hospital. "And combat boots," he adds.

"Yeah, sure."

"What was she like? Did she ever tell you anything about herself?"

"Yeah, we sat around and had heart-to-hearts every night," he says sarcastically.

Jordan crouches down on the sidewalk next to him and holds out the ten he's taken from his wallet. Because why not? Maybe he's finally getting somewhere. "What's your name?"

"Mark." He takes the money and shoves it deep into the pocket of his jeans. Doesn't say thanks.

"I'm Jordan. And I'm just trying to help Hannah. So anything you can tell me about her…"

Mark looks around at the empty sidewalk like he's hoping the tent city will magically reappear. "She'd talk about shit that wasn't there."

"What kind of…shit?"

"I don't know, man, I don't remember. Look, she was messed up. Everyone here was messed up. Most of it was drugs. Give me some more money and I can get us some."

"I really don't want any drugs. What else can you tell me about Hannah? Did she have friends? Family?"

"I don't know." He scratches his head. "I think I got lice," he adds.

Jordan slides a couple inches farther away. "Anything you know could be important."

Mark stays quiet until his cigarette's halfway gone. "No parents," he finally says. "Neither of us had 'em. Well I did, but they wasn't worth anything. I got taken away from them. Rust Belt fuckin' misery. She was in some orphanage way uptown. Charles Dickens shit."

Mark looks over and sees the surprised look on Jordan's face. He laughs. "That's just what she told me."

"Do you know what it was called? What neighborhood it was in?"

"Past Harlem's all I know. I roll south of 45th exclusive."

Did Hannah come from a group home in Washington Heights? Or Inwood? If Mark's telling the truth, then Jordan suddenly knows more about her than anyone else at Belman. He doesn't feel like a spy anymore—he feels like a goddamn hero.

Mark was still talking. "Whatever it was, she said it looked like some kind of fucked-up fortress or something."

CHAPTER **88**

I think today's the day," Amy said, walking briskly over to the little window in my room and peering out.

"But the weather's terrible." I pulled my sweater tighter around my shoulders. "I've seen at least ten snowflakes."

"Oh, Hannah." She smiled like I was being cute.

I wasn't being cute. I didn't want to go outside alone.

"Do you still have that coat we loaned you?" Amy asked.

"Maybe," I said. It was very plainly sticking out of the bottom drawer of my dresser. "But my stomach hurts."

I wasn't expecting Amy to buy it, and guess what, she didn't.

"You were fine when they took your vitals an hour ago," she said.

"It must have been something I ate."

Amy came over and touched my shoulder gently. "Hon, no malingering, please."

"I'm sick," I said. Then I added, "In the head."

Amy gave a short bark of a laugh. "Yeah, I've never heard that one before. Come on, put on your shoes."

There was no point in arguing with her. I was going out, whether I wanted to or not. "I'm going to need laces," I told her.

"And a buddy. You know, how in elementary school, when you have to hold hands—"

"You'll get laces when we sign you out. But you don't need a buddy."

"What if I want one? Like…" I pretended to think. "Like, I don't know—Jordan." I could leave the ward if it meant I'd be with him. I'd laugh at his stupid jokes and we'd walk around the neighborhood and maybe we could get coffee or even ice cream like two totally normal people. I mean, I woke up feeling pretty good today. Like I could have a regular conversation with someone.

Preferably Jordan Hassan.

"It's his day off," Amy said. "And you don't need him."

But I want him.

"Come on, let's get you a MetroCard." She literally lifted me off my bed. "You can borrow my hat."

Thirty minutes later, I was standing outside the hospital that'd been my home for the last few weeks. Shivering. Not feeling so good anymore. Not sure I could take any more steps into the world than I already had.

The air was cold and fresh. It wasn't snowing—not even one tiny flake.

"Go!" I heard Amy shouting behind me. "Go."

I hunched my shoulders. The coat smelled like someone had sprayed it with disinfectant since I wore it last.

"Fine," I muttered through gritted teeth.

I made it out to the sidewalk by keeping my head down. *Just walk*, I said to myself. *Just put one dumb foot in front of the other. One, two, three, four, five…* When I got to the corner, a city bus pulled up beside me. I turned and gave the hospital one last look, and then I got on.

Inside it was warm and steamy, and there were a bunch of free seats. I felt self-conscious in my borrowed clothes. I hadn't remembered to brush my hair or wipe the yogurt stain off my pants. I knew that if anyone looked closely at me, they'd be able to guess where I'd come from. But no one looked at me at all. They just stared at their phones.

The doors shut, and the bus lurched into traffic.

I didn't have a plan for where I was going to go or what I was going to do. I told myself that all I had to do was keep it together until it was time to go back to my little white room.

I stared out the window as we drove west, watching people walking their dogs, or waiting to cross the street, or going into or coming out of stores. It was like having a front-row seat to the world's most boring movie.

After we crossed the bridge to Manhattan, I transferred to a bus going uptown. I got another window seat. By now I had a pretty good idea of where I was headed, but I didn't want to admit it to myself.

It was too weird.

Too crazy.

Jordan always told me not to use that word, but he wasn't around to stop me.

When I got to 116th Street, I slipped out the back of the bus and found myself outside the gates of Columbia University. I took a deep breath and passed right through them.

CHAPTER **89**

I wasn't trying to stalk him—I was just trying to even the score. Jordan Hassan knew where I slept, how I spent my hours, what ratings I got on my daily mental status exams. I lived my life under a magnifying glass, and he could look through it any time he wanted.

Meanwhile I could list everything I knew about him in about fifteen seconds. He told bad jokes, had a bizarre affection for puzzles, and claimed to read the *New Yorker* on the subway (I didn't believe him). His grandfather was born in Egypt, he grew up in New Jersey, and in another couple years he was going to med school. Where? "Wherever I get in," he'd said.

These were tidbits—fragments—puzzle pieces. Not nearly enough. I wanted to know so much more about him. Not just to keep things fair, either.

It was because when I looked into his agate eyes, I felt seen in a way I had never felt before. He cared about me, I was sure of it. And he didn't think I was broken or bad or defective.

Or maybe he did. But it didn't make him run. It made him want to help.

Someone jostled me from behind, and I realized I was just standing in the middle of the walkway, staring into space, while students in puffer coats and backpacks streamed around me. So I started walking again, and in a few hundred yards it seemed like I'd come to the middle of the campus. To my right were steps leading down to fields gone brown and muddy in winter. To my left, a series of white stone steps led up to a huge, columned building. I would've liked to go inside to get warm, but I didn't have a student ID.

I knew I didn't belong here. I didn't need some bored security guard telling me that to my face.

I sat down on that first set of steps and hugged my knees to my chest.

What's it like, Jordan? Do you take classes in that building there? Have you played soccer on that field? Did you ever sprawl across these steps on a sunny spring day?

I knew that even if I could learn how to stay in the present, I'd never be able to be part of a place like this. I'd always be on the other side of an invisible and impossibly high wall.

I sat there watching students walking between classes as the chill from the steps seeped into my bones. If there was one thing I was good at, it was letting time wash over me. Why mark its passage, when one day was so exactly like any other? The Schedule took time out of our hands entirely. It wrapped us, suffocated us, in relentless, numbing monotony.

I hummed a little. Shivered. The minutes turned into an hour. Two hours. How much longer did I have to stay away from Belman?

I started picturing Jordan coming out of a classroom, in his big dumb puffer coat. And then I imagined myself coming out of a different classroom, right across the quad. A look of surprised happiness would appear on his face. I'd hitch up my backpack and start toward him at the same time he'd be hurrying to get to me. We'd meet in the middle of the walkway, and before I could say a word, he'd reach out and pull me close. I'd be pressed against his chest as his long fingers worked their way under all my layers of clothes. I'd feel them against the skin of my stomach, cold and hot at the same time....

Enough stupid fantasies. I had to get out of there.

I stood up and hunched my shoulders against the wind. If I took the M4 to the Q32, I'd be back in my room in a couple of hours. Amy would congratulate me for going outside, for traveling on my own, for keeping myself together.

I went back out through the gate, passed a hot dog stand that made my mouth water, and missed the bus by a second. And that's when I saw him.

Saw *them*.

Jordan Hassan was crossing Broadway. Beside him was a girl with long, dark hair twisted up into a bun. She was short and conspicuously pretty, with blood-red lipstick and a wide, bright smile.

I froze in horror.

They were coming right at me. There was nowhere to hide.

But they were looking only at each other, and as I watched, this girl tucked her arm into the crook of Jordan's elbow. Then her hand burrowed into the pocket of his jacket. He leaned over and whispered something into her ear. She threw her head back and laughed.

I felt like someone had punched me in the chest. I turned so my back was to them. I couldn't let them see me.

But it started getting hard for me to breathe. The sidewalk had become quicksand, and I was sinking into it. I stumbled backward.

"Are you okay?" someone asked.

I nodded, pushing away their offered hand. I just needed to get on the bus. It'd be here in another few minutes. My fingers twisted themselves into knots. My vision had narrowed to a skinny, darkening tunnel.

Just stay here, *Hannah*, I told myself. *Please, oh please, just stay in the right now.*

FOR INTERNAL USE ONLY

INTERVIEW WITH EDWARD JOHNSON, MTA BUS OPERATOR,
JOB ID 101161,
CONCERNING CUSTOMER INCIDENT ON THE M4 LINE
AUTOMATED TRANSCRIPT REC'D 2-25-23

Supervisor: Please describe the incident that occurred on the afternoon of February 25.

Johnson: Well, I was heading south on Fifth, and I was around 102nd Street maybe. The bus wasn't too full yet and it was a good crew. You know, not too many nutjobs, not too many bums, not too many tourists. Sorry, I probably shouldn't say that.

Supervisor: Probably not. How did the incident begin?

Johnson: I mean, it's like I have a Spidey-sense, you know? From all the years of driving. I could tell something was going on in the back, even before I heard it.

Supervisor: What did you hear?

Johnson: I heard a girl screaming. Hollering and crying.

Supervisor: Had anyone hurt the passenger?

Johnson: No, sir. Everyone was just minding their own business. Like I said, it was a good crew. But then she just went fu— freaking crazy, man.

Supervisor: What did you do?

Johnson: Well, I was *driving*. But I looked in the mirror and I could see Henry—he's one of my regulars—trying to calm her down. Wasn't working, though. Some people were already calling 911. Soon as I could, I pulled over. I called dispatch and they called the police.

Supervisor: When the police came—

Johnson: Poor thing! She looked like she didn't know who or where she was. But she had a set of lungs on her, I can tell you that.

Supervisor: Right. So when the police came—

Johnson: They just took her away. Man, you know what, sometimes it's like I can still hear her screaming.

CHAPTER **90**

When I woke, I was strapped to the bed.

And I'd pissed in it.

It was not a great start to the day.

Apparently, after I got chauffeured to Belman in the back seat of a police car, I tried to attack the receptionist and the lobby security guard. Once they got me to my floor, certain parties wanted to give me an ass-jab, but Amy talked them out of it. Somehow she got me into my bed, and she sat with me until I calmed down. I slept for eighteen hours, and then I walked around the ward like a zombie for the next twenty.

News like this wasn't the kind anyone wanted to hear. I felt ashamed, knowing everyone had seen me like that, even though I was pretty sure they'd seen worse before. From me, possibly—from others, definitely.

"It's like you got really drunk at a party and acted like a total ass but you don't remember it," Michaela said.

"Exactly," I said. I didn't mention that I had never, not once in my life, been drunk at a party. I had never even *been* to a party.

"At Steve Boardman's sixteenth birthday, I lifted up my skirt and started screaming about how I was a slut and a whore,"

Michaela mused. "That's what they told me, anyway. It was the last time I ever drank tequila."

Michaela was lying on the bed that used to be Sophie's. She wasn't always the nicest person in the ward, but I liked her, and I was really glad not to be alone. Then I started thinking about what would happen if Michaela left the way Indy had. Then what would I do?

Don't get better, I thought. *I mean, yes, get better—but just not quite yet.*

Honestly, though, how much longer did I think Belman would keep me? I didn't like the way Dr. Ager looked at me, with a weird mixture of surprise and resignation. Like: *Really? We're still putting up with you?*

I didn't like to think about where I'd have to go when they kicked me out.

"Dr. Ager is wholly committed to your care," Dr. Nicholas assured me when I met with him the next morning.

"Okay," I said, not believing him.

"But I'd like to hear about what happened the other day when you were given a pass," he said.

I stared down at the tile floor, at the faint outlines of an old coffee spill. "I caused a scene on the bus, and the police brought me here," I said.

I was pretending like he didn't already know this, and that this was a legit answer to his question.

Dr. Nicholas scratched his pen across his pad of paper for a little while and then he said, "Did the episode come on suddenly? Was there something that frightened or upset you?"

Was there something that frightened or upset me? Hmmm, let's see. I was forced to leave the ward before I was ready, and then I took a bus ride that just happened to lead me directly toward a place where I could see the man I might be in love with getting cuddly with another girl.

For starters.

And then everything went black except for one tiny pinprick of light, and I fell into that light and I woke up in my other world, and I didn't like what was happening there. That was all I wanted to say about it.

The baron loves another—

Be quiet!

How long can a peasant please a lord?

Stop!

"Hannah? Still with us?"

"Sorry. I was just thinking."

"Can you tell me what you were thinking about?"

I could. I didn't want to. What was the point? When had talking made anything better?

Dr. N put both his palms down on the table and leaned forward. "Hannah, listen to me. I need you to *stop wasting my time*," he said.

His voice was low, but I could hear the sudden anger in it, and it scared me. I thought about scuttling away to the corner. Or maybe crawling under his desk.

If you can't see me, you can't hurt me. That's what I used to whisper to myself, over and over again. The words were a song I sang to myself.

"What is going on? Tell me about this world, or the other one, I don't care. But Hannah, I need you to talk."

I squeezed my eyes shut. There was a rushing sound in my ears. My body tingled and burned.

When I spoke, my voice seemed to be coming from very far away. "I saw the baron, and there was someone else in his arms."

CHAPTER **91**

After the morning meeting, Amy tells Jordan to go sit with Max B., the kid who got admitted last night. "Play a card game," she says. "Hang out with him. He looks freaked."

Of course he does, Jordan thinks. Because who has a good first impression of a psych ward? Literally no one.

Jordan does a quick search for Hannah first, but she isn't in art therapy and her room is empty. Amy catches him on his way to check the quiet room.

"Hello? The new guy's in the lounge." She hooks a thumb over her shoulder. "It's *back that way*," she adds, as if he doesn't know.

"Sorry," he mumbles. He'll look for Hannah again later—maybe on his break, when no one can tell him not to.

Jordan finds Max B. trying to make himself as small as possible in the corner of the lounge. He's seventeen, skinny, with a ring through his septum and a few straggly hairs coming out of his chin. He's pale as paper, with arms that seem too long for his body. He doesn't want to talk, but Jordan manages to learn that he likes *Call of Duty* and he lives on Reddit.

Of course, Jordan knows much more about him already, because he scanned Brittany's intake notes.

```
Voices started c. 3 mos ago. Pt's dog was
talking to him. The TV had messages. "The
voices were everywhere. They never shut
up." Pt stopped sleeping. Voices told him
to hurt himself. On 2/26 pt took knife
from kitchen. Resulting cut required
sutures. Transfer from NY Grace ER 2/27.
```

"How about a game of cards?" Jordan asks.

Max shrugs.

"Let's try Go Fish," Jordan says, pulling a Bicycle deck out of his pocket. A little kid's game—a mindless activity that's popular on the ward for that very reason. You could be tranqed to the point of drooling and still manage a hand or two.

"Are you kidding me?" Max says.

"Nope." Jordan starts to deal out the cards when someone sinks down into the chair next to him.

It's Hannah.

"Hey, you," he says, startled. He's so happy to see her, but the expression on her face makes his heart twist. She's not doing well today, it's obvious. She looks like she hasn't slept. Her fingers pick at the frayed cuff of her sweatshirt.

"Hannah, this is Max. Max, this is Hannah. She might be able to show you around a bit sometime. Right, Hannah?" The hopeful, almost puppyish tone of his voice embarrasses him.

Hannah doesn't even glance in Max's direction. "I saw you," she hisses to Jordan.

"What?" he says. "Saw me where?"

"You say you want to help me, but it's a lie. You don't care. You don't understand. I saw you. I saw you. You were laughing about me." Her words tumble over each other, rushed and slurred. "There isn't room anymore. There are too many wrong things. Everywhere I look, I'm losing."

Jordan speaks softly, tenderly, even as fear swirls inside him. "Hannah, I'm not sure what you're talking about."

Her dark eyes flash. "You aren't who I thought you were. You aren't the one. You don't want to help me. You mock me!" She stands up again and waves her arms around like she's a wizard trying to make him disappear.

Then she spits—the glob lands right next to the pile of cards—and runs away down the hall.

"Jesus," Max moans. "People in here are fucked."

CHAPTER 92

After Hannah's outburst, Jordan makes a decision. He finds Renée, the charge nurse, and gives her his best sad, wan face. He tells her he doesn't feel well and asks to go home early.

Lame as it is, the act works. Renée tells him to get to his bed, stat, and to make sure he drinks plenty of water.

"You bet, boss," Jordan says, keeping his voice weak. He gathers his things and leaves, looking as miserable as possible until he's all the way down the block. Then he breaks into a run, heading for the nearest subway station.

God bless Google and the iPhone: Jordan had figured out what foster care center Mark was talking about in under twenty seconds.

Fillan House is a group home in Inwood specializing in trauma-informed care for children between the ages of seven and seventeen, the website read. *Our trained staff offer twenty-four-hour supervision in a safe and supportive environment, and focus on behavior modification, skill development, counseling, and crisis intervention for youth in need.*

It sounded like a real picnic.

And on the face of it, Fillan House is even grimmer than Jordan could've imagined: a dark, hulking building that looms over Broadway and 196th, on the border of Fort Tryon Park. The steps are covered with scattered take-out menus and fallen leaves, and the massive wooden door is flanked by pots of dead mums.

Jordan jabs his finger into the buzzer, and to his surprise, he hears the lock click. Shouldn't a group home for troubled kids take its security a little more seriously?

He pushes the door open and steps into a huge, echoing foyer with cracked marble floors. There's dust in the corner and folding chairs stacked against the wall and not a soul in sight. Only three of the light bulbs in the old chandelier are shining, and music comes faintly from somewhere. Bach, maybe—something old and baroque.

This place creeps him out. Bad.

"Hello?" he says.

A broad-shouldered young woman in cat-eye glasses comes out of the doorway to his left. "You're late," she says briskly. Then her eyes fall on his empty hands. "Do *not* tell me you don't have the food."

"Food?"

"The khao man gai and the pad kee mao that I ordered an *hour* ago!"

"Oh—ah, yeah, sorry—I'm not the delivery guy," Jordan says.

Her face instantly darkens. "Then you'll have to leave." She starts walking toward him like she's going to shove him outside.

Jordan takes a couple of steps back and holds up his hands. "Actually, if you could wait a second—I'm just looking for information about someone who lived here."

She seems to notice his scrubs for the first time. "Are you a doctor?"

"No, but—" he says.

The woman's mouth tightens. "Then you'd best be going."

"I work at Belman Psychiatric, where your former resident is a current patient." He decides not to mention that he's an unpaid college intern.

"I'm sorry," she says, crossing her arms over her chest. "Our clients' records are sealed. You need to leave."

But Jordan can't—not yet. The keys to Hannah's past are within reach, he can feel it. He can imagine her upstairs in one of those rooms, looking out one of those tiny windows. A scared little girl without a home or a family.

Hannah, what happened to you?

The woman is picking up a phone receiver on the wall. She's getting ready to call security.

Jordan says, "Okay, okay, I'm leaving! You can't talk to me, I get it. But could you give information to her doctor?" He's halfway out the door now, his voice pleading. "To Belman's medical director? If it would help with her care?"

The woman gives an almost invisible nod of her head. "We would share pertinent records with the proper authorities." Her hand goes to the glass, pushing it closed on him. "Doctors, lawyers—police, if necessary."

CHAPTER 93

O n Jordan's way back to the subway, his phone buzzes with a text. It's Ellie.

Where r u?

For a second, he considers ignoring it. His mind is racing about Fillan House—about Hannah. But then he answers.

Inwood—for work

u leading a patient field trip to the cloisters?

He frowns. *idk cloisters?*

didn't you take Art Humanities? it's the museum that looks like a medieval monastery—unicorn tapestries & shit

Jordan stops in his tracks. He turns back to stare at Fillan House. One giant stone monstrosity of a group home *plus* one medieval museum...

In the eyes of an imaginative and damaged girl, maybe it adds up to one grand, imposing castle.

A baron's ancestral home.

"Holy shit," he says.

hello? Ellie texts.

Jordan stands there on the sidewalk, his body buzzing with electric energy. *Oh, Hannah,* he thinks. *It's starting to make sense to me now.*

hello? Ellie texts again. *are we still having dinner 2nite?*

hello hello hello?

CHAPTER **94**

Here comes your boyfriend," Michaela said to me. She stood up quickly, grabbing her untouched breakfast tray. "I guess I'll leave you guys alone."

My heart gave a painful lurch in my chest. "Jordan's obviously not my boyfriend."

"Then why are you blushing?" she demanded. "And how'd you know who I was talking about? Maybe I meant Andy." Michaela gave me a wicked grin. "Anyway, see you in group."

"Don't go," I said, reaching out and catching her wrist. Her arm was so delicate it felt breakable. Her nails were thin and bumpy. "The last time I saw him I freaked out on him."

She shrugged, removing herself from my grip. "Whatever, babe. I'm sure you two will work it out."

"Eat your Corn Flakes!" I called after her. "*And* your banana!" She gave me a wave over her shoulder—another "whatever," just wordless this time.

Jordan eased himself down in the chair she'd just left. His hair was extra tousled this morning; he looked rumpled and adorable. He yawned his way around a "hello."

"Up late studying?" I asked.

"Something like that," he said. "Did I chase Michaela off?"

"I think she just wants to not-eat in peace."

He nodded, jiggling his legs under the table. He clearly had something to say to me, but I had something I wanted to say to him first.

"I think I went a little crazy on you yesterday," I said. "And I'm really sorry."

The tiniest of frowns appeared on Jordan's smooth olive brow. "You shouldn't say—"

"*Please* don't tell me I'm not supposed to use that word. I've reclaimed it, it's mine, and you can't take it away from me." I held out half of my blueberry muffin. A peace offering. "Want some? If you find an actual blueberry, you win a prize."

"I'm good, thanks," Jordan said. He patted his stomach. "Full up on protein bars."

"Your loss," I said. "Anyway…I'm really sorry I yelled at you. And I want you to know that I wasn't stalking you the other day when I saw you on campus, I—"

"You came to my school?" He seemed confused.

"I was just…in the neighborhood. Amy told me I had to leave hospital grounds."

"Sure," he said. "Okay."

I wasn't sure he believed me about not stalking him. Fine, I didn't really believe myself, either.

"Who was the girl you were walking with?" I'd told myself I wouldn't bring it up. Oops.

Jordan looked a little surprised by the question. "She's a friend," he said. Then he smiled. "She knows a lot about muons."

If Jordan Hassan thought that would make me magically approve of whoever this friend was, he was mistaken. "Well, she *should*," I said. "They were all over the news after the Fermilab research came out."

"She's majoring in physics."

This was a whole different ball of wax, but without even blinking I said, "Weird, she didn't seem like a huge nerd."

Jordan pursed his lips like he thought that was a rude thing to say, which of course it was. And I regretted saying it, but not enough to take it back.

Because I was jealous of that girl. Like it-hurts-my-stomach-jealous of her. Not just because she got to tuck her arm through Jordan's—though obviously, that was a problem for me. But the way she walked through the world as if it belonged to her, and she belonged to it.

Because I *didn't* belong.

Because I had to be locked away because of it.

"Want to know what I'm majoring in?" I asked. "Insanity. Minoring in lunacy and time travel."

"Oh, Hannah," Jordan said, shaking his head.

"Oh Hannah *what*?"

"You're really funny."

It wasn't at all what I'd expected him to say. "Funny ha-ha, or funny weird?"

"Well, both. Okay? But mostly the first one. Even when you're being impossible, you're great."

"Do you really mean that?" I asked.

"Of course. You're smart and funny and you've read a million books...." Jordan reached out and absently took the muffin half I'd offered, and when he was done chewing, he said, "Definitely no blueberries in there. But I think you're amazing. Because you've done it totally on your own."

I sucked in my breath. *Totally on your own.* Why was he saying that to me? "I don't know what you're talking about," I said flatly.

"I don't think anyone has taken care of you in a very long time, Hannah." Jordan was suddenly staring down at his hands, like he didn't want to see the expression on my face.

Which would have been one of surprise and white-hot anger. I wanted to scream at him. *It isn't any of your business!*

But also: How did he know? And did everyone know that I had no one else in the whole enormous stupid world?

"I just think you're doing a really good job," Jordan went on.

"I'm not sure you understand how patronizing that sounds. And if I was really doing a good job of taking care of myself," I said quietly, "I wouldn't be locked up in a freaking psychiatric hospital, would I?"

"Or maybe it's the place where you take care of yourself the best."

I stood up. "I have to go."

Jordan got up, too. "Wait, Hannah."

But I didn't wait. I was halfway across the room when I turned back around. "What's her name?"

To give Jordan credit, he didn't pretend not to know who I was talking about.

"Do you really care?" he asked.

I shook my head. It turned out that I didn't.

CHAPTER **95**

Lulu looks around the circle, making eye contact with anyone who can bear it. The ones who can't look just stare down at their feet. That's fine with Lulu. It's fine, too, that Elspeth is wearing only one slipper, and it's fine that Ned stinks because no one can convince him to take a shower. It's also fine that Andy is lying on the floor in the middle of the circle, humming softly to himself. At least he's here. At least he knows he isn't dead.

Lulu finishes her attendance check. Cayden's here, and Beatrix, and Michaela, and Hannah, and everyone else.

It's fine. Everything is fine. Lulu finds repeating this to herself to be helpful.

"Let's start with our daily check-in," she says. "Do I have any volunteers?" Lulu sees a hand wildly waving. "Thanks, Beatrix, let's hear what's happening with you today."

"We're not Beatrix—we switched," she says. "Alex is fronting."

Lulu should've guessed. Beatrix never raises her hand. "Hello, Alex. Nice to see you again."

Alex, Beatrix's most talkative alter, begins a rambling story about a dream he had, which Lulu finally cuts off after a solid five minutes. "Thank you so much for sharing," she says. "Can you write the rest down in your dream journal?"

"Sure, okay, no problem," Alex says amiably.

Lulu turns back to the group. "Who wants to talk about how they're feeling this morning?"

No one speaks. Andy even stops humming.

"We're happy to keep talking," Alex says. "If that would be helpful."

Then Gloria blurts, "My boyfriend broke up with me. The bastard came to visiting hours yesterday so he could tell me to my fat, stupid face."

This sparks a loud and immediate chorus of supportive outrage from everyone in the group—everyone, Lulu notices, except Hannah. She's staring into space, oblivious to what's going on.

Lulu leans forward. "Hannah?" she says quietly. "Are you with us?"

But Hannah doesn't even blink. "Who is it?" she hisses. "Who is it?"

Chapter 96

M y voice came out ragged and raw. "Who is it? Who does the baron court?"

Margery only pressed her lips into a line as she swept dust into the fireplace, making the flames leap and hiss.

"I know I have no right to him," I said. "But he came to me—here, in my room. And the way he looked at me..."

I was too ashamed to go on. Was I supposed to tell her how he'd pressed his body against mine, close and hot like a secret promise? She must have heard what he'd said, she'd been there, listening in the corner. *You are unlike anyone I have ever encountered, Hannah.*

"Why won't you tell me who she is?"

Margery swept more vigorously. I wanted to run over and shake her.

"Please," I said.

When she finally turned to me, her pale blue eyes were full of sympathy. "My dear, you said it yourself: you've no right to him. More than that, you could never deserve him."

Her words would've stung me even if they weren't so true. "But I want him, Margery. I can't explain how hate can turn itself upside down and inside out, but it has. *I want him.*"

Margery set the broom aside and wiped her hands on her

apron. "In my experience," she answered, "what people like us want doesn't matter in the slightest."

"I know," I said. "And yet—I thought he cared for me."

"He does, in his way," Margery said. "But when a countess is recently and tragically widowed, what do you expect Baron Joachim to do? Snub her for a peasant and a thief?"

I couldn't voice my answer. Because of course I expected that.

Or no—I didn't *expect* it. But I had hoped for it.

"Where is the baron's chamber?" I asked.

Margery resumed her sweeping, ignoring me again. It didn't matter. I knew how to sneak around a castle. I could feel my way through the dark.

Which was exactly what I did.

The moon was a silver sliver in the sky when I crept from my room, barefoot on the cold stones. I went down dark hallways until I came to a door just a bit ajar, firelight flickering on the other side.

It beckoned me in.

I pushed the door open. The room was far grander than my own, and my eye was immediately drawn to the bed. It was ornately carved and seemed as big as a ship. The heavy curtains had been pulled back, revealing the sleeping form of the baron.

I tiptoed to the edge of the bed. And as I stood over him, my heart pounding, I saw that he wasn't sleeping after all. His eyes were wide open.

For a moment, we stared at each other. Flooded with longing, I began to tremble. And then he reached up and untied the knot at the neck of my shift. With impossible gentleness, he slid the cloth from my shoulders, and it fell in a white heap at my feet. Looking at me, naked in the firelight, the baron sucked in his breath and let it out with a sigh.

"Come even closer," he whispered.

Without hesitation I obeyed him, lifting the covers and sliding into the bed next to his long, lean body. He rolled toward me, on top of me, and his mouth came down and covered mine in a crush of heat. My arms went around his shoulders and then slid along his smooth back to his hips, pulling them toward me. He moaned into my neck. I thought I might die of desire.

"My name is Hannah Dory, and I am yours," I whispered.

simply don't have time for this right now, Mr. Hassan," Dr. Ager says curtly.

Jordan hadn't been expecting the doctor to jump up and down in excitement at his discovery, but he'd definitely thought she'd be *interested*. But even as he's laying out Hannah's story for her—the group home, the tent city on Twelfth Avenue—she barely looks up from her computer. Instead she's typing as she talks, working a surprisingly fast hunt-and-peck.

"The New York State Office of Mental Health is investigating our program. The records system needed an update a decade ago. I'm short-staffed, the board is breathing down my neck, and I don't know what you're doing in my office when you're supposed to be on the ward." Her words come out quickly, distractedly. She hits the Return key with a bang.

"I'm on my lunch break," Jordan says, but she doesn't seem to hear him. She's typing again.

"You don't even have proof that Hannah stayed at Fillan House, do you? We've discussed this before. You're not a detective, and neither am I or anyone who works at Belman."

"I understand that," Jordan says. "But I think knowing what happened might help her get better—"

"A different prescription regimen is *more* likely to help her. So would honest communication with those who are involved in her care," Dr. Ager says briskly.

"What if she truly can't remember? What if she needs someone to tell her?"

What if it's easier for her to believe she's a time traveler than it is for her to face whatever's in her past?

Dr. Ager runs a hand through her short, graying bangs. She looks tired. Overwhelmed. "And what would happen then? Do you think Hannah would miraculously recover? I'm sorry to say that it doesn't work that way. Psychiatry offers treatments, not cures, and there are no quick fixes. Your professors—not to mention your time here at Belman—should've taught you this by now."

She turns back to her computer and begins typing again. He's been dismissed.

Outside Dr. Ager's office, Jordan slaps the bright white wall in frustration. Max, who is not trying very hard to settle into life on Ward 6, stalks by with a fistful of markers in his hand. He probably stole them from the art therapy room, but Jordan doesn't feel any urge to find out.

"Fuck this, fuck that, fuck you," Max mutters.

"Hi, Max," Jordan says. "We're going to show *Space Jam* in the lounge this afternoon."

Max gives him the finger.

"See ya later, buddy," Jordan says, his voice falsely bright.

Could he ask Amy to call Fillan House? Dr. Nicholas? They'd

want to help. But they wouldn't make the call if they found out that Dr. Ager had told him to drop it.

What had the woman at Fillan said? *Doctors, lawyers—police, if necessary.*

So Jordan pulls out his phone and googles the number for the Midtown North precinct.

Chapter 98

I woke in an unfamiliar bed. I was groggy. Confused.
Naked.

Then the night came back to me in a rush, and I remembered everything so clearly I could feel it all over again: the baron's hands tracing their way up my thigh, the baron's lips at my neck, tickling their way down my ribs, my stomach...

My entire body tingled with pleasure. I stretched luxuriously. Rolled over, reaching out for Baron Joachim.

But he was gone, and I was alone.

I sat up and pushed aside the heavy curtains. "Hello?" I called.

The room was dark and cold. The fire in the hearth had gone out. I wanted to bury myself under the covers and go back to sleep, but I felt an uneasy prickle on the back of my neck.

Where had the baron gone? Why hadn't he woken me?

I got up, grabbing my shift from the floor where it'd fallen and slipping it on. I was shivering, but there was no other dress, no cloak.

I need to find my way back to my room—back to Margery. I hurried to the door. I pulled on the handle.

It was locked.

CHAPTER **99**

K id," Officer Dunthorpe says, his voice flickering in and out over the bad connection, "are you nuts? I'm not your secretary, or your messenger boy, or whatever it is you seem to think I am."

Jordan methodically shreds a paper napkin that reads NICK'S BEST BURGER IN NYC. The napkin lies—it's not the best burger at all. It's only the cheapest. Outside the diner, snow has begun to fall. "I understand this is an unusual request, officer," he says.

"You're damn right it is," Dunthorpe practically yells into the phone.

Jordan picks up another napkin and rips it nervously in two. "I wouldn't ask for your help if I didn't need it. If *Hannah* didn't need it. If you called Fillan House, they'd give you the records. All you'd have to do is ask."

Dunthorpe barks out a laugh. "It doesn't work that way, kid. There's no crime I'm investigating here, understand? Until that girl's back out on the street in my precinct, she's absolutely none of my business."

"But I'm afraid she *will* be back out there," Jordan says.

"Well, when I see her, I'll be sure to say hello."

The phone goes dead.

"I guess that didn't go the way you hoped it would," Ellie says.

She's sitting in the booth across from him, sipping a Diet Coke and picking at the french fries he'd ordered.

"No, it didn't."

She reaches out and takes his hands in her small warm ones. "It's Friday," she says. "You've already clocked out. So how about you stop making work calls and pay attention to me?"

He smiles. "Sorry. Okay." He tells himself that he's not going to think about Hannah until Monday morning.

He can manage that, can't he?

So they finish their greasy diner fries and then go see a Marvel movie, and then they walk into a bar where no one asks them for ID. They drink too much cheap beer, and later they find themselves in Jordan's dorm room, which is empty because his roommate is at his great-grandmother's funeral in Indiana.

They stumble-fall-laugh their way to the bed and collapse onto it. Ellie lifts her arms, and Jordan tugs her shirt up over her head. She isn't wearing a bra, and the surprise of this thrills him. But he hesitates.

"What?" Ellie says, touching his cheek. "What is it?"

What is it? He doesn't know. This is what he wants, isn't it?

Or does some buried part of him wish he was with someone else?

He shakes the confusion out of his head and buries his face in Ellie's neck. He kisses her warm, soft, wonderful skin. She laughs—"It tickles," she says—and then she pulls him closer.

CHAPTER **100**

Jordan rolls over and beholds the peaceful, sleeping face of Ellie Wagner. A bar of pale winter light falls across her cheekbone. Her full lips are parted, and he overcomes the urge to kiss them. He barely slept at all last night—it's a single bed, and Ellie kept stealing the covers—but he should let her get her rest. Because when she wakes up, he has a favor to ask, and she isn't going to like it.

He sits up and rubs his eyes. Beside him, Ellie moans a little and snuggles deeper into the covers. He slips out of bed and pads over to the window. It's another gray March day.

Will Ellie do it? That's what matters.

He pulls on clothes, shoes, and a coat, and slips out the door. He'll surprise her with Starbucks. *Then* he'll ask.

When he gets back to his dorm room half an hour later, Ellie is sitting at his desk, wearing his tattered robe. He bends down to give her a kiss as he hands her the coffee. "That looks good on you," he says.

She holds up a floppy, pilled sleeve. "Please. Try *ridiculous.*"

"You pull it off," he insists. Ellie looks pretty in anything. But as he learned last night, she looks best naked.

She takes a grateful sip of coffee. "Thank you." Then she narrows her eyes at him. "Why are you staring at me like that?"

"I have a favor to ask you," he says.

"Okay. Yes," she says. "Sure."

"Don't you want to know what it is first?"

She shrugs. "I'm assuming it's not, like, to write your Abnormal Psych paper."

"Not that," he says. When he tells her what he wants her to do, though, her entire demeanor changes.

"You want me to impersonate a doctor on the phone to try to get access to someone's medical records? Jordan, that's wrong on so many levels I don't even know what to say." Her voice is shocked. Incredulous. Angry.

"I know it's illegal," he pleads. "But remember what you said the night we met? The laws of physics aren't like human laws, because human laws are decisions. I'm telling you that while this might not be legal, it's the morally and ethically correct thing to do," he says. "I wouldn't ask it otherwise."

Ellie shakes her head at him as she pulls on her clothing. "I honestly can't believe you're trying to use that argument on me."

"But human laws aren't perfect—"

"But you still get in trouble for breaking them! And I happen to think that a person's right to the privacy of their medical records is an excellent law."

"Ellie, I'm just trying to help her."

"Because you're clearly obsessed with that girl," she says. "And honestly, Jordan, it's more than weird. It's kind of crazy."

Then the door slams, and Jordan is alone. *We don't say crazy,* he thinks.

Chapter 101

I called for Margery, but she never came. Hours passed, and I must have slept, because I was awakened sometime before nightfall by the sound of heavy footsteps. I heard the bolt sliding back, and then the door opened, and in came the doctor, Goriot, and all his black-robed consorts. They lifted me from the bed and dragged me into the hallway.

They were shouting at me, denouncing me, accusing me.

Of what, I didn't understand. I started to cry.

Goriot shook his gnarled finger in my face. His face was purple with rage. "The countess would make him richer than the king! You have ensorcelled him, there is no other explanation!" Then he slapped me hard across the cheek, and a burst of light flashed inside my head.

I screamed—and then I was gone.

Everything was gone.

I had spiraled out of darkness into light.

CHAPTER **102**

H annah?" Michaela's concerned face was barely an inch from my own. "Are you okay? You're crying."

I put my hands up to my cheeks. They came away wet.

I blinked. The room was so bright, but I could see shadows in the corner, shadows in the shape of men in black robes. I scuttled backward in my bed. "Behind you," I whispered.

She turned around. "There's nothing there at all," she said. "It's okay, Hannah. It's just you and me, your pal Michaela Louise Adeline Carrington." She smiled, and behind her the shadows slowly faded into nothing.

"I never knew your full name before," I said.

Michaela retreated to the other side of the room and sat down on the edge of the bed. "Did something bad just happen—in the other place?"

"I don't remember," I lied.

"I never remember my dreams, either," Michaela said.

But these aren't dreams.

"What day is it?"

"Like I have any idea!" Michaela said, reaching down and picking fuzz off of her grippy socks. "Actually, no, I take that back.

Your boyfriend's not here, so it must be the weekend." She threw the fuzz at me and laughed.

Then there was a knock on the door, and a nurse in Mickey Mouse scrubs stuck her head in. "You have a visitor," she said.

"Is it my mom?" Michaela said, rolling her eyes. "Ugh, she was just here the other day!"

"I was actually talking to Hannah," the nurse said.

Michaela and I turned and stared at each other.

"What the hell?" Michaela mouthed.

What the hell was right. I had no friends and no family—not in *this* century—and I'd never had a visitor, not in all my time at Belman Psych.

I couldn't think of anyone it could possibly be, unless the baron had somehow learned to time travel, too. Then I almost laughed out loud. Because that idea, I knew, was truly insane.

CHAPTER 103

A very pretty older woman I definitely hadn't seen before sat in one of the visiting rooms, her manicured hands folded neatly in her lap. Her white hair was perfectly coiffed, and she wore a beautiful silver fur coat that I hoped was fake but probably wasn't. She stood up when I entered, though she didn't hold out her hand to introduce herself. Instead she offered me a strange, sad smile.

"My dear," she said, "I had hoped you would be gone."

I had no idea what was going on, but when I started to stammer out something, she shook her head at me and I shut my mouth quick.

"I'm Julianna Belman-Powell. Delia F. Belman was my grandmother."

"Oh," I said as my heart plummeted down into my laceless shoes. I knew why she was here.

A long time ago, Amy had sat me down and explained the situation. *You can stay at Belman as long as you need to. You don't ever have to worry about the cost of it. You have Mrs. Belman-Powell to thank for that.*

In other words, Julianna Belman-Powell had been my fairy godmother, making sure I could stay at a ball that no sane person would ever want an invite to.

But now she was here to tell me that my time was up and they were kicking me out, I was sure of it.

I'm not ready. I'm not ready.

"Did Dr. Ager call you in?" I asked. "I know she's dying to get me out of here."

But Julianna Belman-Powell shook her head. "No, Dr. Ager didn't call me," she said. "Jordan Hassan did."

Jordan Hassan? "Why would he do that?" I yelped. "Does he think I should leave, too?"

"This isn't about discharging you, Hannah." She patted her hair, as if my outburst might've disturbed her coiffure.

"Then what *is* it about?" I asked desperately.

"Jordan called me because he wanted to ask me for my help in getting certain information that he thinks will help you," she said. "But I told him that I couldn't. Not until I saw you first."

"I still don't understand."

But Julianna Belman-Powell clearly didn't think I needed to understand, because she just gazed at me, a tender look on her face. "You've grown so much," she said.

"Uh, yeah. Cell division will do that to a person," I said awkwardly.

Julianna Belman-Powell smiled. "Why do you think you keep coming back to Belman?" she asked.

"Because the police keep bringing me here," I said. It was the kind of answer I'd give to Dr. Nicholas. It didn't satisfy her, though.

She reached out and put her hand against my cheek. Her fingers were cool and dry. "I know you say you're a time traveler, Hannah. But do you know what I think? I think it's easier for you to believe something utterly impossible than it is for you to remember something that you've always wanted to forget."

"I don't know what you're talking about," I said.

"Perhaps you'll know someday, and find a way forward," she said. She stood up. "It's been so lovely to see you. Be well. And don't forget to brush your hair. You'll look so much prettier that way."

CHAPTER **104**

As the subway rockets him south, from Inwood down to Morningside Heights, Jordan holds the heavy cardboard box so carefully you'd think he was carrying a bomb.

He can't believe how simple it was to get Hannah's records in the end. Though Dr. Ager was Belman's medical director, when push came to shove, Julianna Belman-Powell and her money were in charge.

"I will be sending a member of the hospital staff to pick up the files," she'd told Fillan House. "I need you to have them ready by Tuesday afternoon."

And so, an hour after accepting the box from the woman with the cat-eye glasses, Jordan's back in his dorm room. The box is now sitting, unopened, on his bed. He has a moment of terrible hesitation. Of almost what he'd call panic.

Is it his place to open the box? These are Hannah's secrets—not his. Doesn't she have the right to keep them hidden?

He touches the corner of the lid. Keeping them hidden is destroying her, he's convinced of that. Maybe Hannah doesn't want to know what's in her past, but how can she get better if she keeps it all buried?

Once she can acknowledge her past, she can begin to heal it.

That's what Jordan believes, because that's just how human psychology works, everyone knows that. "We are what we are because we have been what we have been, and what is needed for solving the problems of human life and motives is not moral estimates but more knowledge," said good old Freud. He wasn't wrong about that.

And more knowledge is exactly what's in the box.

He's doing this for her own good. He can help her.

Jordan takes out his pocket knife and slices through the tape.

CHAPTER **105**

When he opens the lid, the first thing he sees isn't an intake form or a doctor's examination notes. It's a copy of a police photograph.

In the picture, a small girl lies twisted in a half-filled bathtub. Her mouth is open in a scream and her body is covered in stab wounds. Blood stains her skin, blood darkens the water.

Jordan knows exactly who this is.

It's Mary.

He grabs the trash can next to his desk and vomits into it. When he wipes his mouth, he picks up a newspaper clipping.

THE BRONX SENTINEL

A Lost Child Leads Police to a Horrific Crime Scene

BY ALIYAH JACOBS

Heart-wrenching questions about a sweet 7-year-old girl found lost, sobbing, and bleeding in a Bronx park Tuesday morning were grimly answered today. After being treated for multiple stab wounds at Jacobi Medical Center, little Hannah Dougherty was able to tell authorities her name and address. When officers went to her apartment in the Soundview neighborhood, they discovered a scene of utter horror: a woman, a man, and a child dead, in an apparent murder-suicide.

Alana Dougherty, 32, and her 4-year-old daughter, Mary, were discovered in the bathroom, lying in pools of their own blood. A man identified as Brandon Mills, 39, was found dead of a self-inflicted gunshot wound in the living room.

A senior Bronx police official who spoke on condition of anonymity said, "Going into that apartment—it shook me. I've seen a lot. I haven't seen anything like that."

Neighbors reported that they had heard screaming from inside the apartment, including the words, "No, no, don't hurt us."

But no one, it appears, ever called the police.

CHAPTER **106**

I n Room 5A, Jordan and Hannah sit across from each other. Hannah's on her bed, and Jordan's on the one that used to belong to Sophie. The mattress is barely softer than a camping pad; he wonders how he never noticed that before. The door is open, and Jordan catches glimpses of Andy shuffling back and forth, up and down the hall.

He rubs his eyes. He'd lain awake all night, haunted and sickened by what he'd read. Turning the awful images over and over in his mind. Debating, all over again, whether it was right to bring Hannah's dark past into the light.

No matter how Jordan tossed and turned and fought with himself, he always came to the same conclusion. Hannah deserved to know the past she'd been hiding from herself.

But, he decided, no one *else* did.

That's why none of the Belman staff knows he's in here, or has any idea what he's about to do.

Hannah looks at him quizzically. Her dark eyes seem especially bright today. "Come on, what's up?" she says. Then she smiles. "Lulu always likes to ask me that, but I never like to answer."

He waits another minute. If he eases into the subject, he'll only give her time to run. He's got to come out and say it, as quickly and gently as possible. He read the whole box. He knows everything.

> Reports show that Alana Dougherty had called police about alleged abuse by Brandon Mills on three separate occasions. A restraining order was filed, and Mr. Mills entered inpatient treatment for alcohol abuse.

"Wow, you're a barrel of laughs today," Hannah says. "What happened to the terrible jokes? Why aren't you trying to get me to do a stupid puzzle?"

> Mr. Mills allegedly continued to return to the residence after his discharge from Ludlow Treatment Center. Ms. Dougherty informed social workers that he had "turned everything around."

"I need to talk to you about your family," Jordan says.

Hannah immediately stiffens. "I don't have a family. Not in this world, anyway."

"But you did," he says. "And I know about them. I know about your mother, and I know about Mary. Not your little sister from the Middle Ages. Your little sister from here. I know she was only four when she died."

> On the night of January 10, Mr. Mills gained entry into Ms. Dougherty's apartment while

she was giving her daughter Mary a bath. Mr. Mills was allegedly yelling and threatening Ms. Dougherty. Ms. Dougherty attempted to hide in the bathroom with her children. It is believed that when Mr. Mills gained entry into the room, he attacked all three with a pair of kitchen scissors and a butcher knife.

Hannah seems to be visibly shrinking. Jordan crosses the room and sits down beside her. "I think that if you can let yourself remember what happened, you can learn how to cope with it. You don't have to keep running away. You don't have to keep going to the castle. Do you trust me?"

She blinks at him. Her chin dips. He tells himself it's a nod.

And so Jordan Hassan begins to tell Hannah Dougherty every dark thing that he's learned about her past.

CHAPTER 107

Jordan was sitting close to me on the bed, and he was saying the most terrible things in his soft, gentle voice. He kept saying, "I'm so sorry. I'm so sorry."

He was telling me a horror story, but I was having trouble understanding him because shadows were leaking into the room. They were slipping down from the ceiling, curling up from the floor.

I welcomed them. They were going to take me away from here.

I'm going to the castle. I'm leaving.

I felt myself being pulled down into darkness. My limbs felt stiff, but somehow I was trembling, too. My body was being shaken apart. I was dissolving.

When I opened my eyes again, I was in a room that I recognized. But it wasn't in the baron's castle. It was in the apartment where I lived when I was little. Prickles of fear crawled over my skin, a million tiny spiders.

No, please no, I don't want to be here!

My mother was standing in the doorway to my bedroom. Her face was panicked, and her voice didn't sound like her voice at all. "Hannah, come!" she was saying. "Darling, you have to hide, you can't be here!"

I don't want to remember—

When I didn't move, she grabbed me and pulled me down the hallway, and she tripped over Mary's shoes and almost fell. I hit my head on the wall and started to cry. My mother was crying, too, and shaking, and terrible shouting was coming from the kitchen. I heard drawers being yanked open and things crashing onto the floor. There was a monster inside our apartment. A demon.

Please don't make me see this!

My mother pushed me into the bathroom and she followed me inside, bolting the door and pushing the trash can in front of it. She was crying so hard she could barely breathe. "It's going to be all right, girls," she said. "Just be really quiet, okay? Can you do that for me?" And Mary was in the tub with her little tugboat and crying and I was in my pajamas and crying and outside in the hallway the demon was coming closer. I heard him yelling and cursing us, and he was pounding on the door. And then the door splintered and there was a flash of bright, sharp silver and my mother screamed—

"Stop!" I shouted, and the whole world flashed white like it was full of lightning, and then I was back, and there were strong hands on my shoulders, squeezing me. The hands belonged to Jordan Hassan, and he was holding me tightly and staring at my face.

"Hannah?" he said. "Oh, Hannah, I'm so sorry."

I can't believe it. I don't want to believe it.

But I remember it.

I was shuddering and crying so hard I could barely see. My chest heaved up and down, and every breath hurt me, like I was being stabbed all over again. I buried my face in my hands, and then I felt Jordan's arms encircle me and hold me close. If it weren't for his grip, I would fracture into a million tiny pieces.

The tears wouldn't stop. Waves of darkness and agony crested, broke, and crested again.

"It's going to be okay now," Jordan whispered.

I'd fallen into a black void and his voice was calling me back up to the light. I couldn't get there—couldn't come up—but his arms were keeping me from falling further.

"Hannah? I promise you, it's going to be okay. No one is ever going to hurt you like that again."

The darkness held me down. There wasn't enough air to breathe. All the grief I'd shoved deep down into my subconscious had come loose and it filled every part of me. I was made of pain.

"I'm here," Jordan said. "I'm here, and you're safe."

I couldn't remember the last time someone wrapped me in the circle of their arms and held me. I could've stayed that way forever.

But of course that was impossible. Rules were rules, and touching was against them. Jordan hugged me tight, and then, too quickly, he let me go.

The front of his shirt was wet with my tears, and there was a black hole where my heart was supposed to be. But also—there was a sudden kind of quiet inside my head.

What if hiding a thing could be harder than letting it out?

Letting it go?

Mom, you tried to save us.

Mary, I miss you so much.

I lifted my head and looked into Jordan's eyes. I tried to speak but no words came out.

"I promise," he said, "everything's going to be better from now on."

CHAPTER **108**

J ordan practically skips onto the ward the next day. He can't wait to see Hannah. The hours they spent talking after he'd told her what he learned were hard but amazing. There had been more tears—but there'd been laughter, too.

Why didn't Han Solo enjoy his steak dinner?

It was Chewie.

In retrospect, he probably could've laid off the dad jokes, but those came after they'd walked around the hospital grounds the entire afternoon, feeding the half-tame squirrels and talking about Hannah's past. There was a lot she still didn't remember. But a door had been opened. And more importantly, she was ready to walk through it.

Any worry that he'd done the wrong thing had vanished. Against all odds, he's made a difference. He's given Hannah back to herself. It's going to be a long road to healing. But he hopes their old friend Dr. Freud, who was wrong about many things, will be right about this one: "One day, in retrospect, the years of struggle will strike you as the most beautiful."

But then he turns the corner to go to Room 5A, and reality comes crashing down on him.

Hannah is yelling and sobbing in the hallway. She's clawed at her cheeks with her nails and pulled out fistfuls of her hair. There's a knot of patients staring at her in shock. She's not wearing any pants or shoes. Her legs are streaked with scratches.

"Everybody step back!" Amy yells. "Give us space!"

No one obeys her.

Even Jordan is frozen to the spot. He knows he should help Amy, direct the patients to the lounge, but instead he stands there motionless, horrified.

"He lied to me," Hannah cries. "The baron lied!"

Dr. Ager comes running. "Sedate her," she directs as two nurses grab Hannah's arms and Amy goes to prep a B-52.

Hannah screams and cries. "He lies, he lies, he lies!"

Oh, my god, Jordan thinks. *What have I done?*

DELIA F. BELMAN MEMORIAL
PSYCHIATRIC HOSPITAL
PATIENT LOG

Date: 3/9/23, 11:39 a.m.
Name: Hannah Doe

BACKGROUND: Pt woke early and seemed
disoriented, with labile mood.
Disorientation and emotional dysregulation
increased throughout the morning, and
after meeting with Dr. Nicholas, pt
appeared delusional. Vocalizations loud
and frantic without clear meaning.
References to marriage, castle, and
sickness were made. Pt inconsolable.
Placed in QR in high state of agitation.

RESPONSE: In brief moment of lucidity it
was felt that pt sought PRN for acute
anxiety and fear. Administered lorazepam
and haloperidol. Pt slept.

Vital signs normal.

Chapter 109

I honestly believed he would choose me. Against all wisdom, against all odds. Fool that I was, I trusted him. I looked into his eyes and I thought I saw the truth.

But the truth has many sides to it, doesn't it?

And the deepest, most terrible truth is this: the number of things we understand will always be dwarfed by the quantity of things that we don't.

My name is Hannah Dory, and I am...I am what?

I am a girl who has been banished from a castle. I am a girl who lies shivering in a bed in a village that has no real name; it is called only The Bend, after the arc of the river nearby.

I am sick. Whether the sickness is in my body, my mind, or my soul, I don't know. I lie here in the darkness.

But from my bed, I can hear everything. I can hear the wagons coming from the castle, bringing food for everyone in The Bend. I listen to the neighing of the cart horses, the creak of the wheels, and the joyous shouts from my neighbors. In this matter, at least, the baron was as good as his word.

Your village will have as much as it needs, he'd said, *for as long as it needs it.*

Today, though, there are no carts. Today I hear something

different. The sound comes from very, very far away, but my ears are sharp.

Pealing out over the frozen land, their notes bright and deep, comes the ringing of the castle bells, announcing the joyful news.

The baron has a new bride.

Of course, of course—it could never have been me. But hope is a feeling as wild and uncontrollable as love.

My name is Hannah Dory, and I am eighteen in the year of our Lord 1347. Since the day I was born, my life has been a fight—for the right to food, to freedom, to survival. Such basic needs, and yet none of them came easily.

"Conn," my mother called. "Go give Sally her oats now, and make sure the chickens haven't gotten into the flour."

My name is Hannah Dory, and I am to blame for the death of my sister and the death of Otto Rast. But I have saved my mother, my brother, and everyone else in The Bend.

My mother knelt by the side of my bed with a cup of cool river water infused with Zenna's herbs. "Drink, Hannah," she urged. "Please."

I turned my face to the wall.

My name is Hannah Dory, and I fell in love with my enemy. For a little while, he loved me back.

And then—he let me go.

My name is Hannah Dory, and I am free.

May God have mercy on my soul.

I closed my eyes until the music of the bells faded into nothing.

SEVEN YEARS **LATER**

CHAPTER 110

Jordan Hassan is running late. He was supposed to meet some of his med school buddies at a bar off of Houston Street at seven o'clock, but his train sat in the station at 28th for half an hour. It was probably just regular MTA bullshit, but if there was some terrible accident, he'll read about it in the paper tomorrow on his way to his psych residency at NYU.

As usual, he's trying to do a few things at once, meaning: walk east on Bleecker Street, look at his phone, and dodge knots of people who seem really drunk already. He takes a wrong turn and finds himself on the corner of Grand and Greene on a cold and rainy night, before he even realizes he's walked two blocks past the bar.

In front of him is a small bookstore he's never seen before. He's probably walked past it a hundred times, but why would he notice? He doesn't have time to read anything but *Lancet* articles. But for whatever reason, tonight he pauses. Golden light spills from the store's windows onto the wet sidewalk. Inside it looks cozy and inviting. Much better than a loud bar.

Bells tinkle on the door as Jordan enters. A few people seated in folding chairs turn to look at him.

Shit. He's walked into some kind of reading. He's turning to go back out when he catches a glimpse of the person at the lectern.

She's a young woman with long, shining black hair. Her lips are full, her eyes are dark and lively, and her voice is low and musical. When she speaks, she almost sounds like she's singing.

Shock freezes him where he stands. *It can't be*, he thinks. *Can it?*

After he told her what he'd discovered about her past, Hannah Dougherty had suffered a complete breakdown.

"She's gone to the castle," Amy said grimly. "And I don't know if she's coming back."

Overcome with guilt, Jordan had brought the box of Hannah's records into Dr. Ager's office and confessed what he'd done. Dr. Ager listened with cold fury, and then dismissed him from his internship.

After a few months, he was allowed to return to Belman during visiting hours. The nurses greeted him warmly, and Beatrix asked him if he'd work on a puzzle with her. But Hannah didn't know who he was. Her body was on the ward, and her mind was thousands of miles—or hundreds of years—away.

He kept coming back, though. And once in a while, Hannah almost seemed to recognize him. But then she'd call him Joachim. *Who's Joachim?* he'd ask. She could never answer.

But here Hannah is, in a downtown bookstore, standing before a small crowd of strangers. On the podium is a poster. It shows the cover of a book called *The Girl in the Castle*.

Her head is bent; her hands hold the book open in front of her. "My name is Hannah Dory," she reads. "I am eighteen in the year of our Lord 1347, and God forgive me, I am about to do something extraordinarily stupid."

Then she looks up, and she sees Jordan. At first there's no reaction, but then her mouth drops open. A kaleidoscope of emotions flashes across her face. Surprise. Anger. Happiness. Regret.

Jordan doesn't realize it, but his phone has slipped from his hand and shattered its glass on the floor. The years since he's seen Hannah fall away. He's nineteen again, eager, idealistic, and convinced he can be a savior to a girl kept inside a locked psychiatric ward.

The entire room goes silent. Everyone in the audience is wondering what's going on—dimly understanding that something important is happening, but not having any idea what it is.

Jordan tries to speak, but his throat is closed up tight. If he could talk, though, what would he say? *I'm sorry. I'm so sorry. You were the girl I tried to save and all but destroyed. I never should have told you what I'd found out about your past. I never should have looked for it in the first place. Your history should have been yours to discover— or yours to keep locked away forever.*

If I thought you haunted me back then, it was nothing compared to how you've haunted me ever since. I've dedicated my life to making up for how I hurt you.

He wants to tell her all of this. In front of all these people. But he won't. His words have already hurt her too much. Instead he'll imagine their conversation. His apology. Her listening.

Would you like to take a walk? he'll ask. And since this is his imagination, anything at all can happen.

Yes, she'll say. *Yes I definitely would.*

Their eyes are still locked. Neither of them notices the awkward silence, the dozens of New Yorkers witnessing this strange, improbable reunion.

Jordan takes a step toward her. Then another.

And Hannah smiles, and her whole face lights up like a lamp. Like a blazing fire.

CHAPTER 111

For a second, I didn't know where I was in time. It was a feeling I knew well—but it'd never felt quite like this. The walls of the room wavered. My brain doubted my eyes. And my heart started banging in my chest, thumping against my ribs like they were a cage it could escape from.

Was that really Jordan Hassan, standing there gaping at me in the back of Greene Street Books?

It was.

Whether he was here because of coincidence, design, or miracle, I couldn't begin to guess.

You're here. You've come back.

I stared at him, cataloguing the changes made by seven years of life. He seemed taller and broader, but his hair still fell over his face and into his agate eyes. And his smile, when it emerged, was exactly like I remembered it.

"I'm sorry," I said, realizing that everyone in the crowd was staring at us while we stared at each other. "It's not every day that a person's past suddenly pops up in their present." I glanced down at my book, like I was about to start reading again. *I should, shouldn't I?* But then I realized this was a moment I had to reach out and grab on to.

"Everyone," I said, "this is Jordan Hassan. He knew me when I was down—way down." I laughed nervously. "He was my friend and my confidante. And, to be honest, he really messed me up, too."

Jordan was walking haltingly toward me, but then he stopped, with a look on his face like he wanted to say something. But the stage was mine and I meant to keep it that way.

"I wrote about Jordan," I said. "And it's almost like he leapt out of the pages of my book and into this store." I shook my head in wonder. "I can't believe it," I said. "I can't believe you're here."

"Me either," he says. He throws up his hands. "And I can't exactly explain it."

"Like scientists still can't explain the muon," I said.

And Jordan laughs.

I knew he had wanted to save me. And I had wanted him to be able to.

But being mentally ill wasn't like drowning, even if it sometimes felt like it. Because the thing about drowning is that someone else can save you, whether you want them to or not. And the thing about struggling with mental illness is that you have to be part of saving yourself.

"Anyway, why don't you take a seat, Jordan Hassan," I said lightly. "Listen. I think you might like this story."

He did just as he was told. And then I smiled to the crowd of people who had come to hear me read from my book, and I started again from the beginning.

AUTHOR'S **NOTE**

When I was eighteen years old, I started working at McLean Hospital, the psychiatric affiliate of Harvard Medical School. I applied because I needed a job out of high school, and I think they hired me as a psych aide because they saw I had empathy for people. On paper, the job was to assist in medical care under the watchful eye of doctors, nurses, and psych techs. It turned out that I spent a lot of time chatting with patients, listening to their stories, and making friends I still think about to this day.

I didn't meet anyone quite like Hannah at McLean (and I don't *think* I've met anyone who lived in the Middle Ages), but the truths in this book are based on those I encountered as a psych aide and in medical journals and stories researched before writing *The Girl in the Castle*.

Mental and behavioral health units treat patients with a huge range of issues—including those shown in these pages, such as schizophrenia, depression, bipolar disorder, and complex trauma—using a range of therapies, often involving medication. If you or someone you know is experiencing thoughts of suicide or self-harm, or other mental health issues, you don't have to struggle alone. But don't just take my word for it. You can talk to a trusted medical professional or visit some of these websites to learn more:

- American Academy of Child & Adolescent Psychiatry (aacap.org)
- Crisis Text Line (crisistextline.org)
- Go Ask Alice! (goaskalice.columbia.edu)
- National Alliance on Mental Illness (nami.org)
- National Institute of Mental Health (nimh.nih.gov)
- National Suicide Prevention Lifeline (suicidepreventionlifeline.org)
- Nemours Teens Health (kidshealth.org/en/teens/your-mind)

James Patterson

ABOUT **THE AUTHORS**

JAMES PATTERSON is the most popular storyteller of our time. He is the creator of unforgettable characters and series, including Alex Cross, the Women's Murder Club, Jane Effing Smith, and Maximum Ride, and of breathtaking true stories about the Kennedys, John Lennon, and Princess Diana, as well as our military heroes, police officers, and ER nurses. He has coauthored #1 bestselling novels with Bill Clinton and Dolly Parton, told the story of his own life in *James Patterson by James Patterson*, and received an Edgar Award, nine Emmy Awards, the Literarian Award from the National Book Foundation, and the National Humanities Medal.

EMILY RAYMOND worked with James Patterson on *First Love* and *The Lost*. She lives with her family in Portland, Oregon.

JAMES
PATTERSON
RECOMMENDS

JAMES PATTERSON

YOU CAN STOP WAITING FOR
THE NEXT *HUNGER GAMES*

CRAZY
HOUSE

& GABRIELLE CHARBONNET

CRAZY HOUSE

Becca Greenfield was snatched from her small hometown. She was thrown into a maximum-security prison and put on death row with other kids her age. Until her execution, Becca's told to fit in and shut her mouth...but Becca's never been very good at either. Her sister, Cassie, was always the good twin. But her jailers made a mistake that could get them both killed: They took the wrong twin.

JAMES PATTERSON

THE FALL OF

CRAZY
HOUSE

THE BEST SERIES SINCE
THE HUNGER GAMES JUST GOT BETTER.

AND GABRIELLE CHARBONNET

THE FALL OF CRAZY HOUSE

Twin sisters Becca and Cassie barely got out of the Crazy House alive. Now they're trained, skilled fighters who fear nothing. Together, the sisters hold the key to defeating the despotic government and freeing the people of the former United States. But to win this war, will the girls have to become the very thing they hate?

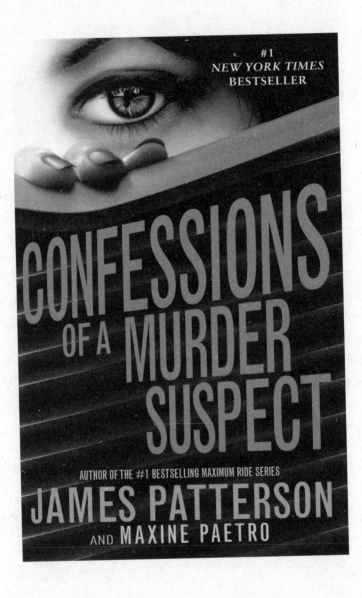

CONFESSIONS
OF A MURDER
SUSPECT

AUTHOR OF THE #1 BESTSELLING MAXIMUM RIDE SERIES

JAMES PATTERSON
AND MAXINE PAETRO

CONFESSIONS OF A MURDER SUSPECT

I've certainly given Tandy Angel a life to be jealous of as part of one of Manhattan's wealthiest and most connected families. But outside of the public eye, Tandy is haunted by the sudden and mysterious death of her sister. I've stripped her of her memory, leaving only fragments that she can't make sense of. Convinced that secrets are being kept from her, Tandy sets out to uncover her dark past. That is, until her parents are found dead and Tandy and her brothers are the prime suspects. With the police and media against her, Tandy knows she must take the investigation into her own hands. But how can she prove her siblings' innocence when she isn't even sure of her own?

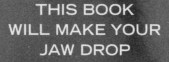

THIS BOOK
WILL MAKE YOUR
JAW DROP

INVISIBLE

THE WORLD'S #1 BESTSELLING WRITER

JAMES PATTERSON
& DAVID ELLIS

INVISIBLE

When I started writing *Invisible*, it seemed like every other TV network was telling the same kind of police stories, robberies, and crime twists. So I wanted to tell a different kind of suspense story, one that would really make your jaw drop. In the novel, Emmy Dockery is a researcher for the FBI who believes she has stumbled on one of the deadliest serial killers in history. There's only one problem—he's invisible. The mysterious killer leaves no trace. There are no weapons, no evidence, no motive. But when the killer strikes close to home, she must crack an impossible case before anyone else dies. Prepare to be blindsided because the most terrifying threat is the one you don't see coming—the one that's invisible.

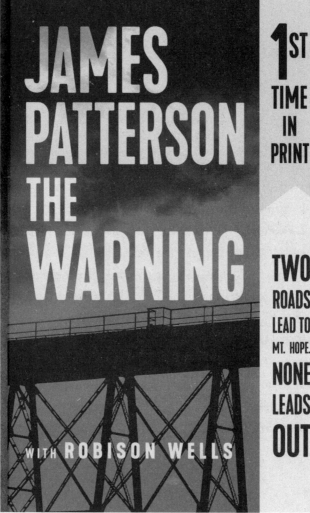

JAMES
PATTERSON
THE
WARNING

WITH ROBISON WELLS

1ST
TIME
IN
PRINT

TWO
ROADS
LEAD TO
MT. HOPE.
NONE
LEADS
OUT.

THE WARNING

Now that we've all lived through a quarantine, this story feels eerily possible. A small southern town was evacuated after a freak accident. As the first anniversary of the mishap approaches, some residents are allowed to return past the National Guard roadblocks.

Mount Hope natives Maggie and Jordan quickly discover that their hometown is not as it was before. While the damaged power plant remains under military lockdown, friends and family start morphing into terrifying strangers. Maggie and Jordan are determined to discover who—or what—has taken control of Mount Hope. Soon they're caught in the crosshairs of a presence more sinister than any they could have imagined.

For a complete list of books by
JAMES PATTERSON

VISIT
JamesPatterson.com

Follow James Patterson on Facebook
@JamesPatterson

Follow James Patterson on Twitter
@JP_Books

Follow James Patterson on Instagram
@jamespattersonbooks

For a complete list of books, visit JamesPatterson.com.